McCarren's Rules
~ Creole Secret

by

DeeAnna Galbraith

McCarren's Rules, Book 2

McCarren's Rules ~ Creole Secret

COPYRIGHT © 2022 by DeeAnna Galbraith

Cover Art by *Kristian Norris*

The Wild Rose Press, Inc.
PO Box 708
Adams Basin, NY 14410-0708
Visit us at www.thewildrosepress.com

Publishing History
First Edition, 2022
Trade Paperback ISBN 978-1-5092-4078-4
Digital ISBN 978-1-5092-4079-1

McCarren's Rules, Book 2
Published in the United States of America

My niece is an avid reader. Mostly electronic but she also likes the paper-print kind. This is her first time in Stella's library, and her gaze is drawn to the floor-to-ceiling shelves full of books. The only break, two long, narrow, leaded-glass windows high up. "This is amazing. And a lot of them appear really old. Must be a bear to dust, though."

Stella looks up, as if seeing the volumes for the first time. "Oh. I don't spend much time in here. Neither did Harlan. It was mostly a cigar and cognac escape for my grandfather and father." She leans her narrow hip against the desk. "This is so terribly inconvenient. I know that sounds rude and wrong, but it just is."

I've known Stella for eleven years. Since I was eighteen. Sometimes she needs a little reminder. "Um, are we talking about the man in the garden?"

She wrings her hands, keeping them from the continual flutter that usually accompanies her speech. "Yes, of course. It's Samuel Guillory. He is—or was—my gardener. You've met him on previous visits, Julianne. And he can't have moved his head forward, because, well, he's dead."

Praise for DeeAnna Galbraith...

She is the award-winning author of *DELTA ON MY MIND, GAMBLING ON THE GODDESS, CHASING GLORY,* and *THE CROWN OF EVERYTHING* (children's book).

GAMBLING ON THE GODDESS:
"This was a really interesting concept, the characters were great and I really enjoyed the mystery part of the story."

~*Kay M., NetGalley Reviewer*

~*~

MCCARREN'S RULES ~ ANGEL FALLS:
"Good book! I definitely enjoyed reading this one! It had a little bit of everything! It had suspense, intrigue, action, drama, and some heartbreak and heartache! It was a great who done it!! Very interesting storyline! I highly recommend it!"

~*Debbie B., NetGalley Reviewer*

Dedication

Dedicated to my sister Sheila. I miss you.

Chapter One

Stella Farrol Neely, hostess of this bridal shower for her niece, Jilly, glides past ornate french tables holding faïence vases filled with hot-house pink and white peonies. She stops to chat with each clutch of guests. I know Stella. She is a tall and slender swan with soft white hair. All elegance and composure outside, unsure of herself and paddling like crazy underneath.

My niece, Rippa Parkes, and I, also guests, are casual types, flat-out plain compared to the other women who wear uniforms of colorful watered-silk dresses or suits and stylish spring heels. I count a number of hats too. Pearls and diamond tennis bracelets are the jewelry of choice as at least half of the guests are Stella's friends, sixty-somethings, or at least admitting to fifty-something.

We are in Stella's overheated house in the Garden District of New Orleans. During Mardi Gras. I glance around the great parlor. The house is over one hundred sixty years old and showing its age. High ceilings produce shadows that hide cracks in the delicate plasterwork, and the hand-painted wallpaper is faded and peeling in places. It was better maintained before the death of her husband, Harlan, but Stella has always been taken care of and now, on her own, prefers not to see things that might be upsetting.

The guest of honor, Jilly, and I were college roommates, *Julianne and Jilly*. We did everything together and promised to be the maid or matron of honor at each other's weddings. She stood up with Raif and me, so it's my turn. She offered to let me out of my promise, just fly in, attend the wedding, and fly home. New Orleans is where I met Raif. Memories here are stacked against me since he died in a skiing accident in St. Moritz almost four years ago. Her offer was tempting, but she's important to me, so I put on my big-girl pants, and here I am.

Besides, Rippa has never been to a wedding or New Orleans or Mardi Gras, and her sheer excitement tipped the scales.

The party-chat level is high but winding down as it's officially over, and the guests are wandering homeward.

Rippa spent an hour this morning getting measured for a refitted bridesmaid dress. A last-minute saving choice as one of Jilly's friends eloped and is terribly happy but unable to perform her bridesmaid duties. Rippa is Jilly's new best friend, having agreed to change from guest to stand-in so as not to ruin the all-blonde bridesmaid/matron-of-honor lineup.

I'm pretty sure Rippa has reached her apex of party boredom. She is nursing a glass of lethal southern punch consisting of alcohol and fruit with sorbet floating on top. Being eighteen, she is legal in Louisiana. She has staked out the window overlooking the garden, mouths *Jules*, and tips her head for me to come over.

I excuse myself from a conversation outlining party attendees' newest baby additions and additions-to-be and wander to her side. "How're you holding up?"

A shudder lifts her shoulders. "I'm okay. Too young to be exposed to all this rest-of-my-life stuff." She holds up her glass of punch. "And I thought this would be, you know, smoother. It's so sweet I can feel the enamel on my teeth dissolving." She points out the window. "I wanted to show you something and see if you think we should bring it to Stella's attention."

"What? I'm all up for a distraction."

"See that guy in the back of the garden holding the hoe?"

I tip my head close to the window, taking in the view. "What about him?"

"He hasn't moved for like, fifteen minutes. Except his head seems to be drooping a little more. It's hard to tell with that big straw hat he's wearing."

"Really? It was raining until about five minutes ago. You'd think he'd step inside."

New Orleans has the same kind of rain schedule as Miami Beach. Frequent, but usually short. In the Pacific Northwest where Rippa and I are from, it rains a lot, and once the clouds move in, trapped by the mountains, they're there for a while. Especially in February.

Rippa shifts a shoulder. "Maybe he's used to the rain, but that doesn't explain his not moving."

"Stella just went back into the kitchen. Let's go ask."

We find her and her sister, Clemmie, directing cleanup for the already semi-harried staff of a catering service Jilly has used before and wanted for this function, even though, as the guest-of-honor, she wasn't supposed to be involved.

"Stella," I say, since this is how she likes to be

3

addressed, "Rippa noticed the man standing in the back of your garden hasn't moved for at least fifteen minutes. Could he be ill or need some help? His head has fallen forward."

Her expression is hard to read. She looks sort of embarrassed, then determination takes its place. "Can y'all step into the library?"

My first thought is that she is going to tell us the man in the garden is some kind of authentic-looking scarecrow. Not a real man.

Rippa and I exchange glances. *What's up?*

My niece is an avid reader. Mostly electronic but she also likes the paper-print kind. This is her first time in Stella's library, and her gaze is drawn to the floor-to-ceiling shelves full of books. The only break, two long, narrow, leaded-glass windows high up. "This is amazing. And a lot of them appear really old. Must be a bear to dust, though."

Stella looks up, as if seeing the volumes for the first time. "Oh. I don't spend much time in here. Neither did Harlan. It was mostly a cigar and cognac escape for my grandfather and father." She leans her narrow hip against the desk. "This is so terribly inconvenient. I know that sounds rude and wrong, but it just is."

I've known Stella for eleven years. Since I was eighteen. Sometimes she needs a little reminder. "Um, are we talking about the man in the garden?"

She wrings her hands, keeping them from the continual flutter that usually accompanies her speech. "Yes, of course. It's Samuel Guillory. He is—or was—my gardener. You've met him on previous visits, Julianne. And he can't have moved his head forward, because, well, he's dead."

I...I know I'm blinking faster than normal, and Rippa and I both suck in breaths, but we recover at the same time. "I beg your pardon?" comes from me and "His head did move," from Rippa.

Stella nods, sighing. "You two are like family, so here's the situation. Samuel came to me about five years ago with the strangest request I ever heard. His uncle, a disreputable gambler, had arranged to have his corpse, I guess the term is extreme embalmed, upon his death and sat at his favorite poker table in front of a deadman's hand." She flaps her own. "A combination of cards, said to be unlucky."

"Probably aces and eights," Rippa says. "But what the heck. Embalmed?"

Stella has to be kidding, Cara.

I was wondering when Raif would weigh in. Cara is his nickname for me. And it's true. He died in that skiing accident, but that doesn't keep him from making comments on the happenings in my life. *Inside my head*. His observations are short and not as frequent as they were in the first couple of years after his death. Rippa caught on early and doesn't think I'm two bricks short of a wall. She thinks it's like a superpower. So I'm okay with it.

Stella looks over our shoulders at the library door. I assume to make sure it's closed. "Yes, and on display before interment. Anyway," she continues, "Samuel wanted the same treatment upon his demise. He diligently saved, as it is an expensive procedure, and asked me to promise that he be stood in the place he loved best. The back of my garden."

Not sure about the extent this disturbs Rippa, but I

am gobsmacked. "Your former gardener is dead and stuffed, standing in your garden? Is that even legal?"

Stella presses her fingertips to her eyelids. "Yes, unfortunately. Samuel is supposed to be out there for a week, and it's only been three days, but I'm beginning to be sorry I ever agreed to it. It didn't occur to me that crazy people would wander by and think it was acceptable to come into my garden to see for themselves. Or have those silly camera self-portrait pictures taken with him. I put up a sign forbidding entry, but they keep knocking it down. Then Jilly's parties and wedding and everything…"

Her hands are fluttering freestyle now. "Samuel worked for this family since God was a small boy and doesn't have any close relatives, just a goddaughter, Honor deGrandpre. She's arranged to have his remains interred at the end of the seven days."

Our friend's gaze slides in a new direction in which, if there were no walls in between, we'd have a close view of the back garden. "If the rain is having a bad effect on his corpse, I'll have to call the company who installed him." She rubs her temple. "So inconvenient."

I can't think of a ready alternative. "That might be best."

"I don't understand," says Stella. "The people who put him there used a sturdy pole and wires and everything. I didn't have the nerve to go inspect him when they were done, and haven't since. I have paperwork around here somewhere."

Rippa's glance takes the same direction as Stella's. "Even embalmed, his remains would probably degrade outside. It rains here all the time."

Stella shakes her head. "I don't think Samuel considered the time of year and his corpse having to deal with wet weather."

She looks as though she's getting perturbed and is already under a good deal of stress, so I take another tack. "Does Jilly know about this?"

"Certainly, but I promised to put Samuel in the very back of the garden, and we hoped he wouldn't be noticed. Y'all won't say anything to the other guests, will you?"

Although the news she just revealed would add a lively boost to the end of the party, I shake my head. "Of course not. But he may be damaged. It might be a good idea to cover him with a tarp at night and if it starts to rain."

She closes her eyes momentarily, and her shoulders droop, then they stiffen, and she singles me out. "It's all rather unsettling, but before I add more people to the melee, could I impose upon you to take a peek at Samuel to see if it's really necessary to make that call? They will probably want to charge me to come out and examine and resecure him."

I step forward and buss Stella's cheek. "You stay in the house and relax. Let Clemmie and Jilly take care of the last guests. If there's anything wrong, we'll let you know."

A deep breath followed by a sigh escapes Stella. "Thank you."

Rippa pats her hand, then follows me into the hall.

I stop and turn. "I said *we* in there, Rip, but if this 'extreme embalming' turns out to be, oh, I don't know, soggy and decomposing, I'm not sure you want to go." *I'm not sure I want to go, either.*

7

"Are you kidding?" She hurries through the kitchen to reach the back door first. "Wouldn't miss it." She glances over her shoulder. "And did you see? She has an actual landline."

I nod. "Not exactly the stone age, but I doubt if Stella will ever feel comfortable with a cellphone." I peer out the back-door window. We can just make out the top of the figure.

A frown furrows Rippa's forehead. "Was Samuel old?"

Old being relative. Anyone over fifty probably qualifies as aged for Rippa. "Yes. You really want to see a man who has been stuffed?" I shudder. Eighteen and not squeamish. I don't recall, but I think I would have been saying *euuuw* a lot and backing far away from the body. Because extreme embalming or not, technically, it is a dead body.

We take off our shoes and put on garden clogs just inside the door. Rippa is down the back stairs and skirting the garden border before I can make it, the clogs I chose being several sizes too big.

"Wait. Don't touch anything."

She stops, looking at the ground near the figure. "As if," she shoots back, then makes a downward circling motion with her finger. "There are lots of footprints around the body. Mostly erased by the rain, but still faint. Don't suppose some kids took Samuel and left a scarecrow in his place?"

The thought makes me shimmy in distaste.

I catch up with her and look for the least invasive path to the body, but Rippa grabs my wrist.

"That's not a taxidermied body. It's a real dead guy."

"What?" I follow her gaze. She's right. Even though the head is drooping, a trickle of dried blood shows on the side where it's protected by the hat. Embalmed remains don't bleed. This guy also isn't Samuel. He was taller and had salt and pepper—mostly salt—hair. This man is maybe four inches shorter and has thick, dark, salt and pepper—mostly pepper—hair.

I don't do dead bodies. Con men, fraudsters, scammers, yes. I investigate the entire range of people bent on committing fraud against insurance companies for a living. Not this. He hasn't moved for some time, but to make sure he isn't still hanging on to life, I take a long step and place my finger over his carotid artery. I can almost feel my capillaries shrink, withdrawing blood supply from my extremities. Possibly why my finger shakes and feels as cold as his skin. Nothing. I shake my head at Rippa.

"Stella is going to hate this," Rippa says, then raises an eyebrow. "But it sure makes the end of the party interesting."

Chapter Two

I sigh. Interesting isn't the word I'd have chosen. "Damn. She'll take it the worst, but none of the family is going to be happy." I glance around. If this isn't Samuel Guillory, are his remains nearby? Lengthening end-of-winter shadows show mostly soggy remains of last year's garden. No additional bodies. My gaze moves to Stella's house. "He's not going anywhere. Let's notify the police when everyone's gone."

Rippa nods. "Okay. But when the cops show and all the action starts, I want to be more comfortable. I'm going to the house to change."

Having been in New Orleans during the citywide madness known as Mardi Gras, I got a hotel room on one of the parade routes and rented a house near Stella's in the Garden District for in-between pre-wedding commitments and pre-Lent craziness. The rental is three doors down.

Rippa is wearing the pink T-shirt dress she bought to wear to Jilly's pre-wedding parties. She only brought the one, as dresses have never occupied space in her comfort zone. She is also tenderhearted enough to not want to give bad news.

I pull the key to the house out of my suit pocket. "Good idea."

Her gaze slides to the body. Hard to tell, since she's never been to a funeral that I know of, how she's handling her first close-up encounter. I don't, however, think she is as offhand as she portrays. She was expecting to see an old man who was deceased and made to look almost alive.

I hand her the key. "Are you all right?"

She pulls her gaze back to mine, pragmatism in place. "I guess so. Not what I expected. And no gore, but way creepy. How about you?"

My own experience is limited to my husband, Raif, on a mortuary table in Switzerland. It was so surreal and soul rending I blocked most of it out. I shudder. "Not what I expected, either." I try a small smile. "We solved the mystery of the drooping head."

Rippa nods, circumnavigates the garden, and takes off. I too cut one more look at the body, then back up carefully until reaching the stone path to the back door.

Sorry you have to deal with this, Cara.

Never a dull moment.

The last of the guests and the caterers have gone. As I enter the kitchen, I see Jilly down the hall in the parlor, tidying up the pile of shower gifts. Stella is sitting at her small kitchen table sipping on something I presume is stronger than the punch served today. Stella's sister, Clemmie Ashurst, and her husband, Davison, are standing nearby. The Farrols are a close family, so I don't need to take Stella aside.

I incorporate calmness into my stance and lean against the counter. "Rippa and I checked out the body."

Clemmie and Davison turn their attention to me. "Is something wrong with Samuel?" Clemmie asks. "He hasn't been damaged, has he?"

In dealing with the news of the new body, I've

temporarily forgotten I also have to deliver the news about the absence of Samuel. "I don't know. There's another issue."

Stella puts down her glass. "Rippa thought his head was drooping, so she and Julianne went out to see if the rain had caused part of the assembly to come loose." She swings her gaze back to me. "What do you mean, another issue?"

There's no other way to break it. "I'm sorry. I've met Samuel, and that's not him out there. It's a dead man whose body has been traded for his."

Stella makes a sucking sound followed by a squeak. She stands. "What are you saying? Are you sure? He's wearing Samuel's clothes, and the body's supposed to look real."

I lay a hand on her forearm. "I'm sure. The man in your garden is decades younger than Samuel. And there's blood. You need to call the police."

Clemmie moves her hand through her short, just-above-the-chin haircut, then touches her husband's arm. "Davison?"

His thumb is on his temple, his index finger rubbing his forehead. "No reason not to believe Julianne, but I'll go check." He pats Clemmie's hand and walks to the back door.

Stella takes a gulp of whatever is in her glass and gasps as it hits her esophagus. "Wait. Do *we* have to go look at him? What about Samuel? Where is he? Do you suppose whoever traded the bodies took him away? I just couldn't stand it. What will happen when his goddaughter comes to pick him up?"

I hold up a hand. "One thing at a time. Hopefully, when the police arrive, they'll find Samuel nearby. The switch probably had to do more with the dead man. That's where their main interest will lie."

"Where is everybody?" Jilly calls from the hall. She pokes her head into the kitchen, grinning. "Didn't expect those few naughty gifts for Hugh and me. Hope nobody was too shocked." She straightens after seeing our expressions. "Oh. Something's going on, and it doesn't look pleasant. Please don't tell me it's going to ruin my wedding plans."

Stella squeezes her eyes, then blinks. "Then don't come in."

Clemmie flaps her hand at her sister. "Oh, hush. Jilly, dear, there seems to be a situation in Stella's back garden. It's in no way related to your wedding." She heads for the kitchen counter, pulling her cellphone from her purse. "I'll call the police from the library."

Jilly looks perplexed, a frown marring her forehead. "The police? What situation?"

Nobody answers her. We're watching the back door for Davison when Clemmie returns a minute later. "They're sending a team right over."

Jilly stomps her foot. "What is going on?"

Davison reenters, looking a little gray around the gills. "There's no mistake." He walks to put an arm around Clemmie. "It's Ames."

I was wrong about who would take it the worst. Clemmie puts a hand to her mouth and leans into her husband. A muffled, "No!" escapes.

Rippa slips into the room quietly and walks to stand by me. "They know who the dead guy is?"

Up until now, it's been Jilly's day. I take pity on her. "Samuel's body has been replaced with a dead man. Somebody your aunts know."

Jilly's face pales. "Oh, my God. Clemmie, I'm so sorry." She sits down hard. "I don't need this right now."

I give her a quick sideways hug. "Sorry."

Stella is regaining her focus. "Ames Renaud? My neighbor?"

"How close did he live?" I ask.

Her gaze finds her empty glass. "The house to the south, other side of the garden. He inherited the house and its contents from his uncle eight or nine months ago. He was nice but standoffish."

Rippa pats Jilly's shoulder, her head tilted toward Stella. "Had you seen him recently?"

Stella nods. "I saw him moving around his back garden yesterday morning when I came out to shoo away people gawking and taking pictures of Samuel. I waved at him, and he seemed so concentrated on something he didn't see me. I don't *think* he saw me anyway. Clemmie and I were much closer to his uncle."

Clemmie uses her husband's handkerchief to dab at her eyes. Davison has always struck me as the southern-gentleman type, although I've been told he was raised above the Mason-Dixon Line.

"Not really," Clemmie says. "You're too busy playing bridge and attending tea socials to notice, but I spent a lot of time with Ames since late last summer. We both loved jigsaw puzzles and worked on them for hours in my puzzle room. He was sweet, and I'm going to miss him terribly."

Davison sighs and lifts an apologetic shoulder. "The police will have their hands full with Mardi Gras miscreants. Even murders get short shrift during these weeks. Especially since Ames has no other relatives we know of. No one to push for a resolution."

"I will," says Clemmie. "He didn't deserve this. Just because he doesn't have anyone else, I won't let it go."

Rippa leans forward eagerly. "Maybe we can help. Jules and me."

Uh-oh, the Parkes women strike again, says Raif with a chuckle.

Davison looks at us doubtfully. "That's a kind offer, but I'm sure the police won't want the waters muddied." He smiles. "Unless they do it themselves."

Chapter Three

A knock on the front door and, like lemmings, we follow Stella into the great parlor. She lets in a man around sixty wearing a suit of muddy brown. I peg him right away as police. I think that color is in the dress code. Lines on his face are a little deeper than my guess at his age. Probably due to his stressful occupation.

He takes in the six of us. "Detective Fontenot, NOPD."

We move back as a group and form an uncertain semicircle, the detective facing us.

He pulls out a small notebook and mechanical pencil. "Can I have your names and relationships to the deceased?"

Stella is the first on his left. "Mrs. Stella Farrol Neely. The deceased was my neighbor to the south."

"Davison Ashurst. I'm Mrs. Neely's brother-in-law. Mr. Renaud was a friend."

Fontenot holds up his pencil to interrupt. "The deceased's first name?"

Clemmie answers. "His full name was Ames Sheridan Renaud. I am Clementine Farrol Ashurst. I prefer Clemmie. Mr. Renaud was a good friend."

Fontenot takes a quick peek at Davison when Clemmie says this. "Um, thank you, Mrs. Ashurst."

"Jilly Farrol. Clemmie and Stella are my aunts. They gave a bridal shower in my honor here this afternoon. I moved out shortly after Mr. Renaud inherited the house and moved in."

Fontenot tips his head at the stack of gifts and mumbles, "Congratulations," as he writes.

Which gives him a point in my book. Establishing rapport by recognizing a potential witness's celebration.

"Thank you," Jilly says.

"Julianne McCarren." I spell my surname for him. "Friend of the family and member of the wedding party." I nod to my left. "This is my niece, Rippa."

Rippa waits for the detective to acknowledge her. "Rippa Parkes. R-I-P-P-A, P-A-R-K-E-S. I spotted that he was a real dead guy first. But to be fair, Jules would have seen it a couple seconds later."

The detective finishes scratching a note. "Before we get into that. Mr. Renaud lived alone? Does anyone know if there is a next of kin who should be notified?"

Clemmie's mouth trembles, and Davison puts his arm around her.

"He was originally from New York," Davison says. "He lived alone and never mentioned anyone to us."

Fontenot makes another note. "Thank you." Then looks at Rippa from under his brows. "How did you know the deceased was a 'real dead guy'?"

"I didn't right away," she responds. And proceeds to give a detailed accounting of Stella's revelation and how we offered to check out Samuel's rigging, ending with… "Jules volunteered to go check. And she certainly wasn't going without me."

Fontenot shakes his head, and his right shoulder twitches. "Certainly not," he mumbles. "Can anyone give me this Samuel's last name?"

Stella fixes him with a gimlet eye. "Of course. I am

not in the habit of employing persons with first names only. He worked for my family for fifty years. His surname was Guillory."

This puts Fontenot in his place. He is dealing with a no-nonsense New Orleans society matron. "Thank you, ma'am."

He gets back to Rippa. "So there was some curiosity about a body that had been extremely embalmed?"

"A little. Mostly we wanted to see if we could fix the drooping head."

"And that's when you found Mr. Renaud?"

She held up a hand. "First, we changed into garden clogs, then, being very careful about where we were stepping, went to take a look."

"Did you know the deceased?"

"Samuel, no. The new dead guy, neither."

"Then?"

"That's when I told Jules it looked like a real dead guy instead of an embalmed one. We both saw the dried blood on his temple. We backed away after Jules checked his carotid artery to make sure he wasn't just hurt. I thought there would be all kinds of stuff going on, so I ran to the rental house and changed out of my party clothes, and Jules came in to tell Stella and the rest of the family."

Fontenot holds up his pencil. "Let me stop you again. We'll have to take the clothes and shoes you were both wearing when you found Mr. Renaud."

Rippa blinks. "Oh. Okay. The shoes were Stella's garden clogs. They're on the back porch. I'll bring the dress back when the rest of your people get here." She makes a wry face and turns to me. "Guess we'll need to go shopping for more clothes for the rest of the parties and stuff."

"Guess we will." I refocus on Fontenot. "I'll go change when you're finished questioning us. Once I told them about the body, Clemmie called it in right away."

Davison looks down at his shoes. "I went out to see if I could identify the body. I'm afraid you'll need to exclude my shoes too. It looked as if the other shoe prints near it were the size a male or males would wear. I was careful not to step on any of those."

Fontenot glances at Davison's shoes. "Thanks. That'll help." He addresses Clemmie. "You said you were good friends with the deceased. Can you tell me a little about him?"

Clemmie reaches for her husband's hand. "Ames was a nice man, if a little strange. Davison and I live right down the street. We tried to get him involved in the goings on in the Garden District, but he wasn't interested. Said he had plant allergies and preferred to work alone, in his library." She sends a sad look to Davison. "Until Ames and I discovered we both loved jigsaw puzzles. We worked on them in the puzzle room in my house. I did see Ames's library once. Books stacked everywhere. Mostly in piles around a big reading chair."

The detective's gaze lands on each of us in turn. "He sounds like a nice, harmless guy who kept to himself. Do any of you know of a reason or person who might want to harm him?"

The whole unexpected murdered man in the garden has us all looking around and shaking our heads. Rippa and I being the least knowledgeable about the deceased.

He nods. "Okay. Then do any of you know why the killer or killers chose to remove the body from his house, take down the extreme-embalmed corpse, and replace it with the victim here, in Mrs. Neely's back garden?"

Also a pertinent question, but with the same responses as before, with the exception of a muted sob from Clemmie.

Fontenot scans the group. "The coroner and the rest of the crime-scene team should be arriving any minute. I need to see the body."

Rippa bounces on the balls of her feet. "I'll do it. Can I, Jules?"

Can't argue with that enthusiasm, Cara.

I'm going to go with interest over bloodthirsty and lift a shoulder. "Not my decision. You're legal age, so it's up to the detective."

Who is clearly not used to dealing with bubbly blonde teenagers who want to get in on the dead-body action. He casts a wary glance at Rippa. "Perhaps Mr. Ashurst would be a better candidate?"

Rippa slumps as disappointment swallows her by inches. "Then can I follow?"

Stella nods. "My property. You have my permission."

The detective peers toward the street at the sound of vehicles pulling up. "I'm sorry, Mrs. Neely. Your garden qualifies as a crime scene. In which case, it doesn't matter who owns the property. NOPD has jurisdiction."

Rippa's "doomed to boredom" stance works, and Fontenot draws his eyebrows together in bafflement. "You interested in crime scenes in general or dead bodies specifically?"

My niece grins. "Yes."

The detective hangs his head and shakes it. "A very discreet distance. No second chances. No throwing up if the body reveals anything gruesome. Understand?"

Rippa lights up. "I promise."

He scribbles something in his notebook, then looks at me. "Your niece mentioned going to a rental?"

"Yes. We have a hotel room on Canal Street but are also renting the house three doors down."

He lifts an eyebrow. "The Sandoval place?"

The precinct that includes the Garden District can't be a frequent spot for homicide investigations. The fact that Fontenot knows the residents is impressive. According to the yellowed documentation framed on the walls of the house, the Sandoval family has been in New Orleans since the Spanish occupied it over two centuries ago. "Yes. Until after the wedding."

"Since that residence is three doors down, you didn't notice the man in the garden when you walked here for the party?"

Good question. "Afraid not. Our flight got in this morning, and by the time we checked into the hotel, got our things together, and changed for the party, we were in a hurry. Besides, he's pretty far back."

The detective scribbles again, then turns to Stella. "A last question, Mrs. Neely. I understand there was a lot of party activity, but you didn't notice a real dead body had been left in your garden?"

She explains Samuel's request and how she had been squeamish about his presence, signing off on the installation without "inspecting" the work. Finished with her contribution, Stella turns and wanders into the kitchen.

Davison follows her toward the back of the house, Fontenot and Rippa in tow. "This way is shorter."

Stella returns with another glass of reddish liquid. I assume it's sherry or a liqueur of some kind.

"Can I get anyone else refreshments?"

No one accepts her invitation.

"So he moved in about eight months ago?" I ask.

Stella frowns in concentration. "About then. His uncle passed away almost ten months ago. The deceased moved in a couple of months later. The first time I saw him, he was hacking away at the beautiful English roses by his front porch. I offered to have Samuel relocate them." A dark expression crosses her face. "He said, 'No, thank you,' and continued hacking away at them until they were barely stubs. His uncle planted those roses when I was a child."

The Garden District is a good place for a person like Stella who lives for greenery.

She is just building up steam. "Many of the fine old plants grown from cuttings by his uncle are gone. So sad. I came out once and asked him if he planned to stay. He said he didn't care for New Orleans specifically and all the plants that made him miserable in particular. He was waiting for some event, then he would put the house on the market and move back to New York."

I agree with Stella. "You'd think he'd get allergy shots or something instead. And wouldn't destroying the garden devalue the property?"

Clemmie glances toward the garden. "The house would still be a valuable listing, no matter the condition. They come up for sale only rarely, and this part of the district is a coveted area."

Stella rolls her head back. "Good Lord, yes. When Harlan died, God rest his sweet soul, I had realtors stop by and knock on the door, asking if I was interested in selling. Which I think is the epitome of rudeness. My goodness, after a spouse dies, it's overwhelming. I had to hire extra help for a week so there'd be someone to answer the door or the telephone to tell those offensive people I had no interest."

Renaud's remarks and the disarray in his library spark my interest. "Do you think he was looking for something? I mean Mr. Renaud. Something that would trigger the event he talked about? If the books in his library were stacked all over the floor, he might have been going through them one at a time, searching for a hiding place for jewelry or a valuable first edition."

Stella is momentarily quiet, but Clemmie frowns in concentration.

Before they can weigh in, Rippa appears down the hall, her step slow. "Harsh. Crime-scene guy says I can't observe *or* ask questions. Too much of a hindrance to their work. *Pffft.* Used the excuse that it's getting dark. I'm still trying to decide if Fontenot knew that would happen."

Speak of the devil. Fontenot follows Davison through the back door. He stops in the kitchen and writes in his notebook, then comes into the parlor to stand in front of Rippa. "Sorry you got thrown out. You were doing good."

Rippa executes a bounce on her toes. "Thanks."

Doing what good? "I'm confused. I thought you were just looking on."

Fontenot nods. "She was. When she pointed out

something shiny that turned out to be a signet ring in the mud, the technicians decided they had too much to do in the amount of daylight left and told her to leave." He shrugs. "Their circus. I couldn't overrule. But she has great observation skills."

This could be our way in to aid in the investigation. My turn to nod. "I've always thought so."

Rippa is beyond pumped. "Jules does too."

A chuckle in my head. *Yes, you do, Cara.*

I smile. "Are some of the team looking for Samuel, Detective?"

His gaze drops to his notes. "My main concern is the murder victim."

"Of course, but Samuel Guillory is the responsibility of Mrs. Neely, and she's very upset."

Stella dabs at her eyes. "Poor Samuel. We have to find him and get his clothing back on."

Davison Ashurst puts a hand on his sister-in-law's arm. "I doubt if the police will let you take the clothes off a corpse to put on another corpse. Even if the clothes were originally his."

Fontenot shakes his head, confirming Davison's assumption.

Stella chews her lower lip, then wads her sodden handkerchief. "I'll bring some of Harlan's things. I will *not* have Samuel taken away in a tarp or whatever those despicable killers put him in. Oh! I can't believe I just said killers in my own parlor."

Clemmie urges her toward the stairs leading to the second floor. "Come on. I'll help you. I'm sure his goddaughter will be grateful."

The detective holds his pen up in interrupt mode again. "A moment, Mrs. Neely. What made you say *those* killers? Do you have an idea of the number of people who perpetrated this?"

Stella blinks and straightens. "Well, of course not. I just put two and two together and assumed it would take more than one person to hold a dead body in place and lash it to a pole at the same time. I think that would be obvious."

Detective Fontenot pulls his lips in and nods, looking chastised by a rookie deduction. Stella two, NOPD zero.

Chapter Four

I suppress a smile and walk to the window to glance at the garden where they're carefully cutting the body loose. I wonder why, since the drooping head is what alerted us to the body in the first place, the rest of the body is kept upright with wire and the head is not. Maybe a hat pulled down over a head bent forward would aid in the length of time the body wouldn't be recognized, or not enough of the original wire was left to secure it.

Based on her activities down there, my niece would do well in the medical profession. Since revisiting the dead body, she seems to be getting used to "creepy."

I'm not that way, totally. Although not too bothered by the scene and it isn't a particularly grisly one, my last dead body was Raif's funeral, and even though it's been close to four years, I haven't completely released my feelings. Don't know if I ever will.

You are getting better, Cara.

I suppose so. After a couple of minutes, my attention is caught by a flurry of activity at the house next door. A female officer heads toward the front of Stella's house. I open it as she reaches the door.

The officer steps inside, hat in hand.

Detective Fontenot two-finger waves her inside. "What is it?"

"There's another well-preserved body of an older man on the floor of the sun porch wrapped in garden sheeting. We'll need identification to prove it's the embalmed man we were looking for. A pair of scissors were also left. It's all being taken into evidence."

Stella is standing at the foot of the stairs, holding a small bundle of clothes. Fontenot looks in her direction.

She clutches the clothes tighter. "I can't believe I'm the best person for this. Clemmie?"

Clemmie nods and speaks low to her husband. Then she says, "My husband and I will make the identification."

"Thanks," says Fontenot.

Stella slumps with relief.

"A question before we go," says Clemmie. "Has Samuel's body been defiled?"

The officer shakes her head. "Not that we can tell, ma'am. He's been wrapped in clean garden sheeting and, due to his original embalming, looks peaceful. But we need a confirmation."

Davison takes Clemmie's hand, and they move to accompany the officer.

"Thank goodness," says Stella, then her eyes widen as she turns to Fontenot. "You won't have to keep Samuel for evidence or anything so awful as that, will you?"

The harried detective rubs his forehead. "Your former gardener was not a victim, but we may have to recreate the circumstances of the body transfer. There also may be evidence on him, the sheeting, or the porch. Right now, I know of no law that applies to holding a legal corpse as evidence. His disposition will have to be determined by the coroner and crime team."

He points to the clothes Stella is holding. "Which means we don't need those right now, but thank you."

I don't envy Fontenot having to untangle those legalities. I turn back to the window to see Rippa has followed Clemmie and Davison and the officer. From the determined look on Rippa's face, she wants to accompany them for the identification. The officer stops and shakes her head, but Rippa points to this house, letting her know she already has permission to watch at a respectful distance. No doubt omitting that she was thrown out of the garden area.

The officer then holds out her arm, ostensibly pointing to a distance at which Rippa will be allowed to observe.

The glee on Rippa's face is evident, even from this vantage point. Quite a combination for a budding investigator. No fear of possible gore at a crime scene and a brilliant mind for making deductions.

I turn to see Stella with a fresh glass of dark amber liquid. Her tolerance for alcohol is amazing. She's sitting quietly by herself while Jilly is talking to the detective. Stella is the less stable or pragmatic of Jilly's aunts. She seems about to float away on liquid courage or completely fall apart.

I walk over. "Things are going smoothly in the garden and next door. Is there anything I can do to help here?"

She gives a watery smile. "Thank you, Julianne. I'm not handling this well, am I? Add to that the selfish things I said earlier. I've known Samuel all my life. He was almost a member of the family. Here as I grew up, here when I got married and moved out, here when Harlan and I came back after Mother died. A touchstone, you might say." She takes a sip, her gaze leveling on the windows that overlook the garden. "I thought I could handle his death and the request to have him put in the garden. I was busy with Jilly's wedding and bridal shower. But this..." Her voice trails off as she points the hand with the glass toward the window. "It's a bit much."

"A bit much" is putting it mildly. If I recall, Stella's husband, Harlan, died of a heart attack on the golf course perhaps a year ago, then Jilly leaving, then Samuel's death, and now... Well, I can't blame her for her reaction.

Clemmie, Davison, and Rippa come through the back into the kitchen. Clemmie and Davison stand talking, and Rippa enters the parlor. She walks to Stella and bends down in front of her. "It was Samuel. His remains are fine."

Stella stands. "Thank you, dear. I'll call his goddaughter and assure her his situation remains the decision of the police as to when his body can be released."

As soon as Stella enters the library, Rippa and I walk over to Fontenot. He and Jilly are just finishing.

"It was Samuel," Rippa says. "He's fine." She grimaces. "As fine as a dead person can be who's been preserved. Stella is contacting his goddaughter."

Fontenot huffs out a breath. "Just as well since I think the coroner may have to call in a forensic pathologist. I'm guessing this is new ground for them."

Jilly's stance is tense. Her shoulders slightly rounded. "Any idea how long that will take? My wedding is in five days, and until then people will be coming and going for events here, in addition to strangers wanting to take a peek at Samuel. Can't you assure me there won't be further interruptions?"

The tightening around Detective Fontenot's mouth suggests the end of politeness to civilians is near. "I'm afraid I can't tell you any such thing, Ms. Farrol. The location of this house and the garden where Mr. Renaud's body was discovered are central to police activity, probably through tomorrow at least. Right now I need to get back to the coroner and the technicians processing the house and garden."

Jilly is not an overly emotional person, but when something, even something as serious as a murder, interferes with the plans for her big day, tears start in her eyes.

Rippa and I walk her a few feet away, and I take her hand. "The bridal shower is over with none of the other guests being the wiser. Rippa and I are the only two who saw anything, and we've already been interviewed. What's on your schedule for the next event that takes place here?"

She doesn't have to consult the big planner she carries everywhere. "A pre-rehearsal-dinner cocktail party in three days. The dinner itself will be held at the hotel where the wedding reception is to take place."

I smile. "Good. After today, they'll probably concentrate on Mr. Renaud's house anyway. That'll give Rippa and me time to see what we can find out. Help the case along."

Jilly nods and sighs, pulling out her cellphone and stepping toward the hall. "I have to let Hugh know. Hopefully, everything will stay on schedule."

Jilly sounds callous at this more or less major interruption in her big event, but she has been planning this wedding for about six years, ever since she met Hugh and decided he was the husband for her.

Detective Fontenot steps closer to Rippa and me. "Excuse me for eavesdropping, but while I appreciate your observation skills, I can't allow you to place yourselves in danger."

Rippa folds her arms, her advocate now tarnished. "Jules has a private investigator's license and works as a contractor for Full State Insurance. Last year she took down a guy wanted for fraud in three states. He pulled a switchblade on her, and she still managed to catch him. We also helped the New York City police uncover a guy responsible for vehicular homicide. I did a chunk of the research on the Russian gang involved. We don't intentionally place ourselves in danger and don't need looking after. We extended our offer today because Mr. Renaud was a friend of Clemmie's and because we're located close to the scene."

Fontenot stands back from the slender blonde, but his stare gives no ground. "I may have chosen my words poorly, and for that I'm sorry. Usually, un-asked-for 'consultation' on an established homicide investigation can be construed as interference. In this case, as you pointed out, the skills the two of you possess could come in handy." He lifts a hand as Rippa's excitement gets the better of her face and a grin erupts. "But...there will be no chasing, confronting, or direct accusations—we are talking about two or more suspects who murdered a man. If there is even a whisper that you or your aunt have crossed the line, you are *out* and may be up on charges. Got that?"

Rippa's eyes widen, but her grin remains.

I'm not swayed by his speech. "We don't intend to

trample on any laws or interfere in the investigation. Just saying if we hear or see anything of interest, we'll let you know. Speaking of which, I don't think it came up during your questioning, but the victim was not a long-term resident of the Garden District. He inherited the house and contents and had only been there for about eight months. He was originally from New York. He didn't like it here and intended to sell the house eventually and return there. If that helps."

Out come the notepad and mechanical pencil. He scratches a note. "Good information. I'll contact New York and have them do a rundown on him. Um, thank you."

That said, the detective's slight frown adds to my assumption that he is, however, not completely convinced. He heads for the front door—wise man that he is. As he reaches it, his cellphone rings. He stops, answers, listens, and mouths *shit*. Turning around, he reenters the parlor. "There's been a double homicide. Since my initial investigation here is wrapped up, I'm on deck. As soon as I assess that scene, I'll try to return."

He hurries out, and Rippa and I go to the window and watch as he trots over to the team in the garden, says a few words to the man in the Tyvek suit with the word *Coroner* on the back, then strolls down the sidewalk.

I raise an eyebrow. "Pretty skinny line he drew for us, but it's better than nothing." I fix my niece with a stare. "You sure you want to dig into this? We're only here for a week."

Rippa huffs a breath. "Shortsighted on my part, jumping in and volunteering both of us, sorry, but yes, I think we could help." She tips her head toward the now-empty sidewalk. "His new attitude hit me as someone who, even if we offered good information, might discount it and us."

I lift a shoulder, remembering a similar attitude from Detective Susan Pavlycheva in New York last year and my own snarky response. "We offer what we have, and if it proves valuable, they usually come around."

Clemmie walks toward us from the kitchen, sadness and exhaustion evident in her red-rimmed eyes. Her gaze strays to the view of the garden but cuts away quickly.

She's followed by Stella, swirling the contents of her bottomless glass. "I do feel bad about Mr. Renaud but also about not being able to keep my promise to Samuel."

"It's all good," Rippa says. "A member of the crime team said it wouldn't take too long, and knowing Samuel's interment is pending, the coroner will do his best to work on him first."

Stella's eyelids droop. "In that case, I'm going to have a lie down."

Clemmie smiles as her sister heads for the stairs. "She's worn out. Probably done for the day." Her smile fades. "We overheard the coroner say Samuel's clothes were modified to be easily put on the body. So the switch was made before rigor set in. Unfortunately, the rain washed off most of the evidence that might be available on the clothing. They think they might get luckier with Samuel since he was wrapped up and inside."

"Did you overhear the estimated time of death?" I

ask as gently as possible.

She nods, her eyes still haunted. "Very early this morning. Possibly between two and three. He also said the exchange was made in a hurry. There are pieces of cut wire and nylon rope in the dirt. It was replaced with regular hemp rope and what looks like a necktie holding his head up. That's why it drooped a little at a time."

Jilly hugs her to her side as Clemmie puddles up again.

"I know it sounds silly, but I'm really going to miss Ames. He was brilliant at working jigsaw puzzles, and we met at least twice a week in my den." She dabs her eyes. "Davison was so sweet to move all his paperwork out and rename it the puzzle room."

Rippa shakes her head. "I don't think it's silly at all. Especially if you worked on those one thousand and fifteen hundred piece puzzles. Those are hard."

A smile breaks through on Clemmie's face. "That's true, although I've been racking my brain, and I don't know if I'll be able to help you two very much. Ames and I were puzzle friends, but that's about it. Except I'm the executor of his will."

Someone he's only known for about eight months? That's interesting. "Why would he do that?"

Davison has approached and puts his arm around Clemmie. "He told her he didn't have anybody else."

Clemmie sighs. "He said it was pretty simple. It's in his safety deposit box along with documents for the house and some personal journals. I have access."

"Detective Fontenot will want to know who the primary beneficiary is," I say.

Clemmie hangs her head. "Ames joked that as his

personal representative, I'd have to inventory the house for the beneficiary as he was too busy working on a different puzzle. Besides, there was only one thing in the house that interested him."

"Let Rippa and me help you with the inventory," I say. "We might be able to find evidence to add to the case."

Enthusiasm bubbles over in Rippa. She grabs Clemmie's hand. "Better and better. We are amazing. You'll see."

Clemmie's smile broadens for the first time since she heard about Ames Renaud's death. "How can I pass up amazing?"

Chapter Five

A stomach rumble reminds me I've only eaten two *petit fours* since coffee and a breakfast cookie on the flight here. I give Clemmie a quick hug. "I think Detective Fontenot is done talking to us, but he knows how to contact me if not. Rip and I are going back to the rental. I'll change, and we'll bring back her dress and my suit and clogs as requested. Then into the French Quarter for dinner. Can we bring anything for either of you?"

Clemmie shakes her head. "Davison is going to fix something and bring it back for Stella and me. I don't want her to think she's here by herself, considering what's gone on today. I'll probably stay the night. If the detective comes back, I'll tell him about Ames's papers."

Rippa rubs her hands together. "Hope there's something to help with the case."

My thoughts exactly, but Clemmie's feelings are too raw to talk about it right now. I nod toward the door. "Let's go."

Outside the air is clear, the rain having washed away some of the oppressive mugginess.

Rippa glances back at Stella's, then takes in the official city cars parked in front of the Renaud house. "This is so exciting. I mean, not the part about Clemmie losing her friend, but that we get to investigate a murder instead of wandering around, getting pushed and shoved by drunk college kids and dodging beads. Probably in the rain."

"You *are* a college kid," I remind, although Rippa doesn't like labels. "Or we could *try* to have some fun, go to Jackson Square and have Tarot card or palm readings, have a voodoo princess make gris-gris bags for us, or even book a ride on one of those steamboat tours."

Her look is skeptical. "I guess. Just seems a lot less exciting. Can we eat first?"

"Definitely."

****

The French Quarter isn't far away, so we lock the rental and walk back to Stella's. Rippa takes the things requested by the detective to the door and is met by Clemmie for the handoff. I wait outside, and although the body is gone from Stella's garden, lights are now on in the Renaud house. Rippa flicks a glance at it as she comes back down the steps.

It's only the second day of Mardi Gras, but as Rippa and I get closer to the celebrating, the noise level is like a wave climbing toward us.

We wind through the crowds toward our hotel. The serious drinking has started, and it looks like some have started way earlier. As we approach a small club with people dancing to zydeco music, couples spill into the street. A tall man with a big smile grabs Rippa's hand.

"Hey," Rippa says, pulling her hand back. "What's the deal?"

"Dance with me, *chère*."

I look past the man at the explicit moves made by some of the other dancers, then at Rippa.

She smiles back at him. "Thanks, but we're on our way to dinner."

He releases her hand and puts his together, giving a short bow. "Okay, *chère*. But you don' know what you're missing." He ducks back into the club.

"Wow," Rippa says. "In our part of the country, you'd expect at least two casual meetings over coffee and a medical history before that kind of invitation. But it does look like fun."

"Yeah. We're way too PC. If I'd not had a couple of drinks and lost some of my inhibitions, I'd have never ended up with Raif."

She grins. "Should I go back and try my luck?"

I remind myself she's eighteen and could drink or dance here as much as she wants. I lift a shoulder. "Up to you, but I'm hungry."

Her mouth twists to one side as she responds in her own offhand manner. "Me too. Maybe later."

We turn the next corner and stop to join a line for a small takeout window.

Rippa looks at the length of the line. "Good food?"

The aroma is enticing. Even from here. "Best bouillabaisse for blocks around."

I remember this place, Cara. The fish was so fresh you could imagine the smell of the gulf coming through the window.

She makes a face. "Fish parts? No thanks. Do they serve any other kind of fish?"

"Fish and chips with a side of deep-fried veggies. Also great and available for the wimp population."

I get the full-force eye roll, then someone in the street breaks into song, and we watch as he attracts a following of other singers and dancers. Soon we're at the front of the food line.

It smells even better this close. We order, pay, and head for our room at the hotel.

****

The hotel room card triggers the door lock, and it flashes green with a small snick. We're greeted immediately by celebratory noises that rise in intensity the farther we get in the room. Expected, since we're on the second floor, but they shouldn't be this loud. Part of the noises are coming from our balcony, the rest from a maximum-decibel party in the room next door. We put our food on the TV credenza, and I head for the balcony door that's ajar.

Two young guys are standing against the railing, hooting and throwing beads. A number of beer cans litter the floor.

"Hey, what's up?" I shout.

One of the revelers turns. "Hey, cute women. And I smell food."

I keep my voice raised. "Our room, our food. What are you doing on our balcony?"

He looks sheepish for about a nanosecond. "Oh, hey. I'm Kyle. We're overflow from the party next door. Hope you don't mind we commandeered your balcony. Got any beer?"

Rippa makes sure her laptop is in the desk where she left it. "Just flow on back to your own party. And no, we don't have any beer."

Kyle shakes his head. "Harsh." He taps the shoulder of the guy who's still throwing beads off the balcony and hooting at the top of his voice to the cheering crowd below.

"Come on, dude. We're being thrown out."

Dude turns a little too quickly and nearly trips over his own feet. "Hey, where did the girls come from? Is there a party in this room too?"

"No, stupid. It's their room, and they don't want company."

It's odd how people one rung up the evolutionary ladder from hominid feel entirely comfortable calling others stupid. Or maybe it's a guy thing.

I reach for the doors. Only eight or nine years older than the revelers, but I feel ancient and prissy. "I'm going to keep these locked. Please take your empties with you."

With the doors closed, it's a little quieter, but not much. Our shared wall is nearly vibrating. I turn to Rippa. "Want to see if there's anything left in the ice machine for our drinks?"

She nods and grabs the ice bucket but stops in front of the closed bathroom door, tipping her head toward it. "Didn't hear over the crowd noise, but the shower's running."

As I approach, the water stops, and an off-key male voice finishes the last line of "Desperado" by the Eagles.

Rippa laughs. "It's just one of the party guys. We can kick him out as soon as he's dressed."

A generous thought, but I'm not so inclined. The bed near the window has been slept in, and a duffel bag sits at the foot. I knock on the bathroom door.

A guy about twenty emerges towel-drying his hair with another towel riding low on his hips. He stops and faces us, grinning. "Busted."

He doesn't look dangerous or drunk and certainly has no visible weapons, but I don't instantly fall for his charm and good looks.

"Want to explain what you're doing in a room I paid for?"

Shower guy holds up his hands. "Sorry. I'll be glad to pay for the use. I came here with friends." He shrugs. "Actually, ex-friends. We had a room two doors down, and they hooked up with some girls yesterday. Long story short, while I was out giving them some space and taking in the sights, they partied too loud, and we lost the room. Don't know where they are, but my flight doesn't leave for four more days. The guys next door mentioned your empty balcony might be a safer place to crash than the street."

During his sad rendition, the noise of the party abates—someone in another room complained? Whatever the case, it's more tolerable.

The towel around our trespasser's hips draws my eye down. He is sporting a maroon and gold pitchfork tattoo rising from in front of his hipbone. He's also got a fine six-pack.

He puts one towel around his neck and hikes up the other before holding out a hand. "Miles Beckett."

I shake. "Julianne McCarren. This is my niece, Rippa Parkes."

His smile widens. "Rippa? That's a cool name."

Rippa holds out her hand for a shake. Her face is a shade of pale pink. "Thanks."

I refocus on the intruder. "About the break-in? The city provides services for stranded tourists. You only had to approach a cop."

"Yeah, probably. But with four days left, I'd already lost the money I put in on the room, and I wanted to stay where the action was. The guys next door offered their bathroom to sleep in, but somebody blew chunks all over it. I started out on your balcony last night, but it was too noisy and hard and got cold." He grins again. "Luckily, the deadbolt wasn't engaged on your balcony door, so I popped the lock. I'd blame housekeeping. Saved me, though. I hadn't slept in a couple of days, so it's all good."

Rippa is still focusing on the physical. "Nice tat. ASU Sun Devils?"

"Yeah." He nods. "Swim team captain."

That she knows a college sports logo so surprises me it throws me out of my mad for an instant, but I regain momentum. "Time out, Mr. Beckett. We can finish this after you get dressed. Then maybe you can explain how you lost all your room money but offered to pay for the use of ours."

His grin dims. "Oh, sure." He heads for the duffel, only to detour a few feet and scrape the fast-food wrappers and drink containers into the room's trash basket. Since there are multiples, it means the room's been used off and on for at least part of today. "Meant to clean up earlier" is directed to the wall. He then scoops up the duffel and takes long, graceful strides into the bathroom and closes the door.

"Goldilocks seems nice," Rippa says. To the same wall.

Good call on the name for the blond, but I'm not feeling charitable. "Hard to tell. Still trying to get past the ooze of charm."

She pins me with a frown. "He explained the situation."

I nod. "Yes. Very much in his favor and soft-peddling the breaking and entering of our room by blaming it on housekeeping. Nice."

My anger is out of proportion. Why? Then it hits me, and tears bank behind my eyelids. Oh, my God. The tall, lanky guy looks very much like the French teen who caused Raif's accident. The Grisons Canton Polizei brought him to our room. He stood there with the same entitled attitude, blaming the accident on "the clumsy American." The kid had been blasting music through earbuds and cut across Raif's path on a steep downhill run. Raif had to turn sharply at high speed and caught the edge of his ski on a lip of ice. The resulting fall broke his neck. Two witnesses placed the blame squarely on the teen. I learned later he had been prosecuted, and the least of his punishments was a lifetime ban from Swiss resorts.

He started crying when you just stood looking at him, Cara.

I turn for the room's door. "I'll be back in a few minutes. Please call the front desk and have them send up someone to make sure he's gone."

Rippa stares at me. "What's going on?"

"Just stay here, please. And make sure he leaves."

I am down the stairs, through the lobby, and out the hotel's front door in about a minute, dodging my way through the early merrymakers. Wow, the feeling linking our hotel room intruder to Raif's death really messed with my head. I take a deep breath. That memory was way closer to the surface than I thought possible after three-plus years. It's been a while since anything hit me that hard.

After four blocks, I turn and head back to the hotel. Guess I can chalk it up to a combination of dead bodies and New Orleans.

Back in the room, I find the bouillabaisse and Rippa are both cool. She cuts me a sideways glance. "He's gone. What was that running out of the room all about?"

"Bad memory playback. Sorry."

A look of compassion on someone so young it amazes me crosses her face. "Oh. Uncle Raif?"

I sit at the table and unpack my soup. "Yeah. Thanks for understanding."

Even cooled, the bouillabaisse is wonderful. Much more satisfying than the sweet cake bites that were served at the bridal shower.

We finish and get to what we came here for. Rippa lights up her high-speed laptop. "Go."

I start with the basics. "Let's talk about motive. The big ones are money, love, sex, and revenge."

She scrunches her nose. "We don't know that much about Mr. Renaud, but we can list things we do know so far."

"Money's a good one. I haven't seen the inside of the house, but you have. The house itself and the prime location in the Garden District are valuable."

She shrugs. "I didn't get far inside, but I saw lots of heavy, dark furniture. The house is probably full of that really antique-y stuff. And Clemmie was right about the library. I peeked over the crime tape and saw those weird stacks of books everywhere."

"Okay, still talking about money, what about inheritance? We don't know who or how many people are in line for the house or its contents. There could be second or third cousins somewhere who thought they were going to get everything, and suddenly the will is read, and Ames pops in from New York and takes over.

Might also tie in with the humiliation. 'How dare you come get what I thought was mine? After you're dead, I'll get my stuff back, and you'll be humiliated.' "

Rippa laughs. "That's a big leap. But you never know. Some of these southern families go back hundreds of years, and they're spread all over. We can't rule that out until we know more." She taps a few keys. "Note to self. Get on one of those ancestor sites and see if someone else is lurking behind his family tree."

"Good idea. What about business people who are always bumping each other off to take over a lucrative operation? Do we know what he did for a living?"

"Not a clue," she says. "But if he had time to do puzzles with Clemmie and wander around his back garden like Stella said, I doubt if he went to an office. Who knows? Maybe he worked remotely and had a job in New York."

I pace the small hotel room, which does nothing but burn a few calories off the meal I just ate. I hold up my finger. "Maybe. Thing is the fraud cases I work always come with a profile. Information to get me started. Here, there's nothing but surprise. 'Hey, my nice neighbor was murdered and his body put on display. What the heck?' "

I stop and turn. "We can speculate all night but won't have anything solid until we find out more. For all we know, it may not even be personal. He got in the way of a home invasion, and when he didn't have anything they wanted, their control got out of hand. The missing piece is the body switch. Unless whoever did it had the time and thought it would be funny."

Rippa shakes her head. "I think it was personal and it has to do with that creepy house he inherited. That's the story I'm sticking with."

She's a great sounding board, but I like to push a little. "How come?"

"Gotta put a pin in somewhere. If it had to do with his old life or other life in New York, it wouldn't have taken this long. Anybody wanting to do him in isn't going to sit around and wait for another body to pop up so they could kill him and trade him out."

"That makes sense, but you can't count on logic when it comes to murder. And his location and/or inheritance might have been new information for the murderer."

"So what's our next step?"

"I think Clemmie is our best bet and maybe Davison. Stella's not going to be much help, even though she was his neighbor. As Clemmie pointed out, Stella really had no interest there."

"Do you think we can stay out of the way of that Detective Fontenot?"

Good question. He acted like a by-the-book cop. "He'll have his hands full, and since we have access from our rental and information from Clemmie, we can at least put together some speculative scenarios for the NOPD. Then dangle those in front of him."

She is nodding enthusiastically.

We are in a hotel room in the center of an exciting city, but my niece is focused on a murder. I test her decision again. "Are you really sure you want to get involved? There's so much more to do here, and you've never been to New Orleans."

She tips her head. "I'm sure. Besides, how many times can you drink chicory coffee, eat beignets at Café Du Monde, and walk around Jackson Square? How about you?"

I laugh. "There's a lot more to do than that, but as far as drinking coffee and eating beignets every day, I can say, unequivocally, every day. Also, Clemmie wants to know why her friend was murdered."

She stands and busses our garbage. "Guess we can take some time to watch a parade or that other stuff you mentioned, but I want to stay involved because, well, according to Clemmie, he was a real nice man. He didn't deserve to die, and he certainly didn't deserve to have his body tied to a stake."

As good a reason as any.

Adding touristy items to our already scheduled pre-wedding activities means we will at least stay busy. "Let's skip to what we know about his social life."

"Huh?" Rippa says. "According to Clemmie, he didn't have one."

"Right. And since he didn't socialize, there might have been a reason."

She frowns. "Like what?"

"Like he didn't want people in his home or knowing his business."

She taps a note into her laptop. "Maybe he was hiding something."

"Yep. Clemmie mentioned there being only one thing that interested him in that house, but she didn't say what it was. Then again, Stella may have known something and not remembered it earlier since her focus seems to have relaxed considerably during the party."

"Yeah, she was pretty sloshed."

I nod. "Unfortunately, that's how she deals with stress, good or bad, these days."

"If we catch her first thing in the morning before

she starts dosing her coffee, she might be able to concentrate better."

"Worth trying. But Clemmie's our best bet. She'll know a little more about his personal life. It looks like a crime of opportunity. Not many murderers bring a weapon that punctures instead of a gun or knife."

"Hadn't thought of that. Could be the police technicians have found whatever was used, and Fontenot hasn't passed that on to us."

"This isn't his only case. Maybe the information just hasn't caught up to him."

She bobbles her eyebrows. "Here's another thing. Clemmie's cute for, I don't know, as old as she is. And Ames, from what everybody says, was only about ten years younger than her. You think there was some hanky-panky going on?"

I laugh. "Not a chance. She gave up a lot to be with Davison."

"Really? Like what?"

I cut my gaze left, then right. "Jilly used to tell me everything about her life. *All*, and I mean *all*, the family gossip. Anyway, according to Jilly, Clemmie's parents tried to raise her and Stella in the same old-fashioned southern mold they grew up in. Clemmie wasn't having it. She had an inheritance from her father's unmarried sister and took off. Her sophomore year in a northern college, she met Davison. The first thing they did, after he convinced her to marry him, was buy a house in the Garden District. They've restored it beautifully, but the parents never forgave her and, even though they lived only minutes away, never visited and remained cold when she came to visit Stella for family events."

Rippa pulls in her lips. "That is so sad and wrong."

"A little. But they had generations of ingrained beliefs and felt betrayed."

"So, in the last ten years, they passed away?"

I nod. "Within months of each other. They carried their ideals to the grave and left everything to Stella."

"That must have hurt."

"Clemmie's a strong woman, and she knows she's paid a heavy price for going her own way. If she hadn't, she wouldn't have Davison. They didn't approve of him."

She tilts her head. "Did Grams and Gramps approve of Raif?"

They were great in-laws, Cara.

I don't even have to think about it. "Yes. They're very different than Clemmie and Stella's parents. To them, whatever makes me and you and your mom happy makes them happy."

"That's nice that Clemmie has Davison. Too bad Stella wasn't lucky enough to find the same happiness. Or she did, and her husband died too soon. Is that where the drinking comes in?"

This surprises me. At Rippa's age I'd been too self-absorbed to notice Stella or Clemmie's personal relationships. "Really don't know. Part of it is probably boredom. She has this big old house that's been in the Farrol family for over a hundred-fifty years, and when she passes it to Jilly, it will be to a generation that may not honor the same traditions. It's pretty much all she has left. No clue, but I'm thinking she doesn't have much income for the maintenance on the house but would never think of selling it."

Rippa stands and peers out the balcony doors. "Sunset here is like watching a curtain drop. It's really weird. I know it's because they're nearer the equator, but so not what we're used to. Ready to get back and see what's happening?"

I nod. "I want to check in with Clemmie before we call it a night."

We double-check the balcony doors are locked and make our way outside, through the noise and music and what passes for dancing, toward the rental house.

Chapter Six

It's dark by the time we get to Stella's. Only one official car is left, and lights are on downstairs in the Renaud house. As we approach, Clemmie walks from there toward Stella's. She sees us and stops.

I step over and give her a hug. "Are you doing better?"

Of course she's not. She's lost a good friend in a horrible way, but her worn-around-the-edges smile is there.

"I'm glad you two are here. Can you come in for tea or something stronger?"

Rippa sucks in a breath. "Leftover punch?"

"Heck, no," says Clemmie. "Margaritas."

"I'm in," from Rippa.

Guess I'm in too.

We are about to head into Stella's when a woman hurries down the sidewalk from the Renaud house. "Excuse me. Is one of you Mrs. Ashurst?"

"I am," says Clemmie.

The woman nods and comes down the garden path to enter the pale glow of Stella's porch light. She is tall, very thin, and dressed in black. She is probably around thirty and pale, with black hair blunt cut about chin length. Some women can carry off this "I'm interesting and edgy" look. On this woman, however, it looks like she dares everyone to challenge her choices. She doesn't hide the fact that she is sizing up Clemmie, Rippa, and me. She points to the Renaud house. "The people in there told me the homeowner is deceased and it is a police matter. They also told me you had access. Is all that true?"

Clemmie nods. "The detective in charge gave me limited access until the end of the investigation. May I ask why you're interested?"

"Because the house must be secured before anything is taken."

Clemmie is shaking her head. "I don't understand what you have to do with Ames's property."

The woman's gaze slides to the house, and her chin tilts up in anger. "It's not really any of your business. Suffice it to say I am the new owner, and I insist the contents not be disturbed."

"You must be mistaken," says Clemmie. "This house hasn't been for sale and…"

"I didn't say I purchased it," snaps the woman. "If Ames Renaud is truly deceased, I am his rightful heir. This house and its contents are now mine."

Clemmie squares her shoulders, frowning. "That's not possible. I'm the executor of Ames's estate. When he asked me to be his personal representative, he never mentioned a daughter or niece or other relative."

Already I don't like this woman. No "Hello, my name is… I need your help." I hold out my hands. "Before we go any further, who are you, and how were you related to Mr. Renaud?"

She shoots me a look of exasperation and grips the sides of an expensive briefcase that she moved from her side and is now held in front, much like a shield. "My name is Sevryn Moffat. Ames Renaud was my father."

Clemmie is momentarily without words. "Ames told me he had no children and had never married."

For an instant, I think of those movies where the man leads a double life. Two personas, one family unknown to the other.

Ms. Moffat slips her hand in a side pocket of the briefcase and pulls out and shows us an everyday white envelope. "My mother passed away last week and left me this letter. It tells of meeting Ames Renaud at a gallery in New York. They spent the next few months together, then separated. She claims he didn't know about the pregnancy. She wanted a child and knew he didn't."

"And now you want all his stuff?" Rippa demands.

Apparently, I'm not alone in taking a dislike to this woman.

Clemmie and I both raise eyebrows at Rippa, but Ms. Moffat glares.

"I came to establish a relationship." She passes the glare to Clemmie. "Are you his latest? That's why he made you his personal representative?"

It's an extremely rude assumption, and Rippa mumbles a very unattractive name under her breath. The woman tries to stare her down. It doesn't work.

Also, Clemmie could take her. Twenty-five years older or not. And I'd be happy to hold her coat.

I lay my hand on Clemmie's arm and face the woman. "From what we are being told, Ames Renaud was a kind, generous man, but it seems as if you're less concerned about your father's death than what you might gain from it. You haven't asked how he died or why his home is being processed by police technicians. Just that you want the house and its contents."

We get the angry chin again. "I assumed it was a gas leak or unattended death. Perhaps falling down some stairs." Her expression sharpens. "As for the house, I'm a realtor in New York and represent high-end clients. In many instances relatives or neighbors decide it's acceptable to take a memento to which they aren't entitled. As I am the new owner in this case, I have the right to protect my property." She nods. "Including if it means fighting the will at hand."

"Your claim will be difficult to prove," I say. "Since Mr. Renaud was murdered and his body went to autopsy several hours ago."

The woman jerks her head, eyes wide as seen by the streetlight. "Murdered? How?"

She seems genuinely surprised. *Seems.*

"The coroner hasn't had time to finalize," says Rippa. "But that's what it's being called by the police."

"Clemmie, who is that person with you and Julianne and Rippa?" Stella is standing on the top step of her back porch in the weak light, leaning toward us and squinting. "If she's a gawker, send her away."

"A visitor. I'll tell you about it later," says Clemmie. She sighs, tilting her head toward us. "Stella's nervous about being in the house by herself. I'll go settle her. Julianne, would you and Rippa take Ms. Moffat to my house and tell Davison I'll be there in a few minutes?"

The woman watches Stella's retreating back, then turns to Clemmie, her father's murder evidently forgotten. "This is not your house?"

Clemmie shakes her head. "My sister's. I live just down the street. We can tell you what we know about the situation and who is in charge of the investigation.

54

Or…" She lifts a shoulder and pointedly looks toward the dark street, indicating the woman could also make the rest of us happy and leave. "Your choice."

The woman nods and pats her briefcase. "Your house would be fine. As the rightful heir of the Renaud house and its contents, I will need a starting place for legal action."

My turn to sigh. Maybe Ms. Moffat thinks if she says it often enough, it'll come true.

Clemmie's shoulders sag as she heads toward Stella's. Generous of her to offer her home to meet. Considering the woman's prickly personality, I'd suggest a coffee shop.

As we head down the sidewalk, I ask Ms. Moffat, "So your intent was to connect with your father?"

She gives no immediate response. Either she's thinking over my question or coming up with an excuse. Hard to tell.

"Yes. Until I read my mother's letter, I was told all my life he'd been killed in a car accident."

"When did you arrive in New Orleans?" I ask.

"Last ni—" the woman starts. "This morning."

Thinks pretty fast on her feet, although she didn't ask if we knew the time of the murder. And where has she been all day? "Drive down?"

She stops and glances back at a low-slung car, its bright yellow evident even for the time of day, parked near the front of the Renaud house. "No. I've spent most of the day in this wretched town trying to find decent accommodations. I was not successful."

"Nice ride," says Rippa. "Fun to drive?"

The woman turns to Rippa, then her gaze bounces to me. "Are the two of you almost finished with your clumsy attempt to interrogate me?"

Could be she's tired and disappointed about not finding "decent accommodations," but imperious snapping is more likely her SOP.

"Just conversation," I say. "But you have to admit showing up soon after the murder of a man you claim was your long-lost father and demanding to take possession of his home and its contents is pretty convenient."

A quick intake of breath from Rippa, but a surprise response from Ms. Moffat. I expect her to try and set me on fire with a laser gaze, but after thinning her lips, she likely thinks better of it.

"I had no emotional attachment to Ames Renaud, and as you tell me he was a nice man, I'm sorry he was murdered. I was raised in the poorest of neighborhoods in New York by a single mother. I have learned from that, and as a realtor, to be quick where a desirable property is concerned. I believe I have a valid claim."

Much nicer, but I don't think Ms. Moffat is done, by a long shot. I give what I hope is a genuine smile. "I'm sure all documents will be taken into consideration."

No response from Ms. Moffat, but I see by the faux gas streetlamps that Rippa's eyebrow is close to piercing her hairline, and I try not to laugh.

We arrive at Clemmie and Davison's and walk up the steps. I knock on the door, and Davison answers with a smile. "Julianne, Rippa, and…"

"Clemmie sent us," I say, nodding toward the New Yorker. "This is Ms. Moffat. We have some things to discuss regarding Mr. Renaud's bequests. Clemmie said you wouldn't mind if we came here rather than standing outside Stella's house."

"Of course," he says, holding out his hand to Ms. Moffat. "I'm Davison Ashurst, Clemmie's husband. Come in."

Hopefully, introducing Davison lays to rest Ms. Moffat's nasty crack about Clemmie being Ames's "latest," but so far, this short introduction to her personality says no.

Ms. Moffat shakes his hand, and we walk into the house. Rippa stops at the entry to the formal parlor.

Davison and Clemmie have traveled extensively and accumulated some very exotic pieces that look to be Moroccan and other colorful pieces from Asia. Colors of gold, black, and dark teal with accents of cherry red dominate the room. A brilliant Oriental rug graces shining wood floors, and some beautiful silk throws hang casually off the backs of chairs. I think of it as a kind of high-end boho and a far cry from most Garden District interiors.

Rippa's mouth drops open. "I love this."

"Thank you. Make yourselves comfortable," says Davison. "May I get anyone something to drink?"

"No, thank you," I say, the earlier offer of margaritas put on hold.

Rippa declines too.

"Do you have any sparkling water?" asks Ms. Moffat.

Davison nods before starting down the hall to the kitchen. "Yes, plain or flavored?"

Ms. Moffat follows him. "May I choose?"

They return, and her calculating glance travels the room while she sips. "The homes in this area are all old?"

She's in for disappointment if she thinks she'll inherit a house like this. "Yes, some in better shape than others."

"The better ones come up for sale rarely," says Davison. "Clemmie and I have done an extensive restoration on this one."

The woman's glance falls on a pot Clemmie bought in Peru. "I see you do a lot of traveling."

Davison follows her gaze. "Not so much anymore, but we still have a few places we'd like to see."

"She says she's inheriting Mr. Renaud's house and stuff," says Rippa.

Davison starts, and he looks more closely at the woman. "Were you a friend of Ames's?"

Ms. Moffat props her briefcase on her lap. "Never met him. I just recently learned he was my natural father."

The sound of the heavy front door opening interrupts, and Clemmie steps into the room.

"How's Stella doing?" Rippa asks.

"More stress than she can handle," Clemmie says. "She took something to help her sleep."

Davison walks to his wife and gives her a quick hug. "Do I understand correctly? The Renaud estate inheritance is under question?"

"I don't think there's a real danger of the original will being overturned," says Clemmie. Then Ms. Moffat is the recipient of a weary smile. "It's sad Ames didn't know he was a father. I think he might have embraced the idea."

I don't think a cuddly father is what Ms. Moffat had in mind. I get a real kick out of southern manners that can be sharp and deadly when wielded by a person like Clemmie who was born and raised in a community like New Orleans.

The woman's nostrils flare. "Clearly my father has been under some controlling duress."

Don't even think about trusting this one, Cara.

Yeah. We're on the same page there.

Clemmie's eyes crinkle, but she shakes her head. "You're wasting your time and money."

The woman sets down her glass. "I'll get the details about the investigation myself. May I freshen up before I go?"

"First door on your left, upstairs," says Davison.

A minute after Ms. Moffat leaves the room, Rippa whispers, "She is not gonna go quietly."

"Ames asked me to do this, and I'm going to see it gets done right," says Clemmie.

"Speaking of quiet." I look up the stairs. "Give me a minute."

When Clemmie and Davison gutted and remodeled this house, they fixed the squeaky stair treads, but I tiptoe anyway, and when I reach the hall, a small flash of light flares in Clemmie's puzzle room. I step to the door. Ms. Moffat is taking a picture of something on the wall with her cellphone.

I cross my arms and block the doorway. "Payback for Clemmie and Davison's hospitality?"

Chapter Seven

Ms. Moffat shows very little embarrassment at having been caught invading her hosts' privacy. She points to the wall by the door, her chin jutting. "See for yourself. People are already stealing things that are rightfully mine. I was taking pictures as evidence."

I stay in the doorway, safe in the knowledge Clemmie would not have anything that did not belong to her. "Not an excuse for snooping. And your claim on the house or its contents is far from proven." I flap my hand in a backward shooing motion, and surprisingly, Ms. Moffat obliges. I tip my head in to see a very yellowed document with hand-inked boundaries and drawing of a house. In the center, in extremely old script, it says *Renaud Land Grant*. "Clemmie and Stella are like family, and as such, I'm telling you to leave. Downstairs. Now." I step back.

She is either firm in her belief she's discovered thievery of her possessions-to-be or, like any ambitious salesperson, is lying with alacrity. My vote lands on option two.

"What's going on up there?" Clemmie calls as we head downstairs.

Ms. Moffat, who is ahead of me, jumps right in with a justification when we reach the living room. "Your décor is so lovely I peeked in your office. There, on the wall, was a very old property description.

Imagine my surprise when it turned out to belong to my father."

Rippa, arms akimbo, frowns. "That's just rude and snoopy."

Sadness at what the day has revealed is etched on Clemmie's face. But southern grit straightens her shoulders. "Not that I owe you an explanation. However, that document used to hang in Ames's hallway, by the library. I admired it a few months ago, and he gave it to me. As I have the original, I had a copy made for him and framed to replace it."

Ms. Moffat's gaze circles the room, possibly searching for an ally. She finds none. "I meant no harm. Old land and property deeds and grants interest me." Still no supporters, so she continues, "The real estate business is cutthroat. It's full of realtors who, given the chance, would walk over your cold, dead body to take a listing. I pride myself at not being taken advantage of."

I meant no harm. A non-apology from someone who has treated Clemmie and her home disrespectfully. Nobody in the room looks sorry for her, and Ms. Moffat's comments put her smack in the ranks of the insensitive as Clemmie winces at the words "cold, dead body."

Ms. Moffat crosses the room, addressing Clemmie on her way. "Thank you for your hospitality. I, or my attorney, will be contacting you. As my father's personal representative, for the time being, please see to it nothing is removed from the house until this legal matter has been concluded."

Apparently, the discussion we came for, the investigation of her father's murder, no longer interests her. She is shown to the door by Davison who returns to the living room.

"Do you want to hire an attorney?" he asks his wife.

"I think we might have to. First, though, I'm going to notify Ames's inheritors and arrange a meeting to see what they think about all of this."

"The realtor seemed very sure of herself," Davison says. "Do you know the date of the will you're holding?"

Clemmie shrugs. "I never checked, but she's only talked about a letter from her mother. Doesn't seem like that would hold much water against a legal document like a will."

"Speaking of which," I say. "Does anyone else think it odd Ms. Moffat didn't ask to see it?"

Rippa nods. "I think that's the least of the questions we're going to have about her. Jules and I started a high-level list about what happened to Mr. Renaud. Didn't get very far seeing as we don't really know anything about him."

Clemmie's color is starting to return to normal. "That's good. We can spend more time on it with what I know after I retrieve Ames's papers."

She looks exhausted, but before I get the chance to excuse Rippa and myself, curiosity gets the better of my niece.

"Do you know who the beneficiaries are?" she asks.

Clemmie shakes her head. "Ames told me it would be explained in his will and journals."

Rippa groans. "Not another mystery in a safety deposit box."

I turn to Davison and Clemmie. "Something that

happened in New York last year involving a missing inheritance."

Before that can be explored, Rippa skips ahead. "Do you think there's anything in the house that might help?"

"I've only been on the first floor," Clemmie muses. "I doubt Ames or his uncle used much more than that, outside of a bedroom." A frown mars her forehead. "He did make a strange request, now that I think of it. He asked me to promise to do a thorough inventory of the house before turning it over to the beneficiary. He said it was specified in the will."

"I'd forgotten," says Davison. "That's a big responsibility. Maybe we should hire professionals. There has to be decades of accumulated *stuff*. Knowing both Ames and his uncle, I would question if it's ever been gone through."

Clemmie puts her arm around her husband's waist. "I promised *I* would do it. I'll have time since Ms. Moffat seems bent on starting a legal challenge."

Rippa starts to quiver. "Jules and I want to help. Can we?"

"That would be great," Clemmie says, holding up a hand. "As long as your help, and my commitment to Ames, don't interfere with Jilly's wedding functions."

Rippa pauses only fractionally. "Forgot about those. Okay. We'll have to replace the clothes Fontenot took, but otherwise our time is yours."

Where it's been a long day for all involved, and I'm personally ready to let my energy reserves drain, the same circumstances seem to have given Rippa an energy boost. Hence, signing me up without asking. Which also trades any sightseeing or Mardi Gras celebrating for spending the next several days in a hot, dirty house.

I pull Rippa toward the door. "Since she's high already, we'll pass on the earlier offer of margaritas. When do you plan to start? Tomorrow?"

Clemmie nods, a hint of a smile on her mouth. "Hopefully. According to the last crime-scene investigator I spoke to a short while ago, the house should be released in the morning. I'll leave a voicemail for the detective, requesting permission. We'll need keys to get in anyway."

"I've got it," Rippa says in triumph. "I'll order a dress online and have it shipped overnight. Problem solved."

Clemmie walks us to the door. "Davison and I are early risers. I'll get some basic inventory sheets put together in the morning and call you when I get the keys. Unless you'd like to have breakfast with us?"

"Very generous," I say. "But Rippa is going to have at least one beignet and New Orleans coffee at Café Du Monde. It's one of my favorite spots, and although it's open round the clock, it gets crowded early, so we'll pass on your offer and wait for your call."

Outside, Rippa is still soaring. "This trip is turning out so great. I mean it's sad about Clemmie's good friend and all, but digging into the mystery is crazy interesting."

Guess I have to face it. Her interest and skill levels are real, most likely my fault, and expanding since this is at least the second time she's talked about investigating the murder.

We walk down the block toward our rental, and as

we pass Ames's house, a flicker of light inside draws my attention. It's not stationary.

Rippa stops, pointing. "Did you see that? Somebody with a light is in there. Let's go find out who it is."

I turn what I hope is a look of disbelief on her. "Really? The occupant was murdered within the last twenty-four hours, and now someone is creeping around inside. No. I'm calling the police."

Rippa purses her lips. "You don't think it's one of the investigative team who might have forgotten something?"

"Nope. Why wouldn't they turn on the interior lights?"

I take Rippa's arm and pull her toward the shadows bordering Stella's yard and away from the light cast by the streetlights. When the call center answers, I give my information and the address. "Yes. We'll stay here. No, we won't go in or interfere with anyone coming out."

"How about this?" Rippa whispers, nodding toward the Renaud house. "I'll watch the front and wait for the police. You can see the back door from behind that flowering hedge. I can see you from here."

It's full dark, and Stella's garden forms a natural border with her neighbor's. "Smarter than going inside with or without a flashlight."

The light is now flickering on and off. I'm wondering if it isn't our new acquaintance from New York.

Rippa asks, "Do you think it's that creepy Ms. Moffat?"

"I have no idea, but since the house was locked, it looks like a break-in. Okay, do not move from next to this tree and wait for the police. I'll go where I can see the back door."

This is not as easy as it sounds. If whoever is in the house glances out the window while I am sneaking behind Stella's hedge, I could be in trouble.

This is poking the bear, Cara.

Raif's right. McCarren's Rules outline McCarren responses to dicey situations. *Don't hang out with bears. If you come across one, don't poke the bear. If a bear pokes you, outthink it.*

I guess trying to discover who's in the Renaud house crosses a safety line, but it also falls under the category of investigating, which Rippa and I promised to do, and she is watching out for me.

The person inside is not being very careful. When I reach my spot, I'm close enough to hear the faint scrape of small furniture being bumped or drawers being opened, although I can't see anyone.

A patrol car comes quietly to the curb, and I'm about to step clear when the back door of the Renaud house opens, and a tall figure dressed in dark clothing slips out, vaults the banister, and runs the length of the back garden, disappearing through the hedges.

"Jules," Rippa says in a stage whisper, "they want to talk to you."

I make my way to the sidewalk. "He's gone."

"The person you thought you saw inside?" a tall officer asks.

"I didn't actually see anyone until he left. Just a penlight or cellphone light moving around."

A smirk overtakes his official "I'm dealing with the public" face. "Maybe the power is out, and it was the homeowner."

Rippa smirks right back. "That would be interesting since the owner lived alone and his murdered body was found this afternoon. Detective Fontenot has been assigned the case. Oh, and the house was locked when the crime-scene investigators left a short while ago."

Immediate posture improvement comes over both officers. "How long ago did you see this person leave, and are you sure it was a he?" the senior of the two asks.

"About two minutes ago," I say. "He slipped out the back door, vaulted the banister, and sprinted down the garden. He's long gone. And he didn't run like a female."

In-Charge Guy turns to his partner. "Check out the back door while I get some information." Genuine interest colors his tone. "Do you ladies have identification?"

We produce our IDs, and his eyebrows rise at our address in Washington State. "Here for Mardi Gras?" He looks at the Renaud house. "What's the connection?"

The partner returns. "Back-door glass broken inward, and size of footprints heading out of the garden indicates male."

I recite the reason for our presence and gloss over our involvement. I hesitate but give him Clemmie's contact information. Although the intruder probably won't be back, she and Davison need to know, and the door needs fixing.

The cop gives us back our IDs and takes down our hotel and Sandoval house addresses. "Thank you for calling. We'll make sure Detective Fontenot gets the information. And the house will be secured until it's determined who has interim responsibility."

Rippa and I head toward our rental.

She casts a glance at the cops talking. "So, if it was a guy, it couldn't have been Ms. Moffat. That and she wouldn't have had the time to change, break in, and wander around before we saw the light."

"*And* we assumed she came alone."

Chapter Eight

Rippa stops walking. "Omigosh. That's true. She could've been snooping around Clemmie's while her partner was scoping out the house."

"More likely, it was the murderer who came back looking for something."

"Probably not evidence. I overheard those crime-scene guys say there wasn't much inside or out. It looked like the victim didn't even put up a fight."

Makes me glad I never met Ames Renaud. I wouldn't have to associate the dead body with a living person. "Sad, but it sounds like someone thought he had something they wanted, and he couldn't or wouldn't tell them how to get it, and it all went wrong."

"That makes sense. Like Stella said, Mr. Renaud didn't even like it here. His allergies made him miserable and—how did she put it? He was waiting for some event, then he would sell the house and move back to New York. Maybe other people knew about it too."

"Had to be a very profitable event. If he sold the house and contents alone, and I'm counting the antiques inside, he'd make a tidy chunk of change."

She rubs the side of her nose, her thinking mode. "But he never left the house, according to Stella. At least rarely. So that must have had something to do with it."

"Yeah. It keeps coming back to the house."

****

Café Du Monde is crowded, but there are two empty tables, and we lay claim to one. Rippa orders her coffee au lait and mine black. The chicory is a new taste for her, and I laugh at the face she makes. We're served three beignets each. They are crisp and hot, and the powdered sugar makes little puffs with each bite.

A lot of damp napkins to clean up, and Rippa slumps in her chair. "Those rank right up there on my list of nommie pastries. Thanks for insisting we stop."

More people are waiting for a table, so we stand and walk across Decatur to Jackson Square. It's relatively quiet since the only time loud noise doesn't punch the silence is now, when revelers squeeze in a few hours of sleep in a desperate attempt to get a rested run at the new day. Still lots of people around for eight o'clock in the morning, though. Some of whom look like they've been up all night.

People work too hard at having fun, Cara.

That they do.

We wander the perimeter of the square, peek inside St. Louis Cathedral, which is stunning, and agree to disagree on the talent of one of the sidewalk artists. We are about to head toward the Garden District when we're approached by a slender girl with gold, green, and purple ribbons woven into her hair.

"Read your palm? I'm very good."

Rippa shakes her head, but I'm determined to give her another city experience.

"Come on. My treat and I'll go first."

The girl smiles and takes my offered hand. Her smile wanes, and her eyes cast down. "I'm sorry for your loss, even though the bond continues."

Um, she really is good. Rippa makes a small gasp.

The girl restores her gaze. "You have amazing strength of will and a power to find things others can't always see." She smiles again. "Although you don't use this gift nearly often enough, you're getting better."

I've always thought the same thing, Cara. This girl is authentic.

The rest of my reading is boilerplate, and when Rippa takes a turn, she is told she will be successful in an upcoming romance.

"That settles it," she says. "Right after we solve this murder, I'm looking for a boyfriend."

The girl blinks at this but happily takes her money and walks toward another tourist.

I laugh. "Luckily, that reading reduces the pressure."

Not to be put off, because she's only asked once this morning, Rippa heads unerringly toward the streetcar that arrives in the Garden District. "Let's go check in with Stella. See how she's doing."

"Subtle. Are you really that eager to work in a hot, dirty house sorting through who knows what all day? The weather is beautiful. Makes me want to take in the waterfront."

A sound between a heavy sigh and a low growl accompanies her eye roll. "Might be some really cool old stuff, yeeeesss."

****

As we approach her house, Stella stands by her back steps talking to three tall, dark-haired twenty-somethings. Two guys and a girl. I start to comment when I realize Rippa has stopped walking and is in full

71

gawk mode.

"Who's that?" she asks.

"Which one?" I know Rippa's facial expressions, but when she turns to me, eyes wide, this is one I've never seen. Never mind the ASU swim god. The girl is smitten.

"The gorgeous guy standing next to that girl."

"Go see, if you're that interested."

She draws her gaze back to Stella and the three others. "Okay, I will."

I tag along to see how Rippa is going to insert herself into the conversation.

She walks up to Stella and says, "Hi."

Simple as that. Stella, with her ingrained southern manners, immediately takes pains to introduce us. She nods toward the boy Rippa has her laser sights on. "This is Étienne Chappelle. Samuel trained him to take over my garden chores."

Étienne turns full face toward us, and I have to admit he's classically handsome. Reminds me of a trip I took with Raif to Florence where we saw the recently restored Michelangelo's *David*. Étienne is tall with dark, curly hair in need of a trim, chiseled features, and a nice, lean, muscular body. As if some poor milquetoast of a guy unwillingly donated his share of maleness so the young gardener would be blessed with extra. I can see why Rippa is keyed up.

I don't feel as generous. His outgoing vibe is one of posing. Of cocky assurance that he is the center of interest.

Stella tips her head. "This other young man is his cousin, Aldo Chappelle."

Aldo is not so lucky. He is also tall and dark with

curly hair, but his facial features are hard, with a large nose that looks to have been broken and badly mended at some point.

Before Stella moves on to the girl, Aldo speaks. "I was sorry to hear about Mr. Guillory. He was a friend and a fine man."

Her expression softens. "Thank you, Aldo. Samuel was almost a member of my family."

She faces us, a graceful hand toward the pretty girl. "This young lady is Honor deGrandpre, Samuel's goddaughter." Her head tips to indicate us. "This is Rippa Parkes, a member of Jilly's wedding party. And her aunt, Julianne McCarren, a long-time friend of Jilly's and also a member of the wedding party."

With her concentration on Étienne, Rippa doesn't pay much attention to the stunning Honor deGrandpre standing beside him. She reminds me of the Cuban-American singer, Camila Cabello. Slender and graceful, with shining dark hair piled on her head, she exudes confidence. Étienne's occasional glance in her direction contains his heart. Not sure if he is aware, but his cousin risks an occasional wistful glance at the beautiful girl too. My gaze bounces back to Étienne, and his stare has morphed into something different than heart. It's want. Which is disconcerting.

Stella's gaze returns to the handsome boy. Her cheeks flush. "Étienne is here to work in the garden. I completely forgot he was due today."

"Oh, your gardener," says Rippa. "That's fascinating."

"Pleased to meet you," he says with a smooth, slightly French accent. "I hope you enjoy your stay in our charming city." He takes Rippa's hand and leans over it, not quite kissing the backs of her fingers. I swear I see an involuntary shiver from Rippa. We receive nods and smiles from the other two.

Rippa giggle-sighs. "We're here to help with an inventory of Mr. Renaud's house. Did Stella tell you what happened?"

A frown mars Étienne's forehead for an instant, and he reaches for the girl's hand. "Yes. My poor Honor. Samuel meant a lot to her. And the police haven't notified Mrs. Neely that it's okay to work in her garden. I was hoping to get in a few hours today."

The girl pulls her hand back and faces Stella. "My godfather spoke often of your kindness. Will you let me know if you hear he's being released? We need to make arrangements."

"Of course, dear."

Étienne frowns at the girl but tips his head toward Stella. "Aldo was going to help me sort the tools that need attention. Is that okay?"

Stella nods, her glance taking in the garden. "I'm afraid with all the people trampling through, it will need some extra help."

A sharpened purpose reshapes Étienne's face as he brings his attention back to Rippa and smiles. "I have a lot of interest in early southern and pre-Civil-War-Era architecture. Do you think Mrs. Ashurst would mind if I got a tour of the house?"

I get the feeling Rippa would hand over the keys without question, so I jump in. "I'm sorry. Mrs. Ashurst has already had to deny access to others interested in viewing the contents. She made it very clear that during the inventory only she and helpers would be allowed in the house."

Rippa passes me a quick, squinty-eyed look, as if she doesn't approve my barring handsome guys from the house, then lifts a shoulder and nods to Étienne. "Maybe in a couple of days. When will you be back?"

Étienne's smile falters for an instant, then blooms again at Stella. "When I return to work in Mrs. Neely's garden." He steps off the path to pull a leaf off a bush. "This goldflame honeysuckle needs culling and pruning or you may lose it."

Plant knowledge aside, I'm left wondering how this guy knows Clemmie is the one who has say over access to Ames Renaud's house.

Rippa has no such reservations. "I can ask Clemmie if it's okay for you to go through the house sooner."

"That's very kind of you," says Étienne.

My cellphone rings. It's Clemmie.

Rippa cants her head toward me. "Wait, Étienne. If you have a few minutes, you can ask Mrs. Ashurst. She's on her way."

His smile is disarming as he tips his head toward the back of the garden. "Aldo can't stay long. I have to take him to work. I'll get your number from Mrs. Neely and call you soon."

He throws another smile over his shoulder as he walks away. It's aimed at Honor, but Rippa is standing in the line of sight, and a peek tells me she thinks it's for her. Wow.

I also find it interesting that this is his chance to ask Clemmie directly and he chooses to leave.

Clanging bells sound nearby, and Honor glances at the streetcar coming through the Garden District. "I have a class this morning, Mrs. Neely, so I have to go.

Again, thank you for calling. Let us know when you hear about Samuel."

As Honor hurries away, I turn my attention to Stella. Gray shadows color the soft skin under her eyes, and she looks ready to fold.

"Are you okay?" I ask.

"Tired," she says. "I was already nervous after the events of yesterday afternoon. Then when the police knocked on my door asking if I saw anyone entering Ames's house, I…" She shakes her head. "I just don't do well by myself."

"Since Jilly's gone, you have a lot of room. Have you considered a renter? Maybe a retiree with your same interests?"

Her eyes light for an instant. "I've considered the option, and it may come to that. Jilly was paying me a monthly amount to help with household expenses. That has stopped, of course. And I don't have The Colonel to keep me company."

She turns toward her back steps as Clemmie approaches. She looks as wrung out as Stella but busses her sister's cheek. "Why don't you have a lie down?"

Stella nods. "I will. After I have some refreshment."

Refreshments before nine in the morning. Sad comment for a woman who's nearing the end of her tether.

A frown mars Rippa's forehead. "Stella had a military officer living here? Did he die?"

I grin. "Yes, he died. About a year and a half ago. No, he wasn't an officer. He was an ancient beagle. And he loved chicken."

The light bulb goes on over Rippa's head. "Got it.

Oh, that's so sad."

I nod at Clemmie. "Is there anything Rippa and I can do to help with your or Stella's commitments for the wedding? We're feeling guilty that all we have to do is get dressed and attend functions. You two and Jilly have done all the work."

She sighs. "Stella got the southern charm, and I got the linear thinking. However, we both got spine. So I'll keep your offer in mind. Right now, help with the inventory is what I need most."

"I vote for the thinker every time," Rippa says quietly, and Clemmie smiles.

"Thank you for reporting the light in Ames's house last night. Detective Fontenot called me. I asked if I could have the locks changed and offered to get an extra key for police access. He said yes." She looks at the house behind us. "I'm going to have the locksmith change Stella's locks too. For her peace of mind. He'll be by later this morning. Oh, and the crime-scene tape is still up across the library door. The detective wants a last inspection before releasing it. Otherwise, we're free to inventory the rest of the house. He's contacted the patrol unit at the house, and we'll be allowed in."

Clemmie's carrying a canvas bag and three clipboards. She hands Rippa and me each a clipboard. "I want to make sure any valuable antiques are logged. They seem to be the most likely objects thieves would be interested in. I also plan to get Ames's will and both his and his uncle's journals out of the safety deposit box and find out why he thought them interesting enough to lock away until his death."

Still facing the Renaud house, Clemmie lifts a shoulder. "A question about what you saw last night.

Could it have been that rude, infuriating Moffat woman?"

"Different body type," I say. "More than likely a tall, slender male."

And until a minute ago, two tall, slender males stood right here.

"Speaking of whom, do you know Étienne Chappelle?" Rippa asks Clemmie.

Zero to sixty without a car. Right to Rippa's new favorite topic.

A smile flickers across Clemmie's mouth. "The young man taking Samuel's place as Stella's gardener?"

"Yes. Isn't he nice?"

I'm getting eye strain from curbing an eye roll. Rippa is usually a great judge of people.

Maybe she's right, Cara.

Going with my gut on this one. Have to disagree. And this is new territory for my niece and me. I get the feeling she's not afraid of logic as a weapon in my battle to convince her Étienne is not a good choice for a crush. Even a temporary one.

"I've only spoken to him a couple of times," Clemmie says. "But he seems nice."

Rippa looks over Clemmie's shoulder. "He's interested in old, southern, even pre-Civil-War architecture and would like to get a tour of Mr. Renaud's house. Would that be okay?"

Clemmie shakes her head. "Sorry, dear. Not for at least another three or four days. We need to finish the inventory, then I have to go through Ames's papers. I don't even know yet if there's a family burial plot or when they'll release his remains." Her voice dips on the word *remains*, and her shoulders curve inward. Then she straightens. "And at the very least, find out if that New York woman has any legal rights to Ames's estate. Until all that's done, I don't feel comfortable having strangers in the house."

Rippa's expression shrinks. "He's not exactly a stranger. I mean Stella said Samuel recommended him and trained him, so it's like he's almost family or something."

Clemmie pulls in her lips and shrugs. "Stella may know him better, but I don't. I'm going to have to insist nobody but the people I allow, and you two, be let into the house. It's just too new and too strange right now. Please understand."

Rippa nods and plays with the edges of the sheets on her clipboard. "Okay."

Clemmie changes her attention to her papers. "I divided off sections of the house. Old Mr. Renaud, Ames's uncle, never got around to making a full inventory, but I found a list of the furniture, accessory pieces, and artwork he had covered by insurance policy riders at one time." She shows us a piece of yellowed paper with spidery handwriting. "You'll find copies with your paperwork. I also have access to his safety deposit box in case of emergency." Her mouth wobbles. "Guess his death qualifies."

Rippa pats her arm.

"I'd also like to have pictures to accompany our inventory," Clemmie continues. "As there weren't any to go with the last one."

"Are cellphone cameras okay?" I ask. "Ours take pretty good shots."

"Of course," says Clemmie. "That's what I'm

going to use. As long as the descriptions match, they should be more than enough."

"We can forward them to you at the end of each shift. Where would you like us to start?"

"Upstairs?" Clemmie says. "I'm more familiar with the first floor."

"Sounds good," I say as Rippa and I follow her around back of the Renaud house.

A young policeman is standing guard. He gives Rippa a smiling appraisal before addressing Clemmie. "Are you Mrs. Ashurst?"

Clemmie nods.

"Detective Fontenot has the results of the break-in investigation, ma'am. He says we can release the property to you, and if you have any problems, call right away."

"Thank you," Clemmie says.

He gives a two-finger touch to the brim of his hat, directed right at Rippa. "Ladies."

An overt effort to get her attention, and Rippa's non-committal smile and polite shoulder shift indicates no interest.

We walk through the back door and sidestep broken glass on the floor.

"I'll sweep that up," Clemmie says. "Davison is going to fix the broken door window later today, and I don't want him or the locksmith to step on it." She holds out the canvas bag. "Brought some bottled water and protein bars for breaks."

We're standing in a very dated kitchen. Just clean enough to avoid old food smells. "Thanks," I say and look around. "Which way?"

Clemmie blinks. "Oh. Through the kitchen and

down the hallway past the library. There's a small, demi-lune table near the foot of the stairs."

I turn to Rippa. "I'll start in the front bedroom if you'll start in back. If either of us needs help moving furniture, we give a shout."

"Done," says Rippa as we walk toward the hall. "I also might need help identifying what's valuable and what's not. I have no idea what a demi-lune table is."

"Shaped like a half moon," I say as we pass a dark, cavernous, formal dining room. "And I seriously doubt if there are any reproductions in here."

Rippa points to an antique push-button light switch near the foot of the stairs. "What's this?"

"Light switch. There are still lots of them in older homes and European hotels."

She presses the top button, and several brass sconces illuminate the stairs and a chandelier at the upstairs landing. "Cool."

We walk up the stairs that end at a four-bedroom configuration. Two large in front and two smaller in back. Rippa walks to the back, and I hear, "Wow."

I follow her voice and poke my head in. "What?"

"The quilt on this bed is amazing." She slaps it in the middle, and a cloud of dust billows. She looks around. "All of this stuff should have been covered by dustcloths or stored. Cleaned up, this quilt alone is probably worth a lot of money."

I step in and look closely at the starburst in the center as I wave at the dust hanging in the still air. "I agree. Put it on the list."

She writes, then pulls out her cellphone and takes a picture, then points a thumb over her shoulder. "I peeked into the other bedroom back here. Door's open.

It's smaller and looks like the one Clemmie's friend occupied. It's not super clean but habitable."

Glad we agreed to do the upstairs. Clemmie won't have to face going through Ames's things. We can just box them up.

I return to one of the front bedrooms and walk into a wall of stuff. Decades and decades' worth of furniture, curios, old linen chests, and lots of boxes. I huff a breath. This is going to take some time to get through. Old Mr. Renaud had hoarding down to a science. This side of the house was a bad choice on my part. At least the beds are visible in the rooms Rippa has.

About an hour and a half into working, I've forged a path to the window. The room is now minus eight boxes of book club selections—*no first editions*—and magazines taken downstairs for transport to a recycle station. I've also overcome a stuck window sash, and from the sound of the squeak when it slides up, it's the older kind with a rope and pulley inside.

Hoping to ease the stickiness of my sweaty T-shirt, I raise the window for fresh air, fresh being a relative term. It's hot and dirty inside and humid outside. It also smells like rain. Living on the wet side of the mountains in the state of Washington, I know that smell. Even though the window stuck, it now won't stay open. I search for something to hold it up and find an old picture frame. I fit it in and begin to turn when I see the locksmith van has pulled up. Clemmie is standing, talking to the driver as I watch through bubbled wavy glass that's made a circus-mirror reflection of the scene.

I hear a muffled yell from Rippa. "Hey. Stop that."

I hurry into the hall. Rippa is almost to the bottom of the stairs.

When I reach the first floor, she has hands on her hips, head forward in attitude, confronting Sevryn Moffat.

"I saw you take that," Rippa says. "None of this belongs to you. Put it back."

Ms. Moffat does not like being caught. Her chin comes up in defense. "I'm taking a sample piece to have authenticated."

"That's what this inventory is for," Rippa replies.

I know thievery when I see it. "What's this about?"

Rippa tips her head at the realtor. "She put something in her bag."

Clemmie has approached, a frown in place. "As I said last night, you will not be allowed in this house until the terms of the will, which includes a full inventory, are met. Now, replace whatever you took and leave, or I'll call the police."

I pull out my cellphone. "I'll be glad to call Detective Fontenot."

We get a look meant to bulldoze us, but the southerner with spine and two hot and dirty Parkes women are not about to give an inch.

"This treatment will be documented for my attorney," Ms. Moffat huffs.

"Go be ridiculous somewhere else," Rippa snaps and holds out her hand.

And good luck finding a law office that's open during Mardi Gras.

Ms. Moffat pulls her tote closer. It's not the same bag she had last night.

"The inventory for this floor hasn't been completed

yet," Clemmie says. "Besides which, if your claim prevails, you'll want an accurate accounting."

Ms. Moffat pulls her lips in, opens the tote, and takes out a small English porcelain of a shepherd and lamb and puts it on the table, not into Rippa's hand, then starts to turn.

"There are two empty spaces in the dust," I say.

She clutches her arm tighter against the tote. "Then it must be something that was taken by the crowd of people from the police that were here yesterday."

"Nope," I say. "They wouldn't risk their job over a knickknack." I echo Rippa's demand. "Put it back."

Damn. Ms. Moffat should give up real estate and go into cryogenics. Narrowed gray eyes pin us with a stare that could freeze flesh.

She reluctantly retrieves a small, exquisite, sterling-silver horse, blackened with oxidation, places it beside the porcelain, then walks stiffly toward the kitchen. Ten seconds later the back door closes with more force than necessary.

Chapter Nine

"Do you think that's all she tried to steal?" Rippa asks.

My niece has no monetary or personal interest in the house's contents, but her moral compass swings true. She is indignant.

"Unless she took something from the kitchen on her way to the hall, she didn't have enough time," Clemmie says. "I've been gone less than five minutes."

"Average time to burgle a house is less than ten," Rippa says, and Clemmie's chin drops.

"Time, and not for lack of trying." I point toward the dark dining room. "The corner of the breakfront inside the doorway has been slid forward, and one of the doors is ajar."

"First the space in the dust, now a door ajar," Clemmie says. "You're very observant, but how do you know it wasn't already that way?"

I lift a shoulder. "There was enough light from the kitchen on our way in to see the breakfront resembled one my grandmother brought from Sweden. When I came down for water a half hour ago, I turned on the light and went in. They are very similar, but the Renaud piece is chock-full of china. Before Rippa caught her, Ms. Moffat probably only took the time to look for a maker's mark on the china and see if there was one visible on the back of the breakfront. Gotta say, if she's strong enough to scoot that forward and most of the way back"—I point to fresh scuff marks on the hardwood floor—"I wouldn't want to tangle with her one-on-one."

"She was either real lucky or peeked in the back door to see if anyone was in the kitchen," Rippa says. "Sneaky."

"Think I'll call Mack," I say. "Ask him a favor. We need to know more about Ms. Moffat, and he has considerable background resources."

At Clemmie's questioning look, Rippa supplies an answer. "Macklin Pierce is the head of security for McCarren Multinational. He helped us investigate Jules's stolen necklace in New York last June. She went back in September to go to a fancy event with him, which is crazy because he's really cute for his age and smart too. I think they should meet more often. You know, in the middle, like Chicago."

Clemmie blinks, her hands clasped in front of her. "I did hear some of that from Jilly. Right now, I need all the help I can get. I don't understand what's going on. First, Ames's death, then that very unpleasant woman, a break-in last night, and now she's back."

Rippa giggles and gives Clemmie a quick hug. "I love the way you said, 'very unpleasant woman.' You make it sound like she's selling something door-to-door and won't leave."

Clemmie laughs. "Can't help it. Sugarcoated upbringing." She looks over her shoulder. "We're going in the right direction, though. In addition to new locks, the locksmith is going to put a piece of thick, clear plastic over the glass once Davison fixes the window." She glances at her watch and nods. "Which should be any minute. He just texted me. If you'll excuse me, I'll check the locksmith's progress on the front door. It's starting to rain."

As soon as Clemmie is out of earshot, I turn to Rippa. "Are you okay? Granted, Ms. Moffat is obnoxious, but 'go be ridiculous somewhere else' doesn't sound like you."

Her gaze bumps over my left shoulder. "Made me mad. Nice people like Étienne aren't allowed inside, and now because of her, Clemmie won't be as willing to let him in."

Wow, again. I tip my head. "The house has been here for around a century and a half, and Clemmie has a legal responsibility to protect the contents as best she can. Why this house and why now? There are other houses in the Garden District where tours are given. How about Stella's? I'm sure she'd show him around. The floor plan is very similar."

She brightens. "That's a great idea. I'll ask Stella later." She wags her index finger. "Wait. How about the Sandoval place? We'd be with him the whole time. I bet he'd like the carved banister and the hand-painted wallpaper. It's been kept up nice. Lots of original details."

"Slow down. We're in the same position as Clemmie. Responsible for the condition and contents of the house as long as we occupy it. The rental agreement specifically states no parties or other guests."

"He wouldn't be like a guest," she blurts, her eyes earnest. "Just a ten-minute walk-through." Blue eyes the exact shade as mine don't look away this time. "Why are you being so negative about this? It was your idea."

"Why are *you* willing to bend the rules for this guy after exchanging a dozen words?"

If stubborn had a poster girl, Rippa's face would be on it. Her finger rubs the side of her nose. "I don't know, okay? You're always saying I'm a good judge of character. Well, I saw a few things I judged as good. He was respectful of Stella and what she was going through. He pointed out her flowering bush needed attention, and he wanted to make sure his cousin got to work on time."

I sigh. Not mentioning that if he came to work, how did he plan to give his cousin a ride right now? And why was he wearing nice clothes and expensive, soft leather shoes to work in a muddy garden? I can be stubborn too. "Sorry, I can't agree, and no, on the Sandoval house."

She and I almost never argue, and I don't want a confrontation, but the set of her jaw is hard to miss. I haven't won anything.

We climb the stairs in silence, but the patter of the rain gets louder at the top.

"Damn." I hurry into the room I've been working in. Rain is blowing through the open window. I close it and survey the floor. It's not too bad, then I see water is still coming in around the window frame. It's warped. The floor's grain is swollen in places, and the floorboards are cupped at the edges. With the rainy weather here, it's only going to get worse. I need to tell Clemmie about this.

We work for another couple of hours and make a good dent in the upstairs bedroom labyrinths until Clemmie calls us downstairs.

She holds out a shiny key. "The new locks are on.

Here's a spare for you two since I may not be able to be here while you're helping. Which I really appreciate, by the way." She grins, smearing a black smudge on her forehead with the back of her wrist. "How much longer do you think it will take to finish the second floor?"

I huff a breath. "At least another day or day and a half for me. If Rippa finishes the smaller back bedrooms, I can use her help up front."

Rippa speaks to a space over Clemmie's shoulder. "Sounds good. Can we lock up and clean up and go find some lunch?"

"I was just about to suggest lunch at my house," says Clemmie. "Davison is an expert at making po boy sandwiches."

"Make mine a half. I never could finish one of those."

Clemmie did not exaggerate about Davison's deft hand at making po boy sandwiches. We sit at their table an hour later, Davison, Clemmie, and I, unable to move.

Rippa is finishing hers. She frowns at the remnants of crusty bread and bits of roast beef on her plate. "Why do they call them po boys? I don't think anybody poor could afford these sandwiches."

"Not meant for poor people," Clemmie says. "The little boys who used to hawk them in the street were poor, so the sandwiches got the nickname."

Davison smiles. "I didn't know that."

She winks at her husband. "Stick with me, Mr. Ashurst, and you'll learn something." She looks at her watch. "Later than I thought. I just have time to clean up and retrieve Ames's will and journals from his safety deposit box."

She nods at Rippa and me. "Do the two of you

have any plans for this afternoon?"

Rippa shifts a shoulder and pats her flat stomach. "I'm all for going back and working on the inventory, for a while at least. Gotta work off these calories."

"Okay with me," I say.

Clemmie blinks, her eyes getting misty. "When we're done, I'll hire a cleaning service. I'm not sure what to do with his personal things. Guess I'll have to keep them until that Moffat woman's claim is settled." She shrugs. "I don't know if he's made arrangements for burial or cremation. I don't know the contents of the will and haven't opened the journals. Ames asked me not to until…"

Davison reaches for her hand.

"I don't know much of anything, do I?" she asks.

"You'll pull it off," Davison says. "You always do."

"I think Ames picked just the right person to take care of his wishes," I add. "And before I forget, you might want to have the eaves over the window in the large front bedroom checked for a leak. The window frame is warped, and rain coming in has started to leave water stains, damaged floorboards, and possibly mold. I know that's not good news, but the sooner the better."

Clemmie smiles and stands. "I'll add that in. Thank you both. In any case, Julianne, it would be wonderful if you and Rippa could work on the inventory just until I get back from the bank. I'd like to share the will and journals with you and get your opinions if anything comes to light."

"Like the paperwork might give clues to why he was murdered?" asks Rippa.

I cringe at the effect her blunt question might have

on Clemmie.

Rippa's gaze drops. "Oh, sorry."

"Being his personal representative, I'm going to have to get used to hearing the word," Clemmie responds with a faint smile.

Good place to change the subject. "Let us bring dinner afterward," I say. "Any takeout you and Davison prefer?"

She smiles. "That would be great. We're partial to gulf shrimp in just about anything."

Fresh fish abounds in Western Washington, but the prawns found there have nothing on gulf shrimp. Nothing like it anywhere. I rub my hands together. "Suits me to the ground."

Rippa bounces up. My bounce comes with a twitch in my lower back. Hours spent on my laptop digging up the dirt on the fraudsters I chase has me regretting my almost total lack of exercise. *Note to self. Get off your butt occasionally.*

We leave Clemmie's to return to the Renaud house, and I stretch my spine as we walk.

Rippa looks over her shoulder. "What if Detective Fontenot said it was okay?"

I clamp my teeth. Étienne again? I want the old Rippa back. The levelheaded, intuitive, smart girl. "Sure," I say, knowing full well, as should Rippa, what his answer will be. "Give it a try."

Squinty-eyed suspicion precedes "I will." She walks a few yards, then stops, challenge taking the place of suspicion in her eyes. "Didn't you tell me you knew right away Uncle Raif was right for you?"

She has me there. Almost the exact words I used when we had long healing talks after his death. Rippa was only fourteen but instinctively let me talk it out. "You're telling me," I say gently, "you felt an overwhelming connection to Étienne when you were introduced?"

She waffles for a second, then her chin comes up. "I don't know if that's exactly what happened, but there was definitely something there."

"What about *him*?"

Her index fingers wave back and forth. "You mean do I think he was interested in me too?" She shakes her head, then continues to walk. "Not yet. He did say he'd call me, though."

He did, but only because he wanted in the Renaud house and saw Rippa as a way to get in. I still want to know why and why now? I don't bring up the tall male running from the Renaud house after breaking in, but my instincts tell me it's possibly related.

My heart goes out to her, but I would really like to deflect her interest in Étienne. "You've never heard the whole story of how Raif and I met. Maybe it's time I told you."

She lifts a shoulder, not meeting my gaze. "Okay, I guess."

"First of all, you're eighteen, and I was twenty-two, just graduated from college."

"What does that have to do with my meeting Étienne?"

"As a sort of comparison. I'm telling you where I was in that point of my life."

"Oh."

We reach Renaud's back porch, and as it's a shade cooler here, I sit on an old wood slider and pat the seat beside me. "I blame Jilly. She talked me into coming down for Mardi Gras to celebrate our graduation. We had a place to stay of course. And Hugh was here. Medical school is torturous, but he managed to squeeze out an evening."

She sits and gives a small smile. "Big draw for her." She tilts her head. "Where was Uncle Raif?"

"He'd just finished a two-month stint assisting a project engineer on a McCarren oil rig in the Gulf."

"No kidding. I never knew he had a job."

I laugh. "Of course. Did you think we traveled all over the world for grins?"

A soft chuckle ripples in my head. *At fourteen that's probably what I would've thought too, Cara.*

"The oil rig was a McCarren Multinational investment," I say. "Your uncle was one of their top troubleshooters."

One eyebrow crests. "So he picked you up?"

That exact moment comes into my head, and I smile. "Figuratively and literally. Jilly, Hugh, and I were in the French Quarter at Pat Obrien's, a famous bar that claimed to have invented the hurricane, when I realized halfway through my second one that the table we were sitting at and the floor wouldn't stay parallel. I tapped Jilly on the shoulder and shouted I was going outside for some air."

Rippa shakes her head. "What do you mean, a hurricane in a bar?"

"Not a weather front. It's a sweet cocktail made with several kinds of rum. Very potent. The effects can sneak up on you."

"Several?"

I sigh. "Jilly either nodded that she'd heard or was keeping time with the music. I managed to work my way outside, but people were packed even thicker out there because a parade had just finished. But I was upright, and that counted, so I slid across the front to get away from the crowded entrance.

"A shout went up, and I was crushed against the building. It took me a few seconds to figure out I was face-to-face with a big guy who made the connection that I was alone. I tried to slide back to the bar entrance when the movement of the crowd slackened, and I felt my purse being slipped off my shoulder. I squeaked something in protest, but the street noise swallowed it. I grabbed the strap and held on for a couple of feet."

"You were being mugged?" asks Rippa, wide-eyed.

I nod. "Guess he figured in all the commotion he could fade into the crowd. I had other ideas. Even through the brain fog of one and a half hurricanes, I was determined to keep my purse. It had all my money and my ID in it." I shrug. "Not very smart. I should've left most of my cash back at Stella's."

She stares, arms akimbo. "That rum must have temporarily lowered your IQ."

"Not my proudest moment. He jerked so hard I fell, the strap wrapped around my wrist."

"You could have been trampled."

I hold up my hand, palm out. "I remember screaming and getting accidently kicked by a couple of people. My wrist and arm hurt like crazy. Suddenly the dragging stopped. I still had my purse and was trying to get on my feet when a strong hand helped me up."

She is grinning. "Uncle Raif."

My grin matches hers. "I thought at first it was Hugh, but I'd never seen this guy before. He half-carried me to the side of the nearest building and, using his arms, caged me in against everyone shoving past. Neither of us moved. He kept turning his face away when he talked, then he apologized for his beer breath."

"He was drunk?"

"I don't think so. As a matter of fact, I'm pretty sure he hadn't had that much to drink. Anyway, I started giggling like a maniac and realized I was about to upchuck, so I sipped breaths to calm my stomach and looked up into a handsome, exotic face with deep brown eyes. I remember blinking, trying to keep him in focus."

"What happened to the guy who was trying to take your purse?"

"I asked that too. Your uncle Raif told me he left him lying down the street a ways. He seemed unconcerned. Then he wanted to know if he could get me some water. I told him that would be great. My head throbbed, and my arm and shoulder were scraped up under my long-sleeved T."

Rippa has uncrossed her arms. "Sounds like you were a hot mess."

"When I got a chance to look in a mirror later, I really was."

"What happened next?"

" 'My name's Raif McCarren,' he says. 'Stay right here for a minute, okay?'

"He's a total stranger who has rescued me, and I have no idea why, but when he asks me to stay there, I don't move. Maybe it was the promise of water."

She is still grinning and nodding. "Why didn't you just go inside with him and find Jilly?"

"The only answer I can give is I felt safe. He kept

his word and came back in about a minute with a beer mug full of water."

"What?" she shrieks. "Are you kidding me? You drank something a total stranger handed you? It could have had GHB in it."

"That did occur to me. But I figured Jilly and Hugh were only a few steps away. If I started to feel any woozier, I would have gone back into the bar. I drank it."

She is saying nothing and shaking her head.

"I felt better, and the crazy thing was he brought a handful of napkins to dip in the water and wipe the dirt off. He told me about coming into town with friends. They were about to enter a nearby bistro when he heard my shouts and saw what was going on.

"I thanked him for helping me and asked if he didn't want to go find his friends. That I could go back in and find mine. I was okay now. He just grinned and said I was better company."

"So?"

"After we talked for a while, he asked if I would like to go someplace quiet. I said yes."

Rippa's mouth gapes. "Were you out of your mind?"

I shake my head again and shrug. "It was one of those things where you just know it's okay to throw caution to the winds. He took my hand and led me back into the bar where I introduced him to Jilly and Hugh. Raif took out his driver's license and handed it to her. He wrote down his cellphone number and told them he was taking me someplace quiet.

"Jilly took one look at him and nodded. 'If my friend is ever sorry she went with you, I will hunt you down and hurt you bad.'

"He agreed to that, then asked if he could stand on their table. Jilly was laughing out loud, and the others at the table scooted back. Raif stood on it, took out a wad of money, and started yelling. He wanted to know if anybody had a hotel room they'd let him have that still had at least two nights left on the reservation. The room had to be nice, and he'd give two thousand dollars for it.

"Jilly started clapping, as did the rest of the people in the bar, when three college girls said they had one and would take the money. The hotel was close by, so Raif and I walked over with the girls, and true to their word we made the exchange with the desk clerk, who made a little extra cash by accepting the exchange and skipping over the waiting list.

"Thinking he was a worker on an oil rig, I told him to stop spending his money, and he shook his head and said, 'No, I got this.' We followed the girls to the room and stood out in the hall while they staggered around giggling and getting their stuff. That's when it hit me what was about to happen."

Rippa's leaning forward. "I would've gotten very nervous the second he mentioned hotel room."

"Oddly enough, my mind didn't go there."

You got me from the very start, Cara.

"How come?"

I peer into the dark, hoping for words that will make her understand. "Hurricanes notwithstanding, there was a pull, a connection. I don't know. It's hard to explain."

She brightens. "Love at first sight. I get it."

Okay, this isn't the direction I wanted this

revelation to go. "Um, what do you mean you get it? The love part came somewhat later for Raif and me. Help me understand how you think my meeting him is the same as your introduction to Étienne."

She rolls her eyes. "Except for the hotel room and the sex, there was a link."

My eyebrows hike. "What do you think happened that night?"

She looks over my left shoulder. "A hookup?"

Still don't want to go there, but I started it. "Let me just say Raif understood my state of mind. While we waited for housekeeping to clean up after the three girls, we sat at the little table and talked. The hotel was completely full, so we waited for nearly an hour. In that time, we learned a lot about each other, and I got a lot more sober."

She claps. "What happened after the housekeeping people left?"

My face warms. Raif never shared about that part of our life, and neither have I. "We had the room for more than one night. We spent the first one talking, laughing, and sleeping in each other's arms. The rest of our time together is personal."

Laughter echoes in my head. *You remember, Cara.*

Rippa's eyes go wide. "Oh. Sounds like he was the perfect man."

"Nope. Neither of us was perfect. We had some very loud, um, *discussions.*"

One side of her mouth hikes up. "Glad to hear it."

Chapter Ten

I stand, pushing at the kink in my lower back, then use our new key to let us in the back door and head for the stairs. Rippa slows, pulling back the corner of one of the boxes I've carried down. "What're in all these?"

"Paperback and cheap book-club editions. Headed for a charity bin."

"All the way to the bottom?" She lifts the flaps and slides the books on top aside. "Anything good to read?"

"I didn't check. The boxes were shallow and contained books. Help yourself."

She lifts out *Les Misérables*. "This title was an option in my junior-year Lit class. I chose something else because it seemed too long at the time." She pulls out a piece of red yarn stuck between two pages. "Weird bookmark."

I walk to the doorway of the library and lean over the tape. "Wait a minute. Come look at this."

The stack of books on one side of the reading chair looks normal. The stack on the other side has red yarn bookmarks.

Rippa peers in. "I get it. The red yarn means he checked the book and didn't find what he was looking for." She turns her head toward the front of the house. "Hold on." And runs up the stairs. She reappears in less than a minute carrying a vintage tapestry bag with wood handles. "Boy, the Renaud men really didn't throw anything away." She opens the bag to reveal a half-dozen balls of red yarn and some knitting needles.

"Who did this belong to?" I ask.

"I don't know. I found it in the closet of the bedroom with that pretty quilt. Maybe when he finished going through a number of books in the library, Renaud carried them upstairs and put them in boxes."

"Guess we'll never know what the intent was. Possibly to get them out of the library or store them until he could take them all to a used-book seller."

She closes the box and draws the back of her hand across her forehead. "I saw a fan in the library we could use in the upstairs hall, but we're not supposed to go past that tape."

It's not really hot, but the humidity gets old fast. It's almost another inescapable presence. Especially as we're used to the cooler temperatures of the Pacific Northwest. I sigh. "There are a couple of floor fans we can bring over from the rental to push the air around. Another hour and Clemmie should be back from the bank with the documents."

I tip my head toward the door. "Let's bring in the fans. When we're done, we can leave the upstairs windows cracked open and lock everything downstairs. It'll be much nicer in here tomorrow."

She gives a hop of excitement. "I've never seen a real will. And reading decades-old journals should be interesting too. Maybe we'll even get a clue about what he was looking for in the books." She lowers her voice. "Or maybe why he was murdered."

Raif chuckles. *You can always tell where her head is, Cara.*

Right. A mystery. Dead bodies and centuries-old

secrets. Have to admit the excitement factor is a lot higher for Rippa than going back to class next week. "There's an old scratched-up table in the hall upstairs. We can put one fan facing the big bedroom and one at the entrance to the formal dining room for Clemmie."

Twenty minutes later we're attacking the rest of the boxes upstairs. Most of which contained books. Same mix of cheap and nicer editions with the red yarn markers. We carry a dozen more loads downstairs.

As we're rinsing the dust off our hands in the kitchen, Stella walks in with a tray and four crystal glasses of tea. She looks around at the well-worn cabinets and appliances. "So sad. This used to be much better maintained when old Mr. Renaud first moved in." She glances down the hall past a faded, and probably dirty, Aubusson runner. "He had a cleaning service and hosted monthly Garden District meetings in the formal parlor."

Rippa nods and plops down, grabbing an energy bar from the table. "Sounds nice. Thank you for the tea. We can use it to wash these down."

Stella swings her gaze back to the kitchen and sits, adding a smile. "You're welcome, dear. Clemmie stopped in to say she's dropping off Mr. Renaud's papers at her house, and she'll be here shortly."

I look at the carefully arranged tray, complete with linen napkins, a porcelain sugar bowl, and a silver spoon. Except for holidays when Mother used to bring out the silver and china, I haven't used cutlery and porcelain this pretty since Raif and I attended McCarren functions. "This is thoughtful and lovely, Stella. How are things going for you? Can we help with tomorrow night's post-rehearsal cocktail party?"

She shakes her head. "All taken care of but thank you for the offer."

Clemmie walks in and sits next to her sister. "Julianne, Rippa, and I are going through the will and the Renaud journals this evening. Would you like to join us?"

Stella stands. "No, thank you, dear. I'm just going to relax. Stop by to say goodnight?"

"Of course," says Clemmie.

Her sister walks out the back door, and a man engages her in conversation.

Rippa rocks her chair back to peer across the kitchen. "Sounds like Detective Fontenot." She's proved right when he enters.

"Good afternoon."

"Good afternoon," we chorus.

"I'm glad to see you," he says, pulling a photo from a manila folder and speaking to Clemmie. "Since there's very little evidence to investigate regarding Mr. Renaud's death, I was hoping the ring Ms. Parkes pointed out at the site would be familiar to you."

She looks at the picture and shakes her head. "I don't recognize it. Why would I?"

"It looks like a man's signet pinky ring," Rippa says, craning her neck to see the photo.

"Exactly," Fontenot responds. "It could also fit a ring finger of a woman. The simple design of vines on either side and the letter S in the middle hasn't been available for decades. We were hoping you'd seen Mr. Renaud wearing it since his middle name was Sheridan."

Clemmie shakes her head again. "Ames didn't wear any jewelry, not even a watch."

Fontenot picks up the photo. "Since the ring was small, the S also might have stood for Stella, but Mrs. Neely says no. Unless one of you has a better idea, it looks as if the owner was one of the perpetrators or someone who came into the garden to see Mr. Guillory's body."

I hold up a finger. "This is a long shot, but speaking of him, could the ring have belonged to Samuel?"

"We can check with the company who *installed* him, but I doubt if they would have left the body in public with a gold ring on it," Fontenot says.

"If the ring is small, it probably wouldn't have been worn by Samuel in any case," Clemmie volunteers. "He had large, work-calloused hands."

The detective shrugs. "Which brings us back to an unknown. Had to check into it, but about what I expected."

Rippa turns her attention to Clemmie. "As long as we're tackling mysteries, there's a dark square on the wallpaper outside the library. Do you know what was hanging there?"

Clemmie stands. "Show me."

We follow Rippa into the hallway. She points to about a fifteen-inch dark square surrounded by faded wallpaper.

Clemmie tilts her head. "Yes. Ames was very proud of it. It was a copy of the land grant to the Renaud family when the New Orleans territory passed from the Spanish to the French. There was a family mystery attached to it." She turns around. "It's odd that it's missing." She points in the direction of her house. "Ames gave me the original."

"Wait," says Fontenot. "What kind of mystery?"

Clemmie lifts a shoulder. "Something to do with Renaud family history. That's all I know."

"And now there's a mysterious death," says Rippa. She points into the library. "That empty frame on the floor next to the chair looks like the one that might have fit."

"Could be important," I say, "considering the stacks of books and the copy of the land grant were the only things disturbed that we know of so far."

Clemmie folds her arms. "Not really. Detective, Ames told me he kept his most recent journals in plastic in his freezer compartment. Since we're going over his and his uncle's journals and family papers, I looked in the freezer, and the plastic bag is there but no journal. Do the case notes show it was taken by the crime-scene people as evidence or something?"

Fontenot skims the notes in his folder. "The empty frame is noted and the missing, um, weapon. Nothing else. You think it was stolen during the home invasion?"

She leads us back into the kitchen, steps to the small, over-a-decade-old refrigerator, and opens the freezer. The three of us gather to take a look. Sure enough, an empty plastic zipper bag with gouges in the ice surrounding it is the only thing there.

Detective Fontenot nods as he scribbles in his notebook. "I'll put it down as a missing item. Do you know what it looked like?"

"No idea," Clemmie says. "If the ones in the bank all look the same, I imagine the missing one does too. I'll let you know." She closes the freezer door.

He puts away his notebook, and his gaze

encompasses the three of us. "Thanks anyway for honoring the crime-scene tape. You'd be surprised at the number of people who walk right through it. Especially considering that's where Renaud was killed."

Clemmie turns and walks quickly down the hall.

"Nice job," Rippa accuses. "You knew Clemmie and Mr. Renaud were good friends."

"Oh," he says, watching her exit. "Forgot that."

Rippa tips her head toward the hallway. "Well, I think you owe her an apology for being insensitive. Now would be good."

Fontenot folds his lips, turns, and walks after Clemmie.

For all that Detective Fontenot is dealing with right now, multiple murder cases, extreme-embalmed bodies, and the insanity that is Mardi Gras, taking the time to apologize to the victim's neighbor puts him in the nice-guy category.

"We only saw a trickle of blood on the side of his head," Rippa says, walking back to the library. "I wonder what they found to convince them it happened in the library." Her gaze moves to the doorway. "It doesn't look like much of a struggle took place, and there's not any blood you can see from here."

I peer inside. She's right. No light was turned on, but this side of the house gets enough afternoon sun that the room looks almost normal. Did the murderer tidy up? Or did the blood just drip inside the chair?

The detective and Clemmie return to the hallway. Clemmie looks pale but straightens her shoulders.

"You're sure this is the site?" I ask.

He nods, picking up the manila folder. "I looked

over the team's reports before I came. I'm sure."

Rippa arches an eyebrow. "If the room's been processed, how come it's still got crime-scene tape across the door?"

"He didn't get a chance to see it yesterday," I say. "Wants to take a look for himself."

Fontenot cuts his gaze across the three of us again. "That okay with you ladies?"

Rippa nods, then tips her head toward the doorway. "When's the tape coming down?"

Fontenot spans his forehead with index finger and thumb, then sighs. "When I verify everything in these reports and photos. Make sure there are no holes. You don't even live here. Why are you so interested?"

"They want to help," Clemmie says. "They have experience, and…" Her voice falters. "And Ames didn't deserve what happened to him. I want closure. For him. Besides, as executor of his estate, I have to inventory everything in the house, and they're pitching in here too."

Fontenot huffs. "I can assure you we're putting the same amount of energy and resources into this investigation as any murder in this jurisdiction."

"Then why haven't the people closest to him been completely interviewed yet?" asks Clemmie.

The detective's eyebrows underline the furrows on his forehead. "I understood there were no relatives, no children, or spouses. I know you were his friend," he says to Clemmie. "Are you saying you have information that may help the investigation?"

"I'm saying I might know the reason he was killed," she responds.

Fontenot shows no exasperation, just curiosity.

"Why are you just sharing this now?"

"Because, in the shock and sheer disbelief of yesterday, I wasn't thinking straight. Wasn't thinking I might know why this terrible thing happened to my friend."

"And what about that creepy Ms. Moffat's claim that she was Mr. Renaud's long-lost daughter?" Rippa asks.

The detective shakes his head. "Room verification can wait. Time for a quiet talk. Can you ladies have a seat?"

Chapter Eleven

Fontenot's interrogation style, if yesterday was any indication, is fairly laid-back. Then again, we aren't murder suspects. And I'm beginning to think a lot of smarts are camouflaged by that drab brown suit.

I learn one more thing about the detective. He has manners. As we return to the kitchen table, he starts pulling out chairs.

"Thank you," I say.

Clemmie slides into hers as if she's used to this courtesy, but each generation becomes a little more relaxed in the niceties.

A real gentleman, observes Raif.

Rippa does a double take as Fontenot seats Clemmie and me, then reaches for the back of her chair.

He doesn't comment on her surprise but pulls out his own and sits, retrieving his tablet and mechanical pencil. "Okay, ladies, it looks as if NOPD needs all the help we can get on this one." He pauses and cuts his gaze from Rippa to me and back. "Aboveboard and without putting anyone in danger. Let's start with you, Mrs. Ashurst. You say you might know a motive for the murder. Please be as specific as possible."

Clemmie clasps her hands on the table. "Ames was a very private person and not easy to get to know. Being raised in a family with strong ties, I stayed with Stella as much as possible after her husband

Harlan passed away. Gardening is a passion of hers, and we spent a lot of time outside with Samuel. After a while, Stella became frustrated with the inattention paid to Ames's garden. As his next-door neighbor and board member of the Garden District Association, Stella was affronted that a homeowner here neglected his duty, his allergies notwithstanding." She shrugs. "I saw someone who I thought of as lonely, and I was determined to bring him out of his shell, if only a little bit."

Fontenot sits quietly, head bent, taking notes. He shows no signs of interrupting or wanting Clemmie to speed up. I imagine this is part training but mostly upbringing.

She smiles. "Some of the gardens here have incorporated small plots of vegetables. I began offering him some from my garden last summer. After a while, Ames invited me in. He wasn't the tidiest bachelor, but I think he began to look forward to my visits. At one point, after the prime vegetable season was coming to an end, I mentioned my jigsaw puzzle hobby. Ames brightened and said he loved puzzles and was working on a big one that involved a secret in his house."

"The house itself? Like a secret passageway?" Fontenot asks.

"Not that," Clemmie responds. "Ames said the house was supposed to contain a several-hundred-year-old treasure left here by a famous person. Maybe in the library."

I choose my words carefully. "That seems to be the center of all the activity."

Rippa clutches the edge of the table. "Who's the famous person?"

"He had no idea," Clemmie says. "This was a well-to-do area of New Orleans, and it could have been anyone from Lafayette to George Washington."

Rippa slumps. "You mean like a letter from George to Martha saying, 'I'm staying here at the Renaud house in New Orleans, and it's very nice.' "

Fontenot says, "I suppose that could be worth several thousand dollars, but I don't think it would be considered a treasure."

Clemmie nods. "Ames and I had a few discussions about what the term treasure would have meant. His belief was it started as word of mouth over a hundred years ago. And maybe further back than that. As far as he could tell, his great-great-grandfather was the first to record the, um, myth or legend or whatever you want to call it. Ames said he, Ames, had made a list of possibilities and how he'd gone about looking."

Fontenot leans toward her. "Like what? Did you see this list?"

I chuckle. Fontenot's eagerness to learn about the treasure nearly matches Rippa's.

Clemmie shakes her head. "I never saw a list. He mostly talked about books. He thought there was a book that contained clues."

"A book that old should be easy to find," I say.

"Exactly what I said to Ames." She sighs. "And that's where the treasure theory got confusing. He claimed the only words the theory contained consistently over time were treasure, book, and Renaud house."

"Still sounds like not a lot of books to go through," says Rippa.

Clemmie smiles. "According to Ames, his great-great-grandfather Renaud was also paranoid. He traveled back and forth to England for his import business. He brought back crates and crates of really old books for the library. His intention being he was the only one who knew which books were in the library when he inherited. He could peruse them for clues at his leisure since someone after the Renaud treasure wouldn't know which were the originals."

"Crazy like a fox," says Rippa. "But he never found it?"

"Not that was ever recorded. According to Ames, he was in his office on the docks when a steamer came in carrying victims of the 1918 Spanish flu pandemic. He died ten days later, leaving two sons and a wife who was bitter at his spending so much family money on old books. She locked the library, which included his diaries. No one since has found the key to the so-called *treasure*."

"Freaking cool," says Rippa.

It is, but I'm not feeling the same infatuation. "Could be an urban myth built onto over the years. With clues added to fit the story."

Clemmie flattens her hands on the tabletop. "I thought so too, but Ames told me his uncle, who restarted the search, believed the family history and wrote that he pulled out all the books published in Europe, first. His housekeeper must have given him a ball of yarn to cut up and use as markers."

The detective looks around the kitchen. "This has all happened here, in New Orleans. Do you know what he did for a living in New York?"

"He told me he was a self-employed accountant and kept the books for several small companies. He worked at home, and it didn't take up much of his time."

The detective shrugs. "That matches the information we found on his laptop. We confirmed with his clients, and they all said he did good work and they were sorry to hear about his death."

That answers the question Rippa and I came up with at the hotel.

Neither Clemmie nor I have mentioned the documents she picked up from Ames's safety deposit box today. Rippa, too, is closemouthed. I think the mystery has gotten her imagination, and she wants to take a crack at it before telling what we know.

Fontenot glances at each of us in turn. Don't think he's completely buying our looks of innocence. His gaze returns to Clemmie. "You said as executor of Mr. Renaud's estate, you had to complete an inventory of the house. Is his will here?"

Clemmie skates the edge of the truth. "Ames kept a safety deposit box. For the will and other family papers."

The detective is scribbling in his notebook again and doesn't look up. "If it isn't in the house, how do you know you're still the executor?"

Clemmie tilts her head. "He had no one else."

Fontenot slides into his next innocent question. "Do you expect to inherit everything, then?"

Really good question and from the widening of Clemmie's eyes, one I don't think has occurred to her.

She blinks. "Not at all. Ames told me everything would go to someone who had no idea they would inherit. And until I read the will, I won't know who that is."

"It couldn't be that creepy woman who claims

she's his daughter," says Rippa.

Fontenot's gaze jerks up. "That Ms. Moffat mentioned earlier?"

"She showed up after you left and while the scene was still being processed," I say. "Introduced herself as Sevryn Moffat, a realtor from New York. Very prickly personality. Got rude with Clemmie and laid claim to the property and its contents. She said her mother gave her a letter on her deathbed naming Ames Renaud as her natural father. When I told her it was convenient for her to arrive at the scene of her father's recent murder, she did seem to be genuinely surprised at how he died."

"Wait. Did she show anyone the letter? Or say how she found him?"

"No one asked to see the letter," I say. "Besides, how hard would it be to disguise your handwriting, write a letter, and declare it came from your recently passed mother claiming your relationship to a murdered man you may have been staking out? Good question on locating someone who's been here for eight months. If she found him in New York, maybe he kept his apartment there, and the landlord gave her his new address. Doesn't explain why she just showed up, although she might have wanted to confront him in person instead of calling first."

Fontenot is scribbling fast. "That's an interesting take on the mystery woman. It's a lot of work for nothing, though, if she can't prove a biological connection." His lips part slightly. "In any case, do you happen to know when she arrived in town?"

"I asked that, and she started to say yesterday, then corrected herself to say, 'this morning.' "

Rippa taps the table with her finger. "She

threatened Clemmie with a lawyer, and when Clemmie offered her home to talk about the situation, the woman snuck upstairs and messed around, snapping a picture of the original land grant and accusing Clemmie of stealing it."

"Did this—" Fontenot checks his notes. "—Ms. Moffat mention where she was staying?"

I shake my head. "Just that she'd spent the day looking for decent accommodations and was unsuccessful."

"So probably a motel on the fringe of the city. Or a nearby city."

"That would be my guess."

Fontenot flips through his pages. "Gotta admit you all have good observation skills." He leans forward. "Any other comments on Ms. Moffat?"

"Her car," I say. "Very exotic. I'd guess Lamborghini. In bright yellow. You might have someone check car rental agencies that rent that make. She didn't seem the type to take in the scenery on a drive down here from New York. Waste too much of her valuable time."

"That's right," Rippa says, folding her arms. "And she got snippy when Jules and I looked at it. She said we were interrogating her and she only came here to connect with Mr. Renaud as he didn't know about her. I think maybe she heard about the treasure and wanted in on it."

The detective scans the group again. "Lots of maybes surrounding her appearance. The one constant is none of you believed her. About her claim, I mean."

Our three heads shake in response.

"Why not?"

Clemmie lifts a shoulder. "All of it. Her showing up within hours of Ames's death, and upon learning that, her focus turned to the value of the estate she now considers hers. She's a realtor and no doubt has researched the address and determined it's in a desirable neighborhood."

The detective bobs his head and pins Clemmie with a stare. "And…?"

Pretty sharp of him to discern there's more.

"And she was a thoroughly disagreeable person. Rude, greedy, and when caught behaving badly, assumes her excuse will be believed."

The look on Clemmie's face, a combination of crooked eyebrow and tucked lips, punctuates her words. "And another thing. Her first name begins with an S."

Rippa tips her chin up. "True on both counts. When Clemmie challenged her, saying there was a will naming another beneficiary, she got kinda mad. Talked about legally stopping anyone from accessing the house."

"She sounds unpleasant."

I smile. Unpleasant was the same word Clemmie used. Very tactful.

"Not done yet," I say. "Ms. Moffat showed here this morning uninvited. Rippa caught her taking two of the smalls from that demi-lune table near the stairs."

"Smalls? Like little things?"

"Exactly," Clemmie says. "Something of value—porcelain, silver, or an antique piece. Ames couldn't have paid much attention to them. They were thick with dust."

"We made her put them back," Rippa says. "She balked at that and said she wanted to have them appraised and they were legally hers anyway. Then she got all bent about Clemmie going ahead with the inventory. Clemmie threw her out and had a locksmith change all the locks."

"Worth an interview," the detective says. "I'll have an officer canvass car rental agencies and motels by phone and see if I can catch up with her. Very interesting that her name begins with S."

"I have a friend in the security business in New York. He's going to run a discreet local background check on Ms. Moffat. I'll let you know what he finds." I scrunch my nose. "Even if it's good."

Glass is half empty on this one, Cara.

Fontenot starts to stand, but Rippa interrupts. "Wait a minute. Is there any information on the break-in?"

He looks surprised, then frowns. "Tall male in dark clothes. No car to follow and a head start on the run? Not much to go on. We're checking to see if those prints match either of the ones made in Mrs. Neely's garden."

"Oh. That's good. Will you let us know the results?"

Fontenot nods. "Yes. Now I need to get on with my review so the tape can come down."

Rippa and I head upstairs. She looks over her shoulder at the hallway below. "Should we carry all those boxes back up? Seems like we would be doing a favor for whoever gets the house to leave them downstairs since it's so hot up here."

"I vote we make sure the rest of the boxes are packed the same, then leave them as is. Let the new owner decide."

"Down with that," says Rippa.

We make it through a couple of boxes each when Fontenot calls out. "Ladies? I have a question."

We troop back downstairs and approach the door of the library.

He makes a sweeping gesture with his hand. "Looking at the disturbed and undisturbed dust on these shelves, it's evident there are a lot fewer books than the spaces indicate. Any ideas?" A smile accompanies his words, and he's holding a book with a red yarn bookmark.

Rippa hooks a thumb over her shoulder at the hall behind us. "Jules and I found books like the one you're holding with the weird yarn bookmark in the bottom of all these boxes upstairs. There are lots more. We figured Mr. Renaud believed in that 'treasure in a book' legend and used red yarn to mark ones he was rejecting."

Fontenot nods. "Otherwise, everything in the reports is accounted for. I can remove the tape." He tears it off and wads it in his pocket, then addresses Clemmie. "Let me know when you get the documents you spoke about, please. I'd like copies." He steps past the three of us. "Thanks for your time. I'll be in touch."

Rippa and I walk into the library, and I see a drip-shaped stain on the arm and seat cushion. Solidifies the reason they ruled this room as the site of the crime.

Clemmie walks into the room and studiously avoids the chair. "I don't think there's any reason to disturb the placement of the books in here. I'll just take pictures of the shelves in sections for the inventory."

"Or Rippa and I can do it," I say. "Take us half the time."

Clemmie smiles in sad understanding. "You two

can tackle it if you finish the upstairs before I finish the dining room and parlor." She moves to the doorway, looks down the hall, then at her watch. "Another hour or so and we quit for the day? I'd really like to see what's in those documents."

****

An hour and a half later, the rooms are nearly done, and most of the dust is washed off. Clemmie, Rippa, and I are gathered around Clemmie's kitchen table.

"How do you think we should approach this?" she asks. "The will doesn't look too long." She points at four small journals, then puts her hand on a larger one covered in green cracked leather. "This belonged to his uncle. The handwriting is tiny, done in fountain pen, and with some French sprinkled in. Ames's are a little easier to understand." She slips a journal off the top. "Here's the last one before the one that was stolen. I think it will be the most interesting."

Rippa's gaze is pinned to the manila envelope also on the table. "Would you read the bequest part of the will out loud first? I'm kinda dying to know who inherits."

"Rippa!" I say.

Clemmie laughs and picks up the envelope to slip out a long document. "I'm kinda dying to know too. Probably some friend in New York."

She scans it for a few minutes, reading the wherefores and other boilerplate material. Her eyes grow wide. "This is interesting. 'Per my uncle's wishes, and therefore mine, and there being no more Renauds in this family line, the entirety of my estate is bequeathed to Honor deGrandpre, heretofore unacknowledged granddaughter of my uncle, Ames Marchand

118

Renaud.' "

"Wow," Rippa says. "I wonder if she knows."

"No hint of it, yesterday," I say. "Though a blessing and a curse."

My niece stares. "What? How could inheriting a big house in the Garden District be a curse? It's an upscale neighborhood."

Clemmie laughs. "Which means upkeep and upgrades to maintain a hundred-fifty-year-old house. Not to mention property taxes and pressure from the community to beautify the house and garden to meet the standards of the Garden District Association."

I nod. "Expensive."

"Very," Clemmie answers. "Probably way beyond the means of someone living at home and going to college. Stella had to pay inheritance taxes on her house, but they've since been abolished, so that's good."

"Unacknowledged. That means Ames's uncle fathered a child he didn't acknowledge as his, and that child is Honor's parent," says Rippa.

"You'd think people were beginning to move beyond that in the 1960s," I say.

"French, French Creole, and Louisiana Creole are still classes apart for a lot of old families, unfortunately," Clemmie replies. "I suppose if there had been other family, she'd never have inherited."

"Sad that it had to happen this way," I say.

Clemmie nods. "Ms. Moffat notwithstanding, I want to tell Honor in person of this right away and let her know I want to help."

Rippa raises an arm. "Yesss."

I am excited for Honor. A girl in her financial

circumstances with tuition to pay deserves a break like this. "It's still relatively early. If you call and let her know the basics and she doesn't mind, Rippa and I would like to go with you."

"Agreed," Clemmie says. "I'll read the rest of the will to make sure there are no codicils. And all Is dotted and Ts crossed."

Rippa bobs her head, then her smile fades. "When are we going to get back to the journals to look for clues to the treasure?"

Clemmie pulls in her lips, but her eyes sparkle. "How about after dinner?"

"We still have tomorrow to work on the inventory before the rehearsal dinner and cocktail party," I say.

"Sold," Rippa says, then reaches for her phone as the minions alert her to a call.

I wonder who. Maybe Ben calling from California. We haven't heard from him for a couple of days. When our former houseguest chose to go to college at UC Davis, we thought he would be more homesick, but he's fit right in.

Rippa's eyes widen as she reads the screen. "Hello? Oh, hi." Her face turns pink, and she stands, absently smoothing her hair with her free hand as she turns from the table. "Dinner, tonight? Okay, what time?" She pauses. "Great. Meet you at the Sandoval house at five thirty. Bye."

Not Ben, then. "That guy Miles from ASU? He was cute." *In an entitled way.*

She frowns. "What? No. It was Étienne." She says his name with almost reverence but without meeting my gaze.

Étienne. The guy whose worshipful glance

centered on the beautiful Honor deGrandpre just yesterday is asking Rippa out? That makes no sense. Unless he wants something. I need to be careful here. "Um, no doubt you'll get to see some real New Orleans sites. You know, outside the tourist stops."

Her smile returns. "Yeah. It'll be fun. He's so great."

Clemmie taps the stack in front of her and addresses Rippa. "Will you have time to go with us to Honor's house, then to your date and get back to help sort through these journals?"

Good questions and a look close to panic crosses Rippa's face. She glances at her cellphone. "It's only two thirty. If we leave soon, we can make that visit and get back in time for me to get ready." She gives us a pleading look. "If I'm back by seven thirty, can we go over them then?"

Clemmie checks her watch and nods. "It could work if Honor is at home and can speak with us."

I toss my hat in. "I need to spend some time with Jilly. I'll see if she can slow down long enough to have dinner with me."

Chapter Twelve

A half hour later we're in Clemmie's car. "Honor lives in the Upper Ninth Ward. An area called The Marigny," Clemmie says, driving slowly, looking for the address. "Samuel lived nearby. I gave him a ride sometimes when he worked late at Stella's."

We arrive in a neighborhood that's tidy if a bit worn around the edges. The houses a testament to having borne the insult of sun and rain for decades.

Rippa cranes her head. "Not a real touristy place, but I love the colors."

I agree as we come to a stop. The house Honor deGrandpre's family occupies is a typical shotgun style. Theirs is a faded dark-melon color with cream trim. Tall, navy-blue shutters bookend the windows next to the front door.

We approach, and Clemmie knocks.

Honor opens the door, smiling. "Please, come in."

We glimpse a narrow, spotless room, my first impression being the sharp smell of chicory coffee and my second of the many shades of red on upholstery and accessories. Inside, the three of us plus Honor almost constitute a crowd. Scratch that. I see a small woman with dark hair, shot through with gray, standing stiffly near the back doorway.

Our hostess glances at the woman, then concentrates on us. If Clemmie had come accompanied by the king of Mardi Gras in costume, Honor would no doubt present the same manners. "Would you like some coffee or tea?"

"No, thank you," Clemmie says. Rippa and I shake our heads.

The young brunette's smile widens. "Thank you for coming." She turns to the older woman, whose arms are now crossed, and pursed lips shape her mouth. Honor motions for the woman to come forward. "This is my great-aunt Arielle. *Tante*, this is Mrs. Ashurst and her friends Julianne and Rippa. Am I correct on your names?"

"Good memory," I say.

The woman stands rooted to the spot, frowning. "There are too many of you."

"*Tante*" is Honor's gentle rebuke. "We talked about this. Mrs. Ashurst is here to help me."

The aunt scowls, undeterred. "Where were they when my poor sister, your grandmother, carried your dear mother for that *connard*?"

"Isn't that bastard?" Rippa whispers behind me, but I think Honor hears. Her cheeks tinge pink.

Clemmie sets her mouth. She steps forward and directs her comment to the aunt. "My friend Ames, the man whose home and belongings Honor will inherit, was born and raised in New York. He knew nothing about the situation with your family until shortly before his murder."

"Pah." Aunt Arielle spits the word.

"*Ma tante* loved her sister deeply," Honor explains. "She never forgave Mr. Renaud's uncle for not acknowledging the child."

"Pah," the woman says again. "It was we who

would not have acknowledged *him*."

Clemmie smiles. "Family pride has a long memory."

Tante Arielle chews on that for half a minute, her gaze dropping to the floor, then nods. Her shoulders relax a little as she starts to walk toward us. Before she reaches the center of the room, a man enters behind her. He's tall with an erect posture. His figure is virile, his arms showing ropey muscles and his face deeply seamed from weather. I'd peg him in his mid-sixties.

Tante Arielle tips her head. "This is my son, Pierre."

Honor smiles again. "Hello, *Pepa*. I'm glad you came."

Pierre nods but doesn't speak. His demeanor matches his mother's. Their gazes rest on each of us in turn, slightly narrowed, showing mistrust. And probably annoyance at feeling discomfort in the situation, even though we're here with good news. I don't blame them.

Clemmie's voice is gracious. "Lovely to be in your home. Thank you for having us." She breaks the tension by glancing at a nearby chair. "May I?"

"Of course," says Honor.

Clemmie sits, and Honor holds her hand toward a small sofa next to it. "Please."

Rippa and I join her.

"As I said on the phone," Clemmie starts, "as executor of Ames Renaud's estate, I wanted you to know what's going on."

"What do you mean, 'what's going on'?" *Tante* Arielle says. "It all belongs to her. No?"

"That's what Ames intended," Clemmie responds.

"But a new claimant has come into the picture since his death that may complicate the directive of the will."

"What is this claim?" asks Pierre, his lips barely moving, his voice low and angry.

Clemmie takes a deep breath. "A woman named Sevryn Moffat arrived from New York shortly after Ames's death. She says a letter her mother left her on her own death names Ames as her natural father. She's adamant that the estate is hers."

Aunt Arielle resumes her vitriolic tone. "Pah on the whole line of Renaud men. We are glad to be rid of them. Taking advantage of poor women, then running away."

Clemmie stands, red suffusing her face. "Ames Renaud knew nothing of this woman. He was a friend of mine and an honorable man. He could have died intestate, and everything would have gone to the state. He wanted Honor to inherit."

"*Tante*," says Honor, her tone pleading. "These women are guests, and we will listen to what they have to say."

Tante Arielle's nod is barely perceptible. Her son gives no sign of agreement or disagreement.

Clemmie sits again and folds her hands. "Part of my duties as executor is to inventory the estate. It's turning out to be a bigger project than I thought." She holds her hand toward Rippa and me. "Rippa and Julianne are helping. I've disallowed Ms. Moffat's presence in the house since I believe you're the intended beneficiary."

"Where is this Moffat woman?"

Our attention is drawn to Honor's *pepa*. His stance radiates animosity.

Clemmie shakes her head. "We don't know. She showed up, said she'd come from New York, and made her claim. Since it's Mardi Gras, we're assuming she's probably somewhere on the outskirts of town. Everything else is usually booked solid."

Pepa's tight nod accepts her answer.

We join Clemmie as she stands. "That's all the information I have right now. I wanted you to be aware of the will and the other claim. I know you have a busy schedule, but of course you can contact me and go through the house and contents any time. Oh, and there's a leaky window due to warped eaves and window frame on the second floor. I'm having it repaired before there's more damage."

Honor's face stills. "How much will that cost?"

Clemmie smiles. "Ames had an account at a local bank. The money in it is part of the estate. I'll make sure all the outstanding bills are paid, including the window repair. If you'd like, I can also have an antiques dealer evaluate the contents of the house."

"No charity," *Pepa* all but growls.

"As he says," *Tante* Arielle responds, her nod as tight as her son's. "But thank you for putting Honor's mind at rest."

Color spreads on Honor's cheeks, and she lifts a shoulder in a silent apology. "Did you say antiques?"

"Yes," Clemmie says. "Some beautiful old pieces. You may want to keep one or two for yourself or your family." She smiles. "In remembrance of Ames."

"I like that idea," Honor says, then glances at her family. "May I have a copy of this will?"

"I should have thought of that," Clemmie says. "I'll make a copy tomorrow. Would you like to come to the house and pick it up?"

Before Honor can answer, *Tante* Arielle speaks. "Does that woman have a copy?"

I'm impressed. Honor's family misses nothing. Although there's a bit of paranoia involved. Deservedly.

"She hasn't said so, and as Ames had no knowledge of her, I doubt it. I certainly haven't given one to her."

More stiff nods from *Pepa* and *Tante* Arielle.

Honor turns a happy face to Clemmie. "I can arrange to come by tomorrow afternoon."

"Good," Clemmie says. "Can you make it early? We all have a pre-wedding function to attend and need to get ready. Also, there are some books we've separated that can be donated if you approve. If you could take a few minutes to go through them?"

"I'll make the time," she says and shows us to the door.

****

In the car, Rippa leans forward. "That's her whole family? It's small."

Clemmie nods. "Let me see if I can do the history justice. Arielle had a sister and brother. The brother, I think his name was Baptiste, was Samuel's best friend. Samuel never married but was close to the whole family. The sister got pregnant by Ames's uncle. She had Honor's mother but passed away shortly afterward. Years later, Honor's mother and father and Baptiste took a small family boat out to help during Katrina. They were all lost."

Rippa and I suck in air. "Wow," she says. "So sad."

"About time they got some luck," I say. "Unfortunately, some probate cases can drag on for years with the attorneys getting most of the money. Especially if Moffat can afford to hire pricey representation and she's assigned a friendly judge."

"That whole Moffat claim could be a con," says Rippa. "Like Jules said, she could've written the letter herself and…"

"There's a connection, but we don't know how strong. It may come down to a DNA match. If both women are related, we can only hope the terms of the will prevail."

"I'll talk to an attorney friend," Clemmie says. "She specializes in mediating settlements."

I catch Rippa glancing at her phone. "Giving yourself time to get cute for your date?" I tease.

She narrows her eyes and wrinkles her nose at me. "It's just a casual thing. He knows I'm only here for a few more days."

This is a surprise. Especially since she's been acting like a giggly thirteen-year-old with a crush on a member of a boy band. "I stand corrected."

Chapter Thirteen

I come through the back door and down the hall to see Jilly pacing the living room. "Hi. Where's Stella?"

The bride-to-be whirls, slamming her wedding-planning book shut. "I didn't hear you. Um, she's upstairs having a lie down."

I peer at my tall, slender friend. She's pale and has lost pounds she can't afford. Stress kills her appetite. Every mid-term and final exam in college resulted in a weight loss. "Hand it over."

Feed her, Cara, says Raif.

My thought exactly.

Jilly's grip tightens on her book. "What?"

"Hand over the magic book and come into the kitchen. Nobody will get hurt."

Her whole body slumps. "That bad?"

"That bad. When did you eat last?"

She doesn't answer immediately, so I pry her fingers from the book and head for the kitchen.

"I know breakfast was hours ago, but bacon, eggs, and toast with jam is what I do best. And you're going to eat every bite."

A long sigh escapes as she sits and lightly presses fingertips to her eyelids, then her gaze follows as I lay her precious planner at the far end of the table. Out of reach, but she can still see it.

"Any wrinkles in your plans?" I ask as I start the

meal I have threatened to feed her.

"Nothing overly serious. Other than poor Mr. Renaud."

I read her slight pause. "What else?"

She lifts a shoulder. "The room we reserved a half year ago at a boutique hotel for Hugh's brother and sister-in-law is in jeopardy. The guests who were supposed to be leaving tomorrow want to extend their stay, and management is agreeing with them. A bird-in-the-hand kind of thing, I guess.

"The silk ballet flats I ordered to wear at the reception came yesterday but in the wrong size."

Another sigh. "The florist will only fill half the bouquets I ordered for the post-rehearsal cocktail party tomorrow night. They said they only received a partial shipment and the rest are being used for a big wedding." She swallows, then sniffles. "They want to backfill with cheaper substitutes. I'd pay less, of course, but I don't want the cheaper ones, and more expensive flowers aren't in the budget."

"And they're not sorry," I quip, stirring eggs. "Because your order is smaller, they feel justified in treating you differently. If you'd cancelled at the last minute, they would've charged you for the flowers anyway. Makes me mad."

I put a cup of coffee and a plate in front of her, but her gaze strays to her book.

"Thanks, Jules, but I really have everything under control."

I rarely pull out the battering ram, the McCarren name, but in this case it's justified because Jilly has played fair, and others have not. "I have an idea." I sit next to her and hand her a fork. "Give me the details for the hotel and the florist, and I'll take care of them."

She has a forkful of egg halfway to her mouth. "What?"

"You heard me. Give me the details, and I'll fix them."

Happy tears fill her eyes. "But I didn't invite you here to work. I want you and Rippa to have a good time."

Her sentiment is genuine. Besides the strain of the pending wedding, Jilly tries to hide an edge of guilt. She had Hugh and a future with him, then Raif and I met and got married. All good. We both had our soul mates. Then Raif died, and although that was nearly four years ago, I know she still thinks it seems wrong that she has so much. I'm convincing her slowly that I'm okay.

Maybe I should have given you more than three days after you said yes, Cara.

Nope. All I wanted was Raif and a JP.

I snap my fingers. "I can't have a good time knowing you're miserable. Now, stop getting your toast soggy and eat. Write down what I need to know while the florist is still open and the day manager of the hotel is still on duty. Then go take a nap."

"You're the best." She retrieves her magic book, tears a clean sheet from the back, and notes the information I need. She clutches the book to her chest. "Are you sure?"

I pull out my cellphone. "Positive. But only if you put the book down and eat."

****

The hotel and florist are within two blocks of each other, and I pick the hotel first, knowing Mardi Gras probably has the staff going full tilt. I step to the counter. "May I speak to Mr. Revere?"

The girl behind the reception desk, whose name tag reads *Tiffany*, gives me a none-too-subtle glance, taking in my casual clothes. "Do you have an appointment?"

"No. Please tell him Julianne McCarren of McCarren Oil would like to speak to him."

She's not impressed but picks up the desk phone. "I'll let him know, but you may have to wait. We're very busy."

I smile sweetly. "I'll just stand *here*."

If Tiffany hasn't heard of McCarren Oil, Mr. Revere probably has and hustles forward from a short hallway behind the pretty reception desk. "Ms. McCarren? What can I do for you?"

I look around at the crowd in the small lobby. "May I speak to you in your office?"

His nerves are beginning to show as he rubs fingers against thumbs. "Of course." He turns to the girl. "Hold off on business that needs my attention for a few minutes." A slightly open mouth shows her surprise as the manager leads me back to a small, well-appointed office, where his official smile comes out. "Please, have a seat."

I've already contacted McCarren Multinational's Travel Group. As I suspected, this hotel is a favorite of the partners and inspection teams who come to New Orleans to visit the McCarren offshore oil rigs in the gulf.

We stayed here a couple of times, Cara. It's very nice.

Raif's right. The rooms were comfortable, the food excellent, and the service impeccable. I get right to the point with Mr. Revere. "Thank you. I'm in New Orleans as a member of a wedding party of a very good friend. She made reservations six months ago for her fiancé's brother and his wife. Now she's being told the room will not be available due to an extended-stay request of the occupants. I find this hard to understand as your reputation has always been outstanding. Surely, there's an acceptable alternative. An empty suite being held for VIPs, a room being used by a staff member so they won't have to put up with the Mardi Gras traffic, something of that nature."

I've hit the nail on the head as the manager's gaze lands on his desktop, then springs up to meet mine. His conciliatory smile doesn't slide into place fast enough. "I'm sure there's been a miscommunication, Ms. McCarren. We'll be happy to upgrade the reservation to a suite. Our compliments." He stands. "If there's nothing else, I'll walk you back to reception to work out the details."

I try not to let my smugness show as Tiffany is interrupted and told about the change. Occasionally, I feel like an app that runs in the background until ready to activate, then use the McCarren name as a bludgeon to overcome unfairness.

You did a good thing, Cara.

At the flower shop, I use Stella's name and her capacity as a member of the board for Garden District Association residents. Garden District seems to be a magic term. Turns out the owner is more than happy to substitute the bouquets Jilly ordered with more expensive ones in the same color palette and same price. I leave, a happy camper.

Back at Stella's, I write a note for Jilly, who is still

napping, and walk to the rental. I wonder if it would be useless to order food and request delivery. The sun sets quickly this far south, and I don't have the energy to fight the dinner crowds. That speculation ends as I come through the door.

Nerves have prevailed again, and Rippa is pacing and glancing at her cellphone. On hearing me, she jumps, and my heart goes out to her.

"Just making sure I'm in sync with the grandfather clock," she says, her gaze betraying her and cutting to the front door.

Her time has not been wasted. She looks pretty in a pale turquoise long-sleeved T-shirt, bleached jeans, and navy sandals. Her complexion glows, and her blonde ponytail shines.

"You look nice," I say, wanting to tie her to a chair so she won't be hurt by Étienne.

My selfish moment ends as a knock sounds.

Étienne's smile accentuates his handsome features as Rippa greets him.

"Hi. Come on in. Sorry I can't show you around. I know you're interested in really old city architecture, but we're renters and can't have guests."

His eyebrows draw together in puzzlement at her disclosure. I'm guessing because his lie about why he wants to get into the Renaud house has come back to bite him on the butt.

"Oh. Yes. But thank you for thinking of me."

As if she's thought about much else.

When they turn to leave, his glance flicks to me. "I'll take good care of your niece."

I hope my smile conveys the threat that if he doesn't, he will be one sorry man. "You two have a good time."

****

I wonder again what it is about Étienne that puts my hackles up but don't have time to dwell on it. I still have to pick up a gulf-shrimp dinner for Davison, Clemmie, and me. I also invited Jilly in my note to her, but she's been spending all her spare time with Hugh. I'll get enough for four. If Jilly declines and Rippa doesn't eat a big dinner, she can have the leftovers later.

My next chore is a call to Mack. We keep up with each other's busy lives by email, but I have to admit I enjoy hearing his voice. He might still be in his office, but I call his personal cell instead.

A smile infuses his voice. "Julianne. Good to hear from you. Are you and Rippa enjoying New Orleans?"

"We are, but a body was discovered in the garden of the house where Jilly's aunt lives. We're staying in a rental nearby. Anyway, guess who wants to solve the murder?"

Wonderful tenor laughter greets my question. "Sorry. I hope the deceased wasn't anyone close to your hostess. As far as who wants to solve it, it's in Rippa's blood, and you're partially to blame."

"I hate it when you're right. And now that I've complimented you, I need a favor."

"Sure," Mack says cheerfully.

"You didn't even ask what the favor is."

Another laugh. "You can't want to borrow money. And I know you don't want me to introduce you to a handsome New Yorker who likes to dance. So what can I do for you?"

My turn to laugh. I need this. The thing with Rippa and Étienne has tied me in knots. Then there's the murder and finally, Jilly's frantic pre-wedding issues. "Getting back to the murder—" A chuckle interrupts. "Anyway, the dead guy was a friend of Jilly's other aunt, and the aunt is his executor. The will says a local girl inherits everything. But on the day the body was found, a realtor from New York showed up claiming she is the natural daughter he never knew about, and she plans to fight the will. This woman is a real pip. She is nasty, sneaky, and hard-edged."

"And you want me do a background check on her."

"Yes, please. Her name is Sevryn Moffat. The spelling of her name is unknown. I'd like her business reputation, legal problems, financials if you can, and any industry gossip. Good or bad."

"I'll start with McCarren's Real Estate Group. See if they know anything. How soon do you need this?"

"Sooner the better."

"Aha. Then you'll owe me."

"Excuse me?"

"How about stopping by New York on your way home? Just for a few days. I'll take you dancing."

Go, Cara. You'll have fun.

The sight of Rippa's heart in her eyes when she left with Étienne makes me put all else on hold. "Got a thing about Rippa being by herself after the wedding. Think I have to pass, but thanks."

"Is she okay? I mean last time I looked, she was a very together girl."

"That's out the window. She met a guy. Good looking, a little too polite in my book, and I think he's using her, but she doesn't see it that way. I'm afraid by the time we leave, she might need me to talk it out."

"Got it. She's resilient, though."

"True. Hey, why don't you invest in a pair of hiking boots, and we can take on the trails in the Olympic Peninsula this June?"

"I will if you plan on being back here in September for the Annual McCarren Foundation Fundraiser. As my date. And wear that silvery blue dress."

"Done."

"Regular work hours are over for the day. I'll get on this first thing tomorrow and let you know what I find. Oh, if you need someone to come break that guy's beak, I'm your man."

****

Clemmie, Davison, and I sit in their kitchen to gulf-shrimp quesadillas and margaritas. I was right about Jilly. Senior medical residents get a pitiful amount of time for a dinner break, but she chose to spend it with Hugh at the hospital after the profuse thanks I got for fixing two of her issues.

"Rippa on your mind?" Clemmie asks.

My face warms. "Sorry. It's not the company. And yes, she is. I don't expect any physical harm to come to her with Étienne, but he strikes such a sour chord with me. He seems so manipulative."

"I didn't know you were worried," Clemmie says. "I might've shared something I overheard." She glances at Davison. "When Étienne showed up for his first day of work after Samuel passed—Samuel wasn't staged in the garden yet—Étienne demanded Stella pay him a higher wage than they'd previously agreed on."

"He tried to bully her," I say.

Clemmie nods. "He said he was much younger than Samuel and could accomplish the same amount of work in half the time, so he should be paid at twice the rate they talked about when Samuel was alive.

"Stella told him she didn't need twice as much work produced and couldn't afford to pay him that rate. Étienne then said he wanted a reference so he could go to work elsewhere in the Garden District and get the pay he deserved. Stella agreed to give him a reference if he worked with her for a month at the original price so she could find a replacement."

"Confirms the manipulative personality type that struck me," I say. "Good for Stella."

"I came out of the house and stood beside her," Clemmie puts in. "Étienne was pissed but agreed, and Stella's holding her ground."

My restless concern alleviates somewhat. Rippa hasn't spent more than a minute or two in Étienne's company. Although it'll be a hard lesson, she'll figure him out. "There is a bright side. Washington State is twenty-six hundred miles away."

Clemmie smiles. "And we all know Rippa is one smart cookie."

Davison and I are smiling in agreement when someone taps on the front door. He stands and crosses the living room. The door creaks slightly upon opening. "Rippa. Come in."

I look at my watch and quash the urge to stand. She's been gone less than ninety minutes. My fear that something is wrong compresses into a long slide of breath. "You okay?" I ask as she enters the kitchen.

She shrugs. "Yeah, fine. Turns out Étienne is weird about meeting new people."

I frown. "I don't understand."

Her gaze rolls up. "Everything was okay for the first twenty or thirty minutes. We avoided the worst of the crowds, and he showed me this little place we were going to have dinner after a walk along the waterfront. Then we saw Honor."

"Uh-oh."

She squints. "What does that mean?"

I find the last few bites of my quesadilla interesting. "In wanting to get to know and help Étienne, you kinda overlooked his infatuation with Honor. Pretty intense. What happened?"

Her shrug returns. "She was with this nice-looking guy and introduced him. Étienne walked past him like he didn't exist and took Honor's hand. She jerked it away and introduced Étienne to the other guy as an acquaintance of her uncle's."

"Whoa," Clemmie says, and I nod in agreement.

"Yeah, I know. Harsh. Not that I blame her. Anyway, Honor said, 'Nice seeing you,' and left with the other guy. I didn't know what to think."

I shake my head. "Yes, you did. You were already thinking it."

Rippa shoots me a look. "I was done and told Étienne I was leaving, but he said he would bring me back. He wanted to talk more about the Renaud house."

"What a jerk," I say.

"True," says Rippa, stepping toward the table. "Not finished, though. Remember Miles?"

"The hottie with attitude wearing the towel after using our shower?"

Clemmie and Davison exchange a look that speaks volumes in questions.

"The same," Rippa says. "Étienne and I ran into him and a couple of his friends. He'd had a few beers and grabbed me in a hug, telling his friends how we met. Miles held out his hand when they were introduced, but Étienne just mumbled something about drunk tourists and walked away."

"He just left you there?" I ask.

Her mouth twists. "Fine by me. As I said, I was done. He's a jerk, and I'm stupid."

He really did a number on her, Cara.

I sigh and rub her arm. "Not stupid. Vulnerable, maybe, to a good-looking, charming guy who wanted something from you."

Her gaze drops. "I know. Access to the Renaud house. He mentioned it when we passed on our way to dinner."

"What did you say?"

Her shoulders slump. "I told him we only had one more day of inventory and after we finished, Clemmie or Honor might walk him through."

Clemmie straightens. "He knows Honor is inheriting the house?"

Rippa's eyes widen in distress. "Was that wrong? I figured everyone would know in another day. He seemed surprised, then commented on her luck in inheriting a treasure."

"Not wrong, I guess," Clemmie says. "I just think Honor having to deal with the whole Moffat woman's claim, the shape the house is in, and people believing there's a treasure inside, well, it's her choice who she wants to tell."

Her gaze lighting on each of us, Rippa shakes her head. "Think I'll stick to solving the mystery. And apologize to Honor tomorrow for spilling the news. If I'm there when she comes to get the copy of the will."

Clemmie smiles. "I'm sure she'll appreciate that.

Now, more gulf-shrimp quesadillas and margaritas available."

Rippa isn't fast enough, and Davison pulls out her chair.

"I'm starved," she says.

Just like that. My fear that Étienne would transform her into a zombie follower dissolves. Rippa digs in as soon as the plate is set in front of her, proving her sour experience with Étienne hasn't adversely affected her appetite.

Chapter Fourteen

Dinner over, Rippa practically inhales a slice of the key lime pie. I'm certain Ben would be proud of the way she laid waste to the shrimp quesadilla.

"Um, if you were blindfolded, would you even know what you're eating?"

Pink floods her cheeks. "A really delish key lime pie," she challenges. "Made from scratch." Her nod is directed to Clemmie. "Sorry."

Our hostess smiles. "That's fine, honey. I think you're eager to find what's in those journals."

"You so get me."

On that note, my niece grabs her dishes and mine and heads for the kitchen. Davison does the same with his and Clemmie's, chuckling.

Our hostess pushes away from the table. "I'm going upstairs for the journals."

I follow suit. "Excuse me, I'm going to wash up."

When I return, Davison has loaded the dishwasher and excused himself. Clemmie is just sitting down. Something's been bothering me, and now is as good a time as any.

I look at her. "Before we look through the paperwork, I want to discuss the intent of the intruders."

Rippa jumps in. "To force Mr. Renaud to tell them what he knew about the treasure."

I put my hand on Clemmie's shoulder. It's only been a couple of days since she lost her friend. "We're assuming that because there were indications the library was where the incident took place. Now we know the last journal is missing. If he told them about it, mightn't he have told them everything? Fontenot said there were no signs of struggle. So why was Mr. Renaud killed? Anger because the killers didn't get what they came for? Because he could identify them? Either choice makes the killers sound like amateurs."

Rippa puts her chin in her hand. "And we still have the mysterious signet ring, the break-in, and the reason why whoever killed him moved him to Stella's garden."

Talking about the people we're openly labeling as killers sends a cool ripple up my spine. "I just want us to keep in mind what happened may not be over."

Clemmie glances at her husband when he reenters the room. "Davison and I have been talking about that too, and we think the person who broke in might be more than the coincidence the initial police investigation is leaning toward. Their theory, since we couldn't identify anything that was missing, was somebody found out the house was empty and came to see what they could steal. We don't believe that."

Rippa cants her head. "How come? It could be that. Some kid taking a dare. 'Dude. Guy got murdered in there. Dare you to go inside and grab something we can sell.' "

Clemmie and Davison are totally in sync. The same communication style Raif and I had. She's the one to speak. "That's quite a leap and one we haven't considered. I guess we don't exactly *know* different, dear. But given everything we do know surrounding poor Ames's death, that's the premise we're working from.

"And since you two also think whoever killed Ames may not be through, we're considering just Davison and me finishing the rest of the inventory tomorrow." She holds her hands palms out. "Not that you two haven't been wonderful. I would just feel awful if anything happened to either of you."

Before I can assure Clemmie that we would feel the same about her and Davison, Rippa bounces up from her chair. "We have new locks and additional police patrols, and Davison fixed the motion-activated lights in front and back. There are enough deterrents that I think we're okay to finish if we're extra careful." She turns to me. "Am I right?"

This is the sensible Rippa. The one whose curiosity about the murder and subsequent talk of treasure overrides her desire to show a cute guy through the Renaud house.

A year ago, I would've balked at Rippa's question, but her maturity and mad skills on the computer have won me over. "I can live with that. The work has to be done, and three is better than two. Besides, we promised."

Clemmie rubs her fingers up her forehead. "All right. If we agree staying safe is our first priority. And Davison will drop by every once in a while."

Rippa and I bob our heads.

Davison smiles. "Told you we'd be overruled."

Clemmie elbows her husband in the ribs and swings her index finger between Rippa and me. "I can't shake the facts I know about Ames. He was not a stupid man and wouldn't have shared his beliefs in the treasure or the methods he used to find it with anyone else. Especially anyone who might be dangerous. It just doesn't make sense."

I shake my head. "Unless he didn't. You said he kept to himself. He might have been unaware of how much history his house had. It's very old, and what he might have thought of as a family secret could've been known by other locals. The fact that he was the last in the Renaud line then posed an opportunity for them to become interested in what he knew."

Clemmie leans into Davison and smiles. "That's possible. There are secrets, stories, and outright fabrications attached to a lot of homes in the district. Davison and I heard one about the butler's pantry in this house. A walled-in body. Turns out, when we renovated, the previous owners had walled off the pantry because their realtor suspected mold." She reaches for the journal on top. "Hopefully we'll learn something about Ames's house from these."

A folded, yellowed paper slides out as she opens it. Four people in the room and four quiet gasps follow.

Rippa, of course, weighs in before Clemmie has a chance to read. "What is it?"

Clemmie scans it for maybe ten seconds. "It's in Spanish. Mine isn't very good. Davison is the linguist in this family." She hands the paper to her husband.

He pats his shirt, then pulls readers from his pocket. An action that elicits a sigh from Rippa though she foregoes the eye roll.

Davison smiles and squints. "Looks like a very old receipt for the Renaud family mausoleum." His eyebrows rise. "It's in St. Louis Cemetery No. 1."

Rippa slaps the table and leans back. "St. Louis?

Missouri? Why there?"

I cross my arms. "If you'd gone on a few tourist excursions with me like I suggested, instead of getting wrapped up in murder and treasure hunts, you'd know it's the oldest cemetery in New Orleans. It's considered haunted, and the graves of notorious torturer and murderer Delphine LaLaurie and Marie Laveau, voodoo queen, are located there."

The look on Rippa's face is entertaining, as her blue eyes widen. "Wait. What? A murderer and a voodoo queen? Who did that Delphine person murder? I mean torture and murder?"

Raif is chuckling in my head. *Bloodthirsty, isn't she, Cara?*

Side trip. My fault. "Her servants."

The corner of Rippa's mouth pulls down. "Like, I spilled ashes on the rug, and now you're hanging me by my thumbs?"

Disturbing that's the visual she comes up with. "Uh, don't know the details." I wiggle my eyebrows. "We can take the midnight tour if you want."

Think I've hit her spooky nerve. She doesn't answer, and her gaze lands on the books. "Maybe we should get back to the journals."

Davison hands Clemmie the piece of paper. "Didn't you say Ames's will had a Directive to Physician attached?"

Clemmie pushes her thumb along the crease of the paper. "Yes. He wanted to be buried. I assume he knew about the Renaud family mausoleum. It's interesting that he spent almost his whole life in New York, but family was still very important to him. I'll make an appointment with the cemetery management tomorrow.

146

That way I'll be ready when the coroner releases his body."

Her last few words wobble, and Davison leans down to kiss her temple. "Want to get back to this later?"

She shakes her head and picks up the older, dark-green, leather-bound journal. "Not when doing this might help us understand what went on."

The contents echo the story Ames told Clemmie. In spidery indigo ink, sometimes lapsing into French, Ames's uncle outlined how he meant to "reignite the search and claim the treasure for the Renaud line."

"That is so kinda sad," Rippa says. "He figured out all that sorting, then how to eliminate the ones that couldn't be the answer." She tips her head. "When was his last entry?"

Clemmie flips to near the end. "He made notations a month at a time. His last entry was fourteen months ago. I remember Ames telling me his uncle died of congestive heart failure. The timing means this entry must have been within a few months of his death."

Clemmie scans the journal while I take a few notes. "Did Ames ever say he thought he was getting close to the treasure?"

Her eyebrows draw together. "No. And I never asked. Now I assume the boxes of books stored upstairs with the red yarn between pages have been ruled out from his hunt. I don't even know what he used as a baseline for checking them."

Rippa rubs her temples. "It could be lots of things, number of pages or a phrase. Date published would exclude most of them due to the age of the treasure story."

Clemmie passes Rippa and me each a journal from the stack. "Maybe you'll have more luck with Ames's older ones. I'll scan this one, and afterward we can compare notes."

We agree and flip them open. Reading the personal journal of someone who was murdered in the last couple of days seems strange. The entries in the one I'm reading are pretty boring. He complains about the humidity and the garden, then goes on to outline the section of shelves containing the books he has reviewed and excluded. The reasons vary. Too new, book club, too popular, and published in England are the most common. No list of reasons is included, so his evaluations must've come from his own idea of what the treasure could be.

Rippa is slumped in her chair, and Clemmie closes her journal.

"I haven't come up with anything. Neither Ames nor his uncle have shown a clear plan or outline for their search. It's so sad that he wasted all those months and eventually lost his life over some phantom treasure."

"I agree," Rippa says. "If he had a formula or word, like a character named Renaud, that only he and his uncle knew about, that would've been the first thing he told whoever threatened him. But, no. It's like buying a lotto ticket with the machine picking random numbers and hoping to win millions. What was he going to do when he got down to the last book?"

Good question.

Clemmie takes all the journals and piles them on the table. "Unless there's something the three of us missed, and I don't think so, I'm going to give these to

Detective Fontenot along with a copy of Ames's will. I guess they'll be looked over, then probably given back to the estate."

I yawn. "And from what Honor has said, she has no interest in pursuing said treasure, so I guess it will remain unsolved. Hopefully we'll have better luck finding information on the persons who killed Ames."

Clemmie stands and hugs me, then Rippa. "That means so much to me."

Chapter Fifteen

The bedrooms in the rental house are very comfortable, if a little foofy. The bathrooms are more modern, without the fluffy pale-coral rugs I've removed for the duration of our stay. Coffee wafts up the stairs, but I decide to shower first, needing the heat to relax the muscles I overused during the inventory.

After showering, I put on a navy T-shirt and crops. They won't stay clean long exposed to the decades of dust we'll be working in today, but I'll be cooler. Downstairs, I step into the kitchen and roll my shoulder before reaching for the coffee pot.

Rippa laughs. "I feel your pain. Got a twinge in the middle of my back from wrestling with all those boxes of books." She grins and reaches behind herself. "Maybe these will help." She produces a cute, green-and-white, awning-striped sack with Café Du Monde lettering on the side, unfolding and flapping the opening. "They're still warm."

The unmistakable aroma of warm beignets. Life is good. "You are my favorite niece."

"Heard that one before." She hands me the bag. "These come with an apology. I woke up early thinking about that sneaky Ms. Moffat. So, as we talked about night before last, I went to our online family history account and researched Mr. Renaud. Turns out he really was dead last in his line." She wrinkles her nose. "No pun intended."

I peek in the bag. "What's the apology for?"

She reaches in and retrieves a pastry. "Your phone rang while you were in the shower. Being nosy, I wondered who would be calling this early and looked. It was from Mack. Call him back, call him back, please."

No apology or bribe necessary. I pick up my phone. "You get plates. Hopefully Mack has some good information." I put the call on speaker.

"Good morning." The smile in his greeting gives me the stomach flutters. "My contact left me a voicemail last night. Your Ms. Moffat has quite the reputation."

"Not altruistic, I'm guessing."

Mack chuckles. "Aah, not even close. Although she does have a real knack for finding gems in the rough and staging them upscale. Unfortunately, the polish has sometimes hidden bad infrastructure issues."

"Oh, is *that* all?"

"Nope. She's been caught undercutting her fees in private offers to get listings over competitors. Guess that's her version of negotiating. She offers the seller twenty-five thousand dollars in cash under the table for a million-dollar-plus listing."

The math doesn't make sense to me. "Why would anyone with that level of listing be interested?"

He chuckles again. "Money's money. And it usually works best on relatives of the original owners if it's a sale following a death. Makes the inheritor's eyes shiny. Unfortunately, she's been sued twice. Under her original name."

I'm in the middle of swiping powdered sugar from

my shirt front and dry swallow my small bite with a choke. Rippa giggles, and we exchange glances.

She leans in. "Sevryn Moffat is a fake name?"

"Hi, Rippa. Not fake. She had it legally changed from Sharon Moore three years ago. About the same time she rented warehouse space in Brooklyn. It's filled with expensive staging pieces. She and a small crew do the work. Saves paying thousands to have a professional deck out spaces for sale or rent."

"That answers one question," I say.

"Just one?" he teases.

"Rippa caught her sneaking into the Renaud house a couple of days ago. She was...I guess the only word is stealing two expensive smalls. We made her put them back. After she left, I noticed a large china cabinet full of pieces had been scooted away from the wall in the dining room. Staging homes explains her furniture-moving skills. Does she have a good side?"

"She was kind to her mother."

Rippa shakes her head toward my phone. "You're making that up."

He laughs outright. "Not at all. Her mother passed away a couple of weeks ago. According to my source, her last year was spent in a very nice rest home with medical facilities. Ms. Moffat paid a sizable bill each month."

Rippa frowns, an act Mack can't see, but her words reflect her feelings. "She told us she was raised in a really poor area of New York by a single mother. Guess Ms. Moffat's not all bad."

At eighteen, my niece has come to terms with her own mother. My older sister, Piper, a hard-core social justice warrior, is more interested in saving the downtrodden of the world than raising her daughter. Which is good for me. I get to spend lots of time with Rippa. And right now, I see she's wrestling with altering her opinion of Ms. Moffat.

I put my elbow on the island, resting my chin in my hand. "Maybe the letter from Moffat's mother expressed bitterness toward the father, who Moffat found out lived in a highly sought area of New Orleans."

"We can only speculate. Maybe her reputation as a hard...um, driving realtor explains her approach to what she sees as her legal inheritance."

I laugh. "You softy. Rippa knows the word hard-ass. In any case, we're better informed about Ms. Moffat. Thanks."

"You're welcome. Let me know if you need additional resources, discover the murderer, and/or find the treasure. Oh, and my best to the bride and groom."

****

I try to rationalize the sugary intake of three beignets and strong coffee by telling myself I'll burn off the punishing calories and carbs by working on the inventory. Rippa laughs as I eat my pastries leaning over my plate so as not to end up wearing evidence of my meal.

Afterward, with only a few traces of powdered sugar marring my navy outfit, we lock up the Sandoval house and walk to Stella's.

She and Jilly are in the kitchen, chatting over a cup of coffee. Stella looks tired. She's been through a lot these past days. She's not a strong woman and has survived the loss of her parents and her husband in the span of six years. Now she's losing Jilly to marriage and will occupy this house alone. My loss of a young husband seems small, compared.

Someone will be lucky and find you like I did, Cara.

I give Stella a sideways hug. "We're waiting for Clemmie. Working in the Renaud house today. Honor's also coming by to have a walk-through."

Stella's mouth pulls to the side. "That boy, Étienne, is supposed to work in my garden for two hours this morning. I doubt he'll put in much effort if he sees that deGrandpre girl next door. She's very pretty, and he's got his eye on the poor thing."

Rippa's face is still. "Why do you say that?"

"Because of the kind of young man he is, I suppose."

"Really? What are you seeing there?"

Stella sips her coffee. "If you look past the handsome face, he's very selfish." Her gaze finds Rippa. "I don't mean the ordinary kind of selfish because he wants more money for doing the same job Samuel did. I mean his bone-deep belief that he's somehow more valuable than everyone around him. So sad for any relationship he has."

Rippa blinks. "That's a good way of putting it. Don't worry about Honor, though. She's got him figured out."

Clemmie walks into the kitchen. "Who's that?"

A smile blooms on my niece. "We girls have Étienne figured out."

"That's what I heard last night," Clemmie confirms.

Jilly cants her head. "I don't like him, either."

Amazing. An opinion from Jilly not involving cake

flavors, flowers, bridesmaid shoe colors, or the pros and cons of a Juliet veil. I have to know why. "How come?"

She frowns. "A while back, I asked him about the lifespan of the different kinds of flowers I was considering for my reception centerpieces. You know, how long would certain flowers last? He never got back to me. I thought that was rude."

I chuckle. And Jilly the bride-to-be is back.

Clemmie shakes her head, digs in her pocket, pulls out a key, and holds it toward me. "Did you bring yours? I want to turn over at least one to Honor when she gets here."

I grimace. "Too busy stuffing my face with beignets. Sorry. I can go get it."

"When we break for lunch should be soon enough. Ready to go?"

Rippa and I nod, and I lean toward Jilly as we pass. "Mack says to give you and Hugh his best."

Jilly beams. "Thank him."

After we're inside the Renaud house, Clemmie locks the doors and dusts her hands. "Not in the mood for a repeat visit from that irritating woman."

I no longer position the fan upstairs on me. It blows too much dust-infused air my way. I take my handy-dandy picture frame and prop the window open.

Two hours and a dozen documented pieces later, I hear Clemmie talking to someone downstairs and walk onto the upstairs landing. Rippa pokes her head from behind what was once an exquisite, Japanese-inspired three-piece screen. She points toward the stairs and grins. "Break time."

Downstairs, Honor is standing beside Clemmie in the dining room. Clemmie has emptied the china cabinet and mahogany boxes of silverware and stacked everything on a clean tablecloth on the large dining room table.

"So much beautiful crystal and china," Honor says. "And the furniture. I don't know where to look first."

Clemmie smiles. "It's pretty overwhelming. Maybe after you've seen everything, you'd like to bring your aunt and uncle in, and you can all pick out some things your family'd like to keep."

Rippa and I stand in the archway. "You're selling the house and contents?" I ask.

Honor nods. "I decided to hire one of those people who comes in and prices everything and sends out the word of an estate sale. It's worth it to me to have someone else do all the work. I'm worried, though. That woman who says she's Mr. Renaud's daughter. Don't we have to wait to see about her claim?"

Clemmie juts her chin. "Until I hear from a legal source, I'm going ahead with Ames's wishes. And he wanted you to have his estate."

We all jump at a banging on the back door and move down the hall in a clump. The new window Davison replaced is very clean and gives a clear view of the pissed-off face of the woman under discussion.

Chapter Sixteen

Clemmie unlocks and opens the door just wide enough to block the woman's entrance. Rippa, Honor, and I have only a partial view of Ms. Moffat. Mine is the best as I'm standing to Clemmie's right. Her greeting is not cordial. "Yes?"

The realtor notes the affront and, if it were possible, adjusts her gaze to freeze ray. "I'm here to advise you I've hired a local attorney who specializes in will disputes. I'm assured that as a direct descendent rather than an illegitimate offspring of a homeowner and housekeeper several generations removed, I have an excellent chance to gain my rightful inheritance. She's filing a court order to obtain a blood sample from my father's remains to perform a DNA test and a cease-and-desist order for you."

Honor emits a small gasp.

I'm wondering about the lawyer's assurances. Direct descendants like children are left out of inheritances all the time. A legal document such as a will should take precedence over a letter, even if Ms. Moffat proves her blood relationship.

Clemmie pales and tightens her hold on the door jamb. "You've delivered your message. Now leave."

Wow, she didn't even say please. This woman is really getting to my normally even-tempered friend. Telling Clemmie about siphoning blood from Ames's corpse was not a good move on Moffat's part.

Footsteps approach from the side, but I can't see who it is. Moffat turns, and her tight features relax into a smile. Who's made this transformation? The four of us lean forward.

"And who is this delightful creature?"

Étienne.

I glance at Honor and Rippa. Twin eye rolls.

Moffat's shoulders relax, and she practically titters. "I don't believe I've had the pleasure."

Huh. Twin egotists. That's not creepy at all. Actually, it's kind of funny.

Rippa stretches toward me. "Why are you smiling?"

"Enjoying how much they have in common."

Honor murmurs, "If you two are interested, I can give you my educated opinion."

"Yes," we chorus.

Clemmie widens the door opening, and the four of us wait for the drama to unfold.

Étienne extends his hand and leans over Moffat's. I notice the young gardener's are clean. Gloves could be the answer, but he's also wearing the expensive, soft-leather shoes he had on the first time I saw him. Neither peg him as having worked today. Stella's observation that he wouldn't get any done with Honor nearby was spot on.

Moffat must have twelve to fifteen years on Étienne, but she blushes and flutters her eyelashes. "Sevryn Moffat."

"Étienne Chappelle. Charmed, *chère*."

The realtor's gaze cuts to Clemmie and back. "I have to leave, but it's nice to meet someone with manners, Étienne."

Rippa murmurs, "What? No good-bye for us?"

With Étienne this close, I check her for signs of anxiety.

She catches me looking at her, and I get my very own eye roll.

"Sorry." Although I don't know why I apologize for worrying about her.

Étienne turns toward us. "May I speak to Honor?"

She nods and steps past Clemmie. "I'll be back in a few minutes."

"Did anyone else think that interaction was odd?" Clemmie asks.

I watch the older woman's retreating back. "Would not have thought she'd fall for that kind of, um, flattery." No comment from Rippa so I continue. "Speaking of Moffat, I'm going to call Fontenot regarding our visitor and retrieve that bottled fruity tea I left in Stella's back-porch fridge this morning. Anything I can get either of you?"

Two negative head shakes, so I walk through the house, intent on avoiding Honor and Étienne. I go out the front door and head for Stella's. I catch a whiff of early-blooming flowers and enjoy the fragrance, especially the citrusy magnolia. The first week of March would not be this nice in the Puget Sound area. I fan my face. It would also not be this humid, so there's a trade-off.

My eye catches movement near the steps to Stella's back porch. I sigh and head for Sevryn Moffat.

She sees me and stops, her mouth pursed in a sour downturn.

I approach and give what I hope is an irritating

huff. "May I ask what you're doing here?"

Moffat doesn't hide her irritation, either. "Not that it's any of your business, but I contacted Mrs. Neely and asked if I could have a chat."

Very clever. A widow living next door to Ames Renaud could have some insights Clemmie isn't willing to share.

My protective instincts flare. "This isn't a good day. Mrs. Neely hasn't been well, and, aside from that, she's very busy today. In any event, she wasn't close to Mr. Renaud. Please don't bother her. You'd be wasting your time."

"Nevertheless, it's *my* time and, as I've already said, none of your business."

I have a genuine and growing dislike for this woman. And I'm sure it's returned. Although she no doubt finds me annoying, I need to try one more thing. "How about this? I've been in every room in that house for the past three days. Mrs. Neely has never been inside. Why not ask me what you were going to ask her?"

Her gaze sharpens. "If I'm not satisfied with your answers, can I speak to Mrs. Neely?"

I shake my head. "Take it or leave it, but I can guarantee I know more."

Raif jumps in with a dark chuckle. *You might have to add another McCarren's Rule, Cara. Dancing with the bear.*

Maybe. But I intend to lead.

Moffat gives a curt nod. "Okay, I'll see if what you know matches what I've already found out."

This is new. "Which is?"

She tips her head southward. "I've already had a

conversation with the people on the far side of my father's house. They told me there's a rumor it contains a big treasure. In a book, they think. Is that true?"

"Is the rumor true? Yes. Apparently, Mr. Renaud believed there was a treasure."

Her eyes widen. "Then it's mine. Part of my inheritance."

I sigh. "He believed there was a treasure, but nothing has been found although many generations have searched. In any case, there's been no legal confirmation the estate is yours."

The laser ray is back. "Ames Renaud was my biological father. He may not have known it but didn't stick around to find out. It's too late for my mother, but he owes *me*."

Her one-track mind is exasperating, so I don't go down that road. I might if she weren't so prickly and aggressive about it. It, being she is the only one with rights, the only one deserving, or the only one who counts. I take a breath. Maybe I can get some additional information for Fontenot. "If I think of more details, where are you staying?"

An impatient shrug. I can almost see the refusal coming. "There's no need—" She breaks off, looking at something over my shoulder. I turn to see what.

Étienne and Aldo Chappelle are rounding the hedge. Étienne's cousin must have been close by at the Renaud house. Dark looks occupy both their faces. They stalk to stand in front of Ms. Moffat, who now takes a half step back.

Étienne's charm is no longer in evidence. "You're going after my girlfriend's inheritance?"

Uh-oh. I'd challenge that Honor considers herself

his girlfriend. But that's just me.

Before she can respond, Stella comes to the back door. She sees the Chappelles and Ms. Moffat. "Oh. I thought the strange car at the curb was delivering something for tonight's party." She looks around the garden. "Étienne, please remember to trim and pick up where I asked." She returns inside.

Neither Chappelle responds, but I have to give it to Moffat. She straightens her shoulders and tips her chin toward the men. "This is tiresome. Ames Renaud was my biological father. I consider myself his legal heir and intend to pursue my rights. Now, if you'll get out of my way."

Uncertainty replaces menace on the men's faces as she steps around them, walks to the street, and gets into her bright-yellow, exotic rental.

I take the stairs into Stella's house without looking back. Inside, I find an empty kitchen and pull out my cellphone, calling Fontenot.

"Detective Fontenot."

"Hello, Detective. This is Julianne McCarren. I have some information for you about Sevryn Moffat. I believe you wanted to talk to her?"

"Very interested as we've eliminated the usual suspects. Do you know where she is? We've come up empty on canvassing motels in the area."

"I still don't know where she's staying, but I found out this morning that Sharon Moore was the name Sevryn Moffat was born with. She had it legally changed a few years ago."

"Good information. I'll have it verified. You think Sharon Moore's a name she might be using?"

"It's worth checking out."

Fontenot pauses. "Most places require photo ID. If she has one under her former name, that'd be enough."

He pauses again, and I hear papers rustling.

"Here's something concrete. Two sets of footprints were found surrounding the body in Mrs. Neely's garden. They were faint because it had rained. However, there was enough distinction to match one set to the footprints found in back of the Renaud house where you saw the man running away the other night."

"So one of them thinks there may be something incriminating left behind."

"That's a theory."

He's not giving anything away, but the detective's helpful, nonetheless.

I persist although it's like pulling teeth. "Any distinguishing sole prints?"

A small chuckle overrides the office chatter in the call's background. "You don't miss much, Mrs. McCarren."

I decide to take that as a compliment. "Well?"

"Still processing. Why? Have you come across anyone who fits?"

"No solid connection. Just trying to force a square peg into a round hole because I don't much like the square peg. If I find something, I'll let you know."

"Same here."

That done, I retrieve my bottle of tea and look out the back-door window. Both Chappelles are using clippers in the side garden, so I head to the Renaud house.

In the kitchen, Honor and Rippa are giggling at the table while Clemmie looks on.

I sit. "What's funny?"

Rippa shifts a shoulder. "Not funny, ha ha. Funny as in weird. Honor says Étienne's been acting like they're a couple ever since they met. She's told him different several times, but he ignores her."

Since Étienne's the one on my mind, I'm game to learn more. Especially as Rippa's comfortable talking about him. I turn to Honor. "How'd you meet?"

"My uncle, Pierre, who I call *Pepa*, celebrated his sixtieth birthday last October. *Tante* told him we would have a party and he could invite some friends. Samuel, of course, and Aldo, as my uncle and he work at the docks, and *Pepa* had taken a liking to him. Aldo asked if he could bring his cousin, Étienne. *Tante* said, 'Of course.' "

Honor sighs. "Frankly, I think Étienne's got all the signs of being a narcissist or has some level of personality disorder. I'm a psych major, and the more I read up on it, the scarier he gets." She waves a dismissive hand. "Guess it's not so funny after all."

Guess not, since it could be even worse.

Rippa leans in. "Tell Jules what he said to you outside."

Honor looks older than her barely twenty years. "Aldo heard about the inheritance from *Pepa* and told Étienne. He was happy but didn't trust that *others* wouldn't steal from me. And then there was the treasure to look for before *we* sold the house. I stopped him and said, 'There's no we, and the treasure is just a story. Even if there was, it would go with the house. Besides, the woman you just met is challenging the will and could win.' "

"Let me guess," Rippa says. "He's going to save the day."

The brunette shakes her head. "Didn't say anything. He turned kind of gray, then he and Aldo left." She looks at her watch and stands. "Which is what I have to do now or miss the start of my next class." She holds out the house key and smiles. "Thank you all very much for having this done and for everything else you're doing here."

Clemmie walks with Honor to the back door, then comes back to the table. "I don't like Étienne's attitude. It borders on dangerous. I wonder where he went and when he'll pop up again."

"I can help. They came around the hedge toward Stella's as I was talking to Ms. Moffat. Étienne got in her face, but she wasn't having it. Told him to back off and left. Both cousins looked very angry."

Clemmie stands. "Wait a minute. What do you mean they? And what was Moffat doing there?"

"It's okay," I say, quickly. "Moffat invited herself to chat with Stella, but I took care of it. Then the guys showed up."

Rippa glances in the direction of Stella's house. "Sorry, but I think you're both a little off."

Clemmie's questioning look probably mirrors my own. "What does that mean?"

A frown mars the teenager's forehead. "No disrespect, but I figure Stella's only as frail as you let her be. She caught Fontenot off guard. Twice. She had already thought about a renter to replace her income from Jilly, and she was dead-on describing Étienne. Maybe she just needs encouragement or a push in the right direction."

"Astute observation," Clemmie returns. "Stella and I might as well have been raised by different people. I believe in letting others know what you are capable of, and she prefers to hide her light under a bushel."

I laugh at the expression on Rippa's face. "Grandmother Parkes said it was from the Bible. It means Stella prefers to keep her talents and aptitudes hidden. More ladylike not to display them. You've caught on that she's stronger than she looks."

Clemmie's gaze also moves in the direction of Stella's house. "I forget that. Davison and I have been talking about her situation ever since Jilly and Hugh announced their wedding date. I jumped right in and asked Stella if she would like to sell that old house and move in with us since we have plenty of room."

Rippa grins. "Betcha she said no."

Our older friend displays a hiked eyebrow. "Very strongly. Not because she doesn't like the idea of sharing space with us, but she's adamant that she has the responsibility to 'save the family manse' to pass on to Jilly."

"Do you think she'd object to a dignified, private estate sale?" I ask. "She's already interested in having the books in the library gone over to see if there are any editions that might interest a bookseller. Maybe we could help her inventory other things. As I recall, her husband Harlan played golf every chance he got and bought himself only the best equipment. Are his clubs and golf cart still at her house?"

Clemmie doesn't hesitate. "They are. He also collected watches. I've seen him in a Rolex, a LeCoultre, and a Patek Philippe among others. I'm pretty sure she still has those too."

"Whoa. Patek Philippe. I had no idea Harlan had that kind of money. My brother-in-law bought one secondhand, and his wife nearly left him."

Clemmie shakes her head. "He didn't. He inherited it from his grandfather. It's what started his collection. In any case, Stella refused to get rid of any of his things after he passed away. Maybe if we convince her selling some of them would enable her to keep the house, it might work." Laughing, she lifts a shoulder. "It's a start. But I warn you, there are places in that house not looked in for generations."

Rippa's eyes light. "Wouldn't it be great if we found a treasure there too?"

Heavy sigh from me. "Maybe you should think about a minor in archeology."

Wrong thing to say. Rippa bobbles her eyebrows. "Not a bad idea."

My response is interrupted by loud banging from in front of the house. The three of us cut through the formal dining room, and Clemmie opens the door.

A middle-aged man standing back from the door is wearing a T-shirt reading *Hal's Carpenter Pals*. He smiles. "Mrs. Ashurst?"

Clemmie glances at her watch. "Right on time." She turns to us, pulls her mouth down, and whispers, "Totally forgot," then widens the door opening to let him enter. "The water damage is upstairs, the bedroom in the front. Let me show you."

Rippa and I watch as two younger men start constructing scaffolding against the house.

"They must be the guys Clemmie hired to fix the leaking window frame," I say. "Good thing I only have the last couple of boxes to go through and I dragged them over by the door to take pictures. Shouldn't take more than an hour."

Clemmie walks up behind us as Hal goes through the door. "You're okay for time. They're setting up scaffolding and evaluating the window area and soffit today. The real work begins tomorrow for the next two or three days." She glances at her watch again. "Besides, we have about an hour left, then a party to get ready for."

Rippa lets loose an "arrgggh" of teen angst. "I was having so much fun."

The hot and cold is hard to keep up with. "Seriously? A party in New Orleans during Mardi Gras and you aren't interested?"

Her eyebrow wings, followed by "I found a great book in one of the boxes and Honor said I could have it. Remember, I showed you. *Les Misérables*."

Clemmie laughs and gives each of us a quick hug. "You two are great. I really appreciate the time you've spent here when you could've been having way more fun." She winks at Rippa. "Or time to read. I promise no ice cream punch tonight. Plus, some cute groomsmen."

Rippa huffs a breath. "Sorry. It's Jilly's big deal, and she's really sweet. I'll do my best. *Then* get back to that book."

****

Stella's formal parlor is decorated beautifully, and she's in her element.

Jilly has matched Rippa and me with Hugh's two brothers as escorts for the wedding. Patrick, my escort, is married and has brought his wife to the party. Rippa's hope to stay a little while, then sneak away to read ended as soon as her escort, Kyle, arrives. He sticks to her side and spends all his time discussing his upcoming fantasy football picks. I lose count of the number of eye rolls I get when he's not looking. So not in her wheelhouse. She's a good sport, though, and stays to the end.

We're cleaning the last vestiges of the mess in the kitchen when Clemmie comes in the back door. Her features are pale, her eyes almost unblinking. "Our house has been broken into."

Chapter Seventeen

Stella takes a step forward, her hand held toward her sister. "What? Are you all right?"

Clemmie pushes out a deep breath and sits at the table. "We're fine. Davison's checking the rest of the doors and windows and calling the police. I came to tell you in case you see a police car in front of our house."

Too many incidents involving the aunts, especially Clemmie, in the last four days gives me an uneasy shimmer in my core.

Stella hands her sister a tumbler of water. "How did they get in?"

"Broke the glass in the back door." A wan smile. "That seems to be the current mode of entry on this block."

Rippa sits across from her, frowning. "Major suck. Did they steal a lot of stuff?"

"That's just it. Nothing's missing we could see. Big-screen TV, laptops, our chest of vintage silver, my jewelry box, all there. I can't imagine it was random. They were looking for something."

Ames Renaud's murder and supposed treasure have been on my mind for days. I lean in to get Clemmie's attention. "The key to the Renaud house?"

She springs up, scooting her chair backward. "I...I didn't think to check. I'll do that now."

Rippa jumps up too. "Can I go?"

"I think she and Davison will be busy checking their house before the police arrive." I face Clemmie. "Have you cleared the house?"

She's partway turned to leave. "Oh, yes. Um, Rippa, could you give it an hour? There's a big parade tonight, and since there was nothing taken and no danger, we're not sure how long before the police can respond."

Rippa sits again. "Sure."

Clemmie nods absentmindedly. "Okay, thanks."

We've finished cleaning in Stella's kitchen, and Rippa and I are going over our respective emails when my phone rings. It's Clemmie.

"Hi. Good call on the key."

"It's missing?"

"No. It's here, but it's been moved. We have six key hooks in a line by the back door. I've been using the last one for the new key. I found it on the fourth hook. We think it was used, then put back."

"Or maybe copied."

Rippa waves her hand in front of my face and hisses. "What's going on?"

I wave back with my index finger and shake my head.

Clemmie sucks in a breath. "There are self-service key-copy machines at service stations and hardware stores. We were at Stella's for four hours. Plenty of time to make either option happen."

She speaks to Davison in the background. "Julianne thinks it could also have been copied and returned."

I hear a response from Davison, too far away for me to understand.

"Julianne? We're going to wait for the police and ask them to walk through Ames's house with us after we get our break-in on record. If it's not too late, do you and Rippa want to be part of that? You can attest to the contents of the second floor."

I glance toward the Renaud house through the glass on Stella's back door. Dark. "We'll be glad to. Let us know."

"Thank you, bye."

"Bye." I hang up and sigh.

Rippa's eagerness is in my face and almost palpable. "What's copied? Help who?"

I hold up my hand. "Whoever broke in at Clemmie and Davison's messed with the key to the Renaud house. Clemmie left it on a hook by their back door, and someone moved it to a different hook. We're wondering if, in the four hours they were gone, it was *borrowed* and used or copied and maybe used."

Stella sits quietly with her glass of brown-gold liquid. Her gaze follows the trajectory of my earlier one through her back-door window. "But how would they know where Clemmie and Davison kept their keys?"

I follow her line of sight. "Where do you keep yours?"

It's a trick question. From staying here with Jilly and the aunts on a number of occasions, I remember a small, cast-iron fleur-de-lis with two hooks screwed to the side of the wall just inside her bumped-out back door.

Stella sips her drink and knits her brow. "Probably the first place to look if that's what they were after."

"It's got to be the same guy," Rippa puts in. "Either he left something behind when he killed poor

Mr. Renaud, or he knows something about the location of the treasure and keeps trying to go for it."

"Oh, and I forgot to mention," I interrupt. "When I talked to Detective Fontenot today, he said the footprints running from the back of the Renaud house matched one of the two sets of prints found in Stella's garden near Mr. Renaud's body."

Rippa nods animatedly. "And as a for instance, two tall guys who hang around Stella's garden and the Renaud house are the Chappelle cousins."

Wow. Étienne went down like a brick in Rippa's favor. Sounds like he took Aldo with him.

Stella shudders and slides out a breath. "I guess that adds more people to the list of those with a motive to break into the Renaud house. And Clemmie's."

"Don't forget Moffat," I say. "When she was in Clemmie and Davison's house, she followed him into the kitchen for her fizzy water. She could have seen where they keep their keys then."

Rippa sighs. "How would she even know to look for a new key?"

"I wondered that too. Think about when we caught her in the Renaud house. She'd walked through the back door while Clemmie was at the front door talking to the locksmith. Moffat could have seen his truck and guessed what was going on."

Rippa shakes her head. "We're giving her a lot of credit, but since the break-in seems specific to the new house key, that still makes our pool of suspects limited. A tall guy or guys, and Ms. Moffat."

"If the police haven't found anything and the three of you haven't, whatever they're looking for must be very small," Stella offers.

Rippa bounces in her chair. "Yeah. Like a key, or a word puzzle in an old book."

"Maybe," I say. "Or a small gold signet ring the CSIs found with your help."

"If that's it, none of the suspects would know the police have it already."

"And with the initial S, it's one of the reasons they're looking for Moffat." I raise an eyebrow. "Guessing aside. We have to wear these clothes to the rehearsal dinner tomorrow night. If we're going to keep them clean, we need to get to the rental and change into more comfortable, washable clothes to accompany the police and Clemmie and Davison."

Rippa makes it completely out of her chair. "Good idea. I'm ready."

I turn to Stella. "You okay to lock up behind us? Or you can come if you want."

She scans her kitchen, her gaze landing on the bottle holding her cordial. "You girls go ahead. I'll be fine. The party tired me out."

Neither Rippa nor I had much to drink, but we probably look a little strange craning our necks during the two-minute walk past the Renaud house. It's quiet and dark.

A half hour later, now in comfy clothes, we're both yawning as we wait for Clemmie's call in the living room.

Rippa leans back in a dark-brown, tufted Chesterfield chair. I've sat on it once since we got here, and it feels like it's stuffed with horsehair. Which it could be if it's original. Not too comfy.

"Want some popcorn or a snack? Chips, maybe?" she asks.

I always regret eating when I'm bored. "No, thanks. How's your story of the French Revolution coming along?"

Her eyes sparkle. "Great. I feel so sorry for Jean Valjean. He only stole that bread because his sister's kids were starving. And that Inspector Javert guy is so mean and relentless."

Not so great for the protagonist. My phone rings and displays *C. Ashurst*. "Hello."

"Hi, Julianne, can you and Rippa meet us at the back door to Ames's house?"

"Sure. See you in a few minutes."

Rippa and I walk past the Renaud house and approach the back from Stella's side so as not to alarm the neighbors on the other side. The same young cop who tried to catch Rippa's eye after the break-in is standing on the back porch. His partner and Clemmie and Davison are there too.

Clemmie turns to us. "These are the women who did the estate inventory of the second floor. They're going to check for obvious signs of items having been disturbed."

The older cop frowns at the four of us. "You all are saying this might be related to a murder that took place here and to the previous break-in?"

I nod. "Detective Fontenot's the primary."

He scratches a note. "I'll loop him in."

Clemmie steps aside. "This officer's already gone through looking for intruders while the other one checked for fresh footprints outside. Neither found any indication the house has been gone through. Could you two look around the upstairs while Davison and I walk the first floor?"

Rippa and I head down the hall to the stairs. I can't help it; I glance at the demi-lune table to see if the smalls Moffat was interested in are still there. They are. The only dust out of place in the hall is where the boxes of books we brought down the other day were scooted together.

Upstairs it's the same. No signs of intrusion aside from articles moved by me and the window repair guy. I flick the light switch and walk out. Rippa is standing at the top of the stairs.

"You find anything?"

"No. You'd think with the mess up here it'd be hard to tell, but it's not."

We walk downstairs, and her quiet sighs suggest she expected something more exciting.

I tap her ribs with my elbow. "Me neither. No boxes torn through or contents scattered."

She shrugs. "Kinda disappointing."

We reach the bottom, and Clemmie is there with the older cop. She turns, her face a mask encompassing exhaustion and anxiety. "Nothing?"

Rippa and I shake our heads in sync.

The cop slaps his notebook shut. "We'll report the break-in, but with no indication of robbery in either residence, this incident is closed. I'll notify Fontenot."

Chapter Eighteen

The cops walk away, the younger one throwing a smile at Rippa, who gives a tentative smile in return.

Clemmie receives a hug from her husband and sighs. "Catching whoever is behind this would've been too easy I guess."

Davison swipes his jaw and kisses his wife's temple. "I know that look. Your commitment to Ames is mostly done, but you're not going to turn the house over to Honor and walk away."

She smiles. "Can we come up with a few other options?"

"I'm in," Rippa claims.

"Me too. Most obvious would be another new set of keys."

Clemmie nods. "I'll call the locksmith first thing tomorrow morning. In addition, we could hire a security team to guard the house."

"Until when?" Davison asks. "While the house sits empty, it's a target for vandals or whoever wants to get in. If the Moffat woman persists in her legal claim, the court case might go on for an extended period of time."

I wince. "There's no way Honor could afford a long court case. She'd be forced to give up her claim or suffer a big debt at the hands of a probate firm."

Clemmie rubs her temples. "Remember my attorney friend who specializes in settlements? I gave her a copy of the will and a rundown on Ames's supposed daughter's claim. Ms. Moffat doesn't seem the type to hang around ignoring her business in New York. Or pay attorney fees while the case drags on. She may be open to a settlement. That way, Honor doesn't completely lose out. Besides, I found Ames's checkbook. As executor, I can itemize everything it takes to keep the house safe." She lifts a shoulder. "Whatever that ends up being."

"Short-term decision?" I ask.

Davison nods. "We call an emergency locksmith first thing tomorrow and hire extra security for a week. That gives us some peace of mind. At least through the wedding befores and afters. How does that sound?"

"Agreed." From Clemmie. "And the police promised additional drive-bys for the rest of tonight."

I smother a yawn. "Are you going to let Honor know what happened?"

Clemmie's mouth pulls down on one side. "I'll see if she's available right after the locksmith leaves tomorrow. She and the contractor will need new keys." Her gaze takes in the back of the house as she locks the door. "I wish there was some way we could tie this mess to that awful woman from New York."

I hear a hint of confirmation bias—that person should be guilty even though I have no proof. Just because I don't like her. In Moffat's case, hard not to lean in that direction. Even for Clemmie.

"Care for some company to Honor's tomorrow?" I ask.

She brightens. "Of course. Maybe you'd also like to go to the cemetery with me. Not looking forward to it. The detective called to say they'll be releasing

Ames's body to the mortuary soon, so I want to make the arrangements he specified. I've made an appointment to meet a member of the staff at the cemetery at ten in the morning since the office governing that location isn't at the site. She said it was an unusual request, as I'm not a family member, but eventually agreed. I think out of curiosity over Ames's death. I want to see the condition of the Renaud family mausoleum before he's interred and we hold a small service. This saves us time tramping around looking for it. She said we can follow her back afterward to deal with the paperwork."

Not a big fan of cemeteries myself, but this death is still new for Clemmie, and she's a friend. "I'm game. Rippa?"

"Sure. Running errands will fortify us against the onslaught of manicurists. Are there also pedicurists?"

Aaarrggh. Totally slipped my mind. Tomorrow afternoon all the women in the bride's entourage are getting mani/pedis so we all match on fingers and toes with our wedding garb. The colors being pale teal, pale coral, and cream. I glance at my nails. Cleaning and working in dirt and dust for the past three days has taken its toll. I could definitely use a manicure and the hand massage that comes with it.

Clemmie nods. "Thanks. I'll call as soon as I have the new keys."

****

Eight a.m. is a sleep-in for me. Even with the hollow sound of rain on the roof of the rental house causing some restlessness, I feel good. Turns out to be great timing. Rippa is up and has made coffee. I contribute bacon, eggs, and toast.

A chuckle from Raif. *One of your three personal-best meals, Cara.*

Smart-ass. Undeniable, though.

Rippa is deep into something on her laptop. She's eating with one hand and typing with the other.

"What's got your attention?"

"Clemmie let me take a picture of that Renaud land grant Mr. Renaud gave her. I'm tracking down some historical information on it. And on the family."

"You know if the DNA matches, Moffat really is his daughter."

Rippa wrinkles her nose. "More than one Ames Renaud on Google. Maybe she just picked out the one who had the most for her to gain."

"Still can't beat the science."

Heavy sigh. "Oh, well. I wanted to put together the Renaud background as a gift for Clemmie anyway. Maybe even have a color copy of the grant made into a custom puzzle for her."

"Nice idea."

"Thanks. You should be getting a call from her soon. I saw the locksmith truck drive toward the Renaud house just before you came down. It said 'twenty-four-hour service' on the side."

I glance at the time on my phone. "Wow. Serious speed."

Rippa taps a few keys on her laptop and slants me a look. "Pictures of that cemetery look depressing. Sure you want to go?"

Sweet of her to think about the effect it might have on me, since she's very familiar with the dark ledge I occupied for a few years after Raif's death. "I'm good. Besides, when we stop by Honor's, I'd like to take another look at *Pepa* if he's at home. I have enough faith in my own judgment to believe she's not involved in the incidents surrounding the Renaud house, but her family is very tight knit and a little quick to temper from what I saw. The tall, rangy figure running through the garden a couple of nights ago wasn't necessarily a *young* man."

"Kind of a stretch for motive, especially since those footprints were also found in Stella's garden. But we can't rule out anyone at this point. Since the veil has been lifted from my eyes regarding a certain charming guy, I've been thinking he might fit the bill too."

I make an exaggerated smirk. "So you said last night. Veil lifted from your eyes?"

She returns the smirk. "I'm well read."

My eye roll is interrupted by the ringing of my phone. It's Clemmie.

"Hi. Got the new lock keys, and Honor will be available between nine thirty and ten. Have you two had breakfast?"

"Yes. Are you ready for us?"

"Come over and have a coffee, then we'll leave."

"Good. Rippa and I have been discussing the possible identity of the break-in culprit. We'd like your opinion."

We lock up the rental and walk toward Clemmie's. Outside Stella's house, Étienne is raking in the back of the garden, near the spot where we found Ames Renaud. The young gardener's effort seems intent, and he doesn't acknowledge us.

Clemmie and Davison's kitchen smells like strong coffee and baked goods. Rippa oohs and aahs over Davison's brass and copper espresso machine. He grins and obliges with two excellent cups. If we weren't awake before, we are now.

Not to be outdone, Clemmie presents us each with a warm maple bar.

"Thank you," we chorus. Finishing, I ignore good manners and lick my fingers. Rippa follows suit.

Clemmie puts on a light windbreaker, grabs two small envelopes, a large one, and her keys. "Davison's working on securing the house. We need to get moving if we're going to be on time to meet with Honor."

The three of us get into Clemmie's compact, Japanese luxury car and head out. She shakes her head at our conjectures as she navigates the rain-swept streets of the Upper Ninth Ward. "What's the connection? I get that Honor's uncle and Étienne would both want her to have the inheritance, but why the break-ins? It couldn't be a matter of trying to scare off the Moffat woman. She's too tenacious. If she wins, she'll just sell the house and contents as soon as possible and go back to New York."

"Maybe it doesn't have anything to do with the inheritance," I say. "Maybe the goal is to find the treasure before the house is sold and occupied again."

Clemmie makes quick eye contact, then refocuses on the road. "That specific idea hadn't occurred to me. Ames was certain it existed after he inherited his uncle's house and papers. I hate to think he lost his life because of a family rumor passed down for over a century and a half."

I shrug. "The fact that the legend of the Renaud treasure lasted this long actually lends it credence I suppose."

Rippa reaches forward and taps Clemmie's

shoulder. "We talked at Stella's while you were waiting for the police. Maybe the bad guys are looking for a clue they left behind and are afraid the police will discover its importance and how it connects to them. Something small."

Clemmie shakes her head again. "None of this explains the break-in at my house. How would Honor's uncle or Étienne know where I keep the Renaud house keys?"

"Most people have their keys located by their doors for easy access," I say. "Either one could've overheard Honor talking about the locks being changed after the first break-in and decided to try and disassociate the break-in at your house by making it look random. And I don't think whoever broke into your house is done."

We pull up to the deGrandpre home no further along than we were at the start of our trip.

Clemmie turns off the ignition and pulls up a text. "Davison couldn't get a private security firm to watch Ames's house. They're all busy during Mardi Gras. He's going to purchase a self-install system and put it in this morning. No alarm sounds in the house, but it will at the police station, and the owner receives a text notification. That and new locks and keys are the best we can do right now." She hands me a small envelope. "Here's the key and house code. In case you need to get in while you're here."

I slip it into my crossbody as we approach Honor's house.

Rippa whispers, "I keep forgetting my book. Maybe we can pick it up after the mani/pedi party this afternoon."

We're greeted warmly again by the pretty brunette.

"Come in. Thank you for making the trip out here. I've been trying to finish a paper, and this is a real time-saver."

Tante Arielle stands at the back of the room, as before, her stick-like frame in another mud-toned dress. Arms crossed, she brandishes a frown as if to guard against attempts at friendliness. We have something in common. Her great-niece is pretty, smart, and possibly too trusting. And like me, *Tante* Arielle's motto is "do wrong by my niece, find yourself in a world of hurt." Although they are grown, this attitude doesn't change. I give what I hope is a sincere smile.

Clemmie pulls a shiny key and a slip of paper out of her purse and hands them to Honor. "You're welcome, dear. Here's the house key and access code to the new security system."

Honor slips them in her jeans pocket. "Thank you, again." She glances toward her aunt, then back at us. "You've been beyond kind, Mrs. Ashurst, but that Ms. Moffat... She dresses in designer clothes and drives an expensive car. If she is Mr. Renaud's biological daughter and can obviously afford to challenge his will... I mean I'm very grateful, but I can't afford to do anything about it."

Clemmie sighs. "My fault for getting your hopes up. I've been so focused on making sure Ames's last wishes are met I've skirted the bigger issue." She dips her head. "Especially since Ms. Moffat is so unpleasant."

Honor puts her hand on Clemmie's forearm and chuckles. "That's putting it mildly. And however it turns out, I know you've done your best for me."

My earlier conjecture about *Pepa* makes me a little

ashamed. This small family is about as down-to-earth as they come.

Clemmie smiles at the beautiful girl. "You haven't lost yet. Besides, if she does prove her case and you file to appeal, she'd be smart to offer a settlement. Cut down on time and money she'd have to invest."

Honor's eyes widen slightly, and she tips her head. "Something to think about."

We offer our good-byes, and my last glance at *Tante* Arielle is greeted with a brisk nod. I think she's beginning to thaw.

Outside, the air is heavy with rain.

In the car, Rippa leans forward. "*Tante* Arielle seemed a little friendlier."

Clemmie shifts a shoulder and starts the car. "Can't really blame them for not greeting all this with open arms and trust. An unexpected and valuable inheritance out of the blue, then an angry, rude woman rides in on her expensive broom and threatens to take it away."

Rippa giggles. "I like the expensive broom part. Describes Ms. Moffat to a T."

Clemmie's mouth pulls down. "My parents would die of embarrassment at my language."

"OMG," Rippa squeals. "My virgin ears."

Clemmie and I laugh.

"How far to the cemetery?" I ask. "Our visit will probably be the only tourist destination I'll be able to drag Rippa to in your wonderful city."

"Actually, it's fairly close. Maybe five minutes," says Clemmie.

Rippa taps me on the shoulder. "And what you said about tourist stuff is not true. We ate at Café Du Monde, walked across Jackson square, had our palms read, kicked drunk college boys out of our hotel room, wandered in the Garden District, dodged the zydeco guy, and more."

"I stand corrected."

Chapter Nineteen

The rain is heavy as we arrive at the parking lot along one side of the walled cemetery.

Clemmie looks through the windshield, then over her shoulder. "We're a little early. Rippa, there should be a couple of umbrellas in the back seat." Her gaze slides between Rippa and me. "I also want to say again how much I appreciate your company. Ready?"

Checking out the burial site for a friend shouldn't have to be done alone. We nod.

"Good to go," Rippa says, handing the smaller umbrella to Clemmie and the large one to me. "We can share."

The three of us leave the car and walk around the corner to reach the cast-iron gate.

Rippa looks through it. "Are those people attending a funeral?"

Clemmie follows the line of sight to the clutch of people huddled together as the rain slows. She shakes her head. "Tourists. The really interesting tours are the ones that start at midnight."

I pull my shoulders upward. "Jilly tried to talk me into one of those during a spring break. I declined."

Clemmie bobs her eyebrows. "Went once during high school. The guides are really good. Lots of historical knowledge, some of it guaranteed to scare the socks off you."

A woman approaches the gate. She is medium height with dark hair and a nice smile. She holds out her hand to Clemmie. "Mrs. Ashurst?"

Clemmie shakes hands, then tips her head toward us. "These are my friends, Julianne McCarren and Rippa Parkes. Thank you again for agreeing to meet here."

"Hi. Linea Creighton. It's nice to get out of the office occasionally, and I have to confess to my curiosity. We don't usually have two requests for interment in the same family mausoleum within a year. None where one of them has been murdered."

That confirms Clemmie's assumption of at least one reason the manager is here.

Ms. Creighton shows some identification at the gate, and we're admitted. Inside, she stops and turns. "Please stay with me. There is no practical layout of this cemetery, and if you aren't with a guide, finding the site you're looking for is almost impossible. It's also easy to get lost."

It's mid-morning, and the rain has stopped, but as we enter, the gray sky seems to weigh more.

It's very crowded here, Cara.

I bet it is. "Don't get stuck," I mumble.

Rippa looks over her shoulder, her face reflecting concern. "What? You okay?"

I take an emotional inventory and find I am. "Yep. All good."

We move slowly, hindered by the condition of the ground. Some of the walkways are nothing more than shallow troughs filled with water. There is also a fetid odor, no doubt caused by the high-water table, rain, and the rusting iron fences that surround several of the sites.

It appears every other one is in disrepair. Some just long, narrow piles of broken bricks.

I stop at one. "Is this really a grave?"

The manager turns. "Yes, unfortunately. This location, being over two hundred years old, has many gravesites where the family line has ended."

This elicits a brief gasp from Clemmie. She looks from the pile of bricks to the woman. "Ames was the last in the Renaud line. There's nothing in his will about grave maintenance."

Ms. Creighton's face is impassive. She must've heard this before and waits.

"I'd like to discuss maintenance fees in your office," Clemmie says.

"Of course."

My guess is Ms. Moffat will have strong objections to the cost of a burial being subtracted from the proceeds of the estate. She would probably go with a cheap cremation and be done with it. In any case, since the coroner is finished with his body, Ames Renaud has nowhere to go, and Clemmie is determined to fulfill his final wishes.

The cemetery has a haphazard layout with every kind of construction from marble to cement. Even cast iron. A good number are also surrounded by ornate cast-iron fences.

I touch a spike on one of them. "Wait. Why the fences?"

Our guide gives no sign of exasperation at our questions. "Several reasons. They started as property markers. You know, 'Don't trespass on the plot I bought to build on.' They were also for decorative purposes. At first for the Spanish, then the French.

Some say the primary purpose was theft deterrent. Kept thieves from breaking in to look for valuables. Personally, I like superstition as the reason. The properties of iron keeping out bad spirits."

"Ghoulish, but interesting."

We arrive at the Renaud mausoleum. It's much smaller than I thought it would be for a family with an almost two-hundred-year history in New Orleans. The roof is peaked, and the structure is granite but terribly dirty and pitted. Two smallish chambers, one on top of the other, make up the structure.

Rippa voices what I think is an obvious question. "I don't get it. This is the whole family?"

The woman smiles. "No, dear. This is usually more or less temporary. The Renauds also have an ossuary."

Clemmie sucks in another small breath, her gaze not leaving the mausoleum. "Once the flesh decays from the body, in an obscenely short amount of time because of the moisture and heat here, the bones of previous family members are sent to an ossuary for storage. It looks as if Ames and his uncle will stay here, though. Is that correct?"

"Correct," the woman says.

"So the uncle is already in one of the chambers, and the other is unoccupied?" Rippa asks.

Ms. Creighton nods.

Her question answered, Rippa scans our surroundings and points at a tall, white pyramid several sections over. "Is that structure for a burial? Why is it so new?"

Our guide looks a little pained. "Yes, it is. A few plots and mausoleum sites are still available here. That particular one belongs to an actor."

A new bank of dark gray is rolling in, so we quick-step as much as possible to the gate and out to the parking lot.

We follow the woman's car. When we arrive at the office, Clemmie turns. "After the paperwork, lunch is my treat. Solid fortification for the afternoon. No dessert, though. Jilly is serving petit fours and champagne."

Rippa claps. "Now we're talking. But…"

Clemmie grins into the rearview mirror. "You have a problem with bubbly and little cakes?"

"Nope. Just working our schedule. I had the dress I ordered delivered to our hotel. The concierge said she'd have it unpacked, steamed, and hung in our room. I called, and it's there. After lunch if you could drop me off at the hotel, that would save me a trip later."

"That's not necessary. I'll just circle the block while you run inside."

Rippa shakes her head. "Thanks, but I have another errand to run. Some shopping."

I blink. This is news. Rippa's shopping is usually limited to a run to the mall or online for jeans or Ts. "Wait. Why didn't you have the dress sent to the Sandoval house?"

She holds up her index finger. "The front porch is beautiful but exposed. And those tourist trolleys go past lots of times a day. A package sitting there for an extended period could be tempting."

Clemmie nods. "Sad commentary, but smart. Sure. I'll drop you off."

****

The gastropub Clemmie takes us to for lunch is dark, and the music is a little loud. We're saved from this atmosphere when the man at the door greets Clemmie by kissing the air near each of her cheeks.

"Mrs. Ashurst. Lunch with friends today?" He peers through a window. "Sun's out. Let me find you a table in the courtyard."

Clemmie shrugs at us. "Vaughn's the son of a family friend. Davison and I eat here frequently."

"Smells really yummy," Rippa confirms. "I saw where they just served a burger."

Vaughn leads us to a more or less quiet corner of the courtyard and adjusts the table umbrella. Our server is right behind him with menus.

I open mine and scan the selections. "The Gulf seafood looks amazing."

Rippa taps a column in hers. "Sticking with a burger. What's a gastropub anyway? How's this any different from a pub or a bistro or a brewpub?"

Clemmie sips her water. "I think when the term gastro prefaces it, that means trendy, upscale, inventive food. However, it's not always a hit. Don't order the burger with dandelion greens as one of the toppings."

The grimace on Rippa's face as she reopens her menu has us laughing.

Clemmie stops when her cellphone buzzes. She pulls it from her purse. "Davison rarely texts. I need to call him."

I nod as she steps away and taps the screen.

A minute later I glance back. Her lips have flattened, and her eyes close for a moment. Uh-oh. This can't be good.

Rippa focuses on Clemmie as she ends the call and walks back. "Everybody okay?" she asks.

My stomach wobbles. I hate seeing my kind friend

upset.

Clemmie sits. "Everyone's fine. Davison wanted me to know I received a document overnighted from a local law firm. Per a judge's order, I am to cease fulfilling the terms of Ames's will. The beneficiary of the estate is being challenged."

I pat Clemmie's hand. "We knew it was coming."

Our server approaches, and we order.

When she leaves, Clemmie sets her mouth. "I'm getting an attorney. Should have done it already. Just because Ms. Moffat may be directly related doesn't mean Ames's wishes, and those of his uncle, should be completely overturned. Besides which, Detective Fontenot hasn't interviewed her yet. I'd like to see her designer flats replaced with jailhouse plastic slip-ons."

I blink. Clemmie might be taking on a losing battle, but her moral compass is to be admired. "Kinda like to see that myself. Unfortunately, he can't find her."

Clemmie smiles. "I bet her attorney would know how to reach her."

"Brilliant. I'll call Fontenot when we get back to the house."

Rippa taps the table. "Don't forget the treasure. We don't want her to get her hands on that."

Perspective restored.

We're all laughing when our food is served.

****

We drop Rippa off and head to Clemmie's. Inside, Davison has left the legal documents and a note on the kitchen table.

She opens the note first and smiles. "He's at Stella's helping move furniture for the party."

"He's a sweetie."

Clemmie nods. "My mother and father were dead set against Davison, which made me more determined. In a way, I have them to thank for a truly wonderful husband."

She picks up the cover letter. "Here it is. Ms. Moffat's attorney's information." She slides the letter to me. "Detective Fontenot should be able to contact her through her."

Fontenot doesn't answer, so I leave a message. Odds are slim that the New Yorker found out Ames Renaud was her father, scoped out his address, then had him dispatched. Then again, people have been killed for a lot less.

Clemmie looks up from the legal documents, hooking her short, dark bob around one ear. She pushes out a breath. "No getting around this. I'll call Honor and let her know we're at a standstill until it's resolved."

I glance at the document. "I know she's mentioned several times how grateful she is for your help, but are you sure Honor would want you to hire an attorney on her behalf?"

Clemmie rubs her temples with thumb and middle finger. "My voice of reason says no, but my heart, and sense of fairness, says yes. You do have a point, though. I'll tell her my intent and see what she has to say, but I have a feeling the deGrandpre family pride will win."

We look up at the sound of the front door opening.

Davison appears a few seconds later, grinning. "I'm told by Jilly the wedding colors are pale coral and teal." He shrugs. "I see pink and green."

I gasp in mock horror. "Heresy, sir."

Clemmie stands and gives him a kiss below his salt-and-pepper sideburn. "Luckily, you only have to walk Jilly down the aisle. Dodged a bullet there. Only your black tux involved."

He looks at the documents. "Sorry about these. Mostly because Honor and her family sound deserving."

"Knock, knock."

Clemmie turns toward the front of the house. "Back here, Rippa."

Rippa peeks around the doorjamb. "Stopping here and at Stella's before I freshen up for the party." She steps in and swings a silver bag from behind her toward Clemmie. "For making my stay in New Orleans so fun."

Clemmie accepts the bag. "We have different ideas of what constitutes fun, but you are so sweet. Thank you, dear." She spreads the glittered tissue apart and pulls out a small, ornate, sterling-silver candy dish. "An engraved F in the bottom!"

Rippa looks pleased. "For Farrol since your family name is important. I saw two of them in the window of a shop when I was with Étienne. I got the other one for Stella."

Clemmie slides her thumb across the letter. "The Farrols go back five generations in that house. She'll love it."

"Only five?" Rippa asks. "I've been doing historical research on the Renaud house and planned to do some on the Farrol house too. So they weren't the original occupants?"

"From what I recall, a Farrol married into the original family. Grandfather Farrol said there was a

Bible tracing the original owners and the Farrols documented somewhere. He just couldn't remember where."

Rippa nods. "Hey, thanks. I'll do some digging."

I'm always proud of Rippa, but times like this, doubly so. These gifts cannot have been inexpensive, and I know she also wanted to buy for her mom and Ben. Tomorrow's the wedding, but since we're staying a few extra days, I need to find time to get a couple of souvenirs for her too. Maybe a little silver mask for her charm bracelet.

I look at my cellphone. "If you're stopping at Stella's first, I'll meet you at the rental. We're supposed to dress in very comfy clothes for the mani/pedi party."

****

As I'm her matron of honor, Jilly has saved a chair for me next to hers. She, Davison, and the people she hired for the spa treatments have transformed Stella's formal parlor into a tranquil, pastel haven. Still, Jilly looks pale and tired. I give her a hug.

"Almost there. This time tomorrow you'll be dancing with your new husband at your reception. Then two relaxing weeks in Fiji. Are you excited?"

She musters a lopsided smile. "I hope to spend the first week in bed. Sleeping."

With that, she stands and thanks her entourage as the caterers bring trays of petit fours iced in the wedding colors and flutes of champagne.

The undercurrent of party chatter among the guests and spa employees commences, and smiles bloom.

An hour later, the champagne is low, and spirits are still high.

The pre-manicure salt-rub cleansing followed by

hand massage is the highlight of my day. My nails usually go naked, but this pale coral is the perfect color for the fingers and toes of Jilly's blonde line up.

Rippa wanders over, blowing on her fingernails. "I'm waiting for a foot wax. By the way, Jilly, thank you for having me in your bridal party." She nods at a few of the other women in the wedding party. "Your friends have been so nice to me, and I've really enjoyed myself."

Jilly stands and gives her a hug. "Good to hear. So my plan to plant a mystery treasure next door hasn't detracted from your fun?"

Rippa's eyes widen, and she stops mid-blow. "What?"

The champagne has worked its magic. Jilly and I start to giggle. We stop at Rippa's eye roll, then the rest of the room goes quiet. I realize a timid knocking on Stella's front door is the reason.

One of the caterers answers it, and I hear a familiar male voice. Detective Fontenot.

My nails are dry, and Jilly's look of concern at the intrusion prompts me to pat her hand and walk to the door. Rippa is right behind me.

The detective looks relieved at our arrival and starts backing onto the front porch. "Um, pardon my timing. I didn't know I'd be interrupting a lady party. However, this latest development puts a new twist on the Renaud murder." He reaches to close the door behind us, and I notice he is either wearing the same brown suit from a week ago, or this shade of brown is his favorite color.

Maybe the information I provided about her attorney has helped. "You found Ms. Moffat?"

He casts a quick glance at Rippa and sighs. Probably remembering her interest in the case. "Yes. At a motel on the outskirts of the city. She was murdered between eight and nine last night."

I did not see that coming, Cara.

Me, neither.

Damn. Moffat was annoying and rude, and yes, mercenary, but losing her life over a nasty personality isn't right. My stomach tightens. Especially since the people who will benefit the most from her death are so nice.

Rippa huffs out a breath. "Whoa."

Chapter Twenty

Late afternoon sunlight dips under the porch overhang and accentuates the wince on her face as Rippa echoes the same shock I felt. Only out loud. "That is so harsh. Like she was mega mean and didn't care that she was stealing Honor's inheritance, but murdered? How?"

Detective Fontenot flips through his notebook. "Not my case, but since she was a person of interest in Mr. Renaud's case, I have the details." His gaze holds Rippa. "The dry facts aren't as bad as stumbling across a real dead body, but the result is the same. Sure you're okay to hear this?"

Rippa studies her bare toes, breaking eye contact, then pulls up. "Thanks for asking. Um, is it gory?"

"No blood or guts. Looks like it was quick."

That actually makes *me* feel better.

Fontenot continues. "She was found lying across the driver's seat of her rental close to nine o'clock last night by one of the two guys in the room next to hers at the motel. They heard her car pull up around eight." He glances at me. "Good call on the name. She registered as Sharon Moore."

I hear a note of gratitude. "She used Sevryn Moffat when she hired that attorney yesterday to go after Ames Renaud's estate."

The detective glances up from his notes. "Knew

about the attorney from your message. Not which name she used. Thanks."

Rippa rises to her toes to peek at his upside-down notes. "The guys heard her come in at eight but didn't hear her get killed? She seems—seemed—like someone who would make a lot of noise if attacked."

Fontenot tips his chin. "She might have, but they explained that. After they heard her car, they started some multi-player warfare game wearing headphones. The volume with exploding bombs and hand grenades was—" He looks at his notebook. "—'Like really atomic. But we didn't care. Yesterday she was all nasty and screamy because she said our rental car was too close to her parking space.' "

Rippa gives me a sideways glance. Nasty and screamy, indeed.

"Anyway," Fontenot says, "when one of them went out to have a recreational smoke about an hour later, he found her. He thought at first she had passed out, and he wasn't going to try and wake her. After a while, he kicked her foot and, getting no reaction, called 911."

Kind of gruesome being discovered by what sounds like a party guy who initially didn't care enough to check for a pulse. I can only think how pissed she would be at the whole scenario.

Not shy about getting to the point, Rippa blurts, "If she wasn't all bloody, how did she die?"

"Apparent broken neck," Fontenot says. "Bruising on her neck, arms, and wrists. She did not go gentle into that good night. Processing of the scene also indicates possible skin under her nails. Could be a source of DNA."

Despite his French surname and slightly rumpled

appearance, the detective quoting a Welsh poet makes him a romantic in my book. Interesting.

The motion-activated porch light comes on, and I blink. "Weird that nobody else heard anything."

"Not so weird," he says. "She was in the last unit of a cheap motel. Behind it was greenspace, then freeway. Besides, one of the big parades was on in town, and most of the other units were unoccupied. These two guys were probably in their room instead of at the parade route because recreational smoking is illegal and very frowned upon by New Orleans's finest."

I know there's a connection, but I have to ask. "Anything that points to it being random?"

Eye roll from the detective. "Amateur 101. Clumsy attempt at staging a robbery. A good, strong shove would've gotten them past the cheap lock. Her room was tossed, but to make it look real, they should've taken the ruby earrings and bracelet off her."

"Rookie mistake," Rippa says. "Or they killed her accidently and were too squeamish to loot the body."

I know this is coming but take a step back when the detective pins me with a raised eyebrow.

"Your turn. You've kept me informed on the break-in at the Ashurst residence and the extra security measures at the Renaud house. I've read the copy of the will Mrs. Ashurst sent to the station. What can you tell me about the other party in the lawsuit?"

I shift a shoulder. "There is no other party. Clemmie received the letter from Ms. Moffat's attorney this morning. She'd already been told by Honor that she, Honor, couldn't afford to hire an attorney, so Clemmie was thinking about hiring one to protect the final wishes of Ames and his uncle."

Fontenot flips a notebook page. "Now there's no one in the way of Miss deGrandpre inheriting a valuable estate. Can you give me her contact information? Address?"

"I can, but you're looking in the wrong place."

We turn to see Clemmie in the half-light beside the bottom of the stairs to the porch. She looks pale and is holding onto the balustrade. "I didn't mean to eavesdrop. I just went over to make sure Ames's house was secure and saw you three talking. I'm sorry to hear about Ms. Moffat. She was not a likeable person and well...very abrasive." Clemmie inhales, then exhales a couple of times. "That being said, the situation we found ourselves in, although contentious, never escalated to the point of verbal or physical threats."

A slow smile eases from Fontenot as he makes a note. "Thank you for your observation."

Jilly opens the door and favors the detective with a small frown before turning to Rippa. "Excuse me. Rippa, she's ready for your pedicure. You're the last one."

Rippa's gaze bounces from the door opening to Clemmie, then to me. Followed by a heavy sigh. "Fill me in later?"

Her longing to be included in the interview prompts an urge to smile on my part, which I squelch. "Sure. I think we're almost done."

She nods and goes into the house with one last glance behind her. When the door closes, I grin.

Clemmie, who is now on the porch, joins me, tipping her head at the door. "She really wants to be involved."

Detective Fontenot clears his throat. "Mrs. Ashurst?"

Clemmie turns her attention to the detective. "I realize it's only my opinion, but I consider myself a good judge of character. That judgement is no one in the deGrandpre family is involved in Ms. Moffat's death."

His tired gaze bumps between Clemmie and me. "Okay. Say that solid lead is a waste of time for my counterpart assigned to Ms. Moffat's case. Both murder victims have one thing in common. The Renaud residence. Can either of you think of a person or persons with enough interest in the house to kill the owner *and* his disagreeable wannabe beneficiary? And finally, if the house is the motivation, should we warn Miss deGrandpre?"

"You can, to be on the safe side," I say.

Fontenot taps his tablet with his pencil. "I'll talk to the deGrandpre family about the house during my interview, but you both look like you think there's another direction to consider."

Perceptive. I nod. "Miss deGrandpre is a beautiful, smart young woman who has the unwelcome attention of a young man super focused on the supposed treasure in the Renaud house."

"And she doesn't?"

Interesting that he doesn't ask who the guy is first. "No. She's very level-headed. Her plan, if she did inherit, was to sell off the contents, then the house, as is. She's said if there is a treasure, it goes with the house."

"I agree with that," Clemmie says. "The young man Julianne's talking about made several efforts to access the house since the death of Mr. Renaud. Through me and Rippa."

The T-shirt I wore to the mani/pedi party is inadequate for keeping me warm now that the sun is down. I rub my upper arms. "He's also tall and slender, which fits the description of the male running from the house several nights ago."

"Did you give his information to the officers investigating the break-in?" Fontenot asks.

I shake my head. "We had no way of connecting his request to see the inside of the house, due to his interest in historical architecture, with the hunt for treasure."

The detective has been taking notes, again, and stops, frowning. "I need a timeline here. He'd been paying attention to Miss deGrandpre even before she was named in the will?"

"Yes," Clemmie and I chorus.

He looks at me from over the tops of his glasses. "How is your niece involved?"

I pull my lips in and out. "His name is Étienne Chappelle. He's tall, dark, and handsome. Not to mention charming and has a French accent. Rippa fell for the whole package, and he used that to try and manipulate her into getting him access to the house. Even asked her out, but the shine wore off in a hurry when they ran into Honor with another guy during a Mardi Gras event on Bourbon Street. Étienne unceremoniously dumped Rippa and walked off in a snit. Seems he thinks he and Honor are a couple. She has tried to disabuse him of the idea several times. He doesn't accept the fact."

The detective holds up a hand. "Wait. Where did

this Étienne guy come from? Is he a local resident?"

"He's a resident of New Orleans and Samuel Guillory's replacement," Clemmie volunteers.

Fontenot blinks and flips through his notes. "Mr. Guillory was the original, um, embalmed occupant in the back of Mrs. Neely's garden, and this Chappelle kid was taking his place as the new gardener?"

Clemmie cuts a glance toward Stella's garden. "Not for long. Étienne has already demanded double his agreed-to price per hour."

Fontenot shrugs. "An altogether unpleasant guy. But that doesn't make him a murderer."

I hold up my hand, palm out. "True. But his intense interest in Honor deGrandpre and the Renaud house sparked a confrontation with Ms. Moffat. I intercepted her on her way to chat with Stella about her knowledge of the supposed treasure in the house when Étienne and his cousin showed up. He demanded she forget her claim involving his *girlfriend's* inheritance."

A glint of interest lights the detective's eyes. "How did she react to that?"

"Didn't seem to faze her. She basically told them to back off, then left."

"Did either one follow her?"

I smile, remembering the astonished looks on the cousins' faces at being dismissed. "Not that I know of. They just stood there, angry and sort of stupefied. That's a good question, though. If the police were unable to locate her, how would someone without those resources find out where she was? Especially since she didn't use the name Sevryn Moffat when she checked in?"

The detective scratches his chin. "I've seen photos

of the crime scene. A bright-yellow, exotic rental car is pretty distinctive. Maybe a guy bent on doing her harm would look for that. Happen to know if the cousins or Miss deGrandpre saw it?"

"Hard to miss," I say. "It's been at the curb the same time each of them has also been here. They'd have to be pretty lucky tracking it down, though. There must be hundreds of motels on the fringes of the city."

Fontenot nods. "True, but not unheard of." He turns to Clemmie. "I'll need the cousin's name and any contact information you or Mrs. Neely can give me for him, Étienne Chappelle, and the deGrandpre family. It sounds as if considering the family's a dead end. However, we still have to eliminate them."

"Stella's in her kitchen," Clemmie says. "I'll get the information she has about the cousins and meet you back here. She has Honor's cellphone number, but I also have her address. We can walk to my house from here."

"Thank you," Fontenot says with heartfelt meaning as Clemmie opens the door to the laughter and chatter of the "lady party."

Chapter Twenty-One

The early afternoon wedding ceremony the next day is flawless. As is the reception in the hotel ballroom. All of Jilly's efforts and attention to detail have paid off. She and Hugh look happy and relaxed.

I would feel the same if I had taken Jilly's advice and either spent more time breaking in my matron-of-honor heels or bought a pair of matching flats to wear to the reception. Not knowing over ninety percent of the guests, I figured I'd spend the reception at my table, chatting. I didn't count on the number of guys attending stag or a couple of widowers Stella had invited singling me out as an available dance partner. Witness my pretty pale coral dress with chiffon overlay almost wrinkleless by the end of the reception.

I miss dancing with you, Cara.

I smile. At least my toes were always safe with him.

By the time Rippa, Stella, the Ashursts, and I get back to Stella's kitchen for some chamomile tea, I wonder if the toes on my left foot will ever uncramp.

Our hostess blows a breath across the surface of her full cup. "I'm going to miss her terribly, but Hugh will take good care of our girl. What I won't miss is the last several weeks of constant guests, caterers in my kitchen, and the pinch on my purse."

"Speaking of which," Clemmie says. "Have you

had time to consider your options for income? It's been a while since Jilly's monthly rent payment, and with the added wedding expenses, you won't be able to keep up with your house maintenance and property taxes."

Stella takes the fifth by letting her gaze wander around the kitchen. "I'm thinking about it, yes. There are two widows I could get along with as housemates. If necessary."

If necessary being the operative phrase. I would offer a loan to tide her over, but even a hint of that would be a huge misstep in our relationship.

Clemmie must be familiar with this avoidance tactic, but she just changes the subject. "I contacted my friend who's the mediator and attorney. She's offered to meet with me in the morning to help untangle the whole mess with Ames's will and Ms. Moffat's death. At one o'clock tomorrow afternoon, I'd like us all to be present at the cemetery when Ames's body is transferred to his family vault."

Stella looks dismayed, her gaze indirect. "I'm sorry, but Samuel's interment is the afternoon after that. Attending two memorials in two days is a bit much. Especially since I wasn't on familiar terms with Mr. Ames Renaud. As I also have little desire to go to that particular cemetery, you will have to represent the Farrol family."

Clemmie accepts her sister's decision. "That's okay. Davison and I will go."

"That's good for Rippa and me too. The Sandovals were happy to extend our stay up to a week longer. Since we suggested helping Stella go through her library to sort out possible rare editions, we can start that in the morning and attend the interment in the afternoon. Hopefully, the hotel will extend our stay too. Mardi Gras's almost half over, and our hotel package included a ride from and to the airport. I'll work on changing our flight."

Clemmie forges ahead, taking a bead on Stella. "Now that's settled, as long as you're willing to go through the library, you have to seriously think about the other assets Harlan left."

Stella's wide eyes and slightly open mouth indicate her honest confusion. "Harlan's life insurance and other small investments were cashed out almost immediately to cover funeral expenses."

"That's true." Clemmie nods. "But his watch collection, cashmere sweaters, and expensive golf equipment are just moldering in storage when selling them could bring you a good measure of financial relief."

Stella turns her back on the group at the table, her voice small. "Those things give me comfort."

Clemmie walks to her sister and pulls her into a sideways hug. "Except for the golf cart and sets of clubs, maybe you could keep his favorite sweater and the watch he wore most often as mementos."

Stella shrugs but makes no commitment. "That's a possibility."

I love these people, and Stella's distress has me rubbing my fingers into the edge of my scalp.

"Speaking of books," Rippa says. "Now's a good time to get *Les Misérables*. Honor said I could have it, and I left it on the second floor of Mr. Renaud's house. I can't wait to find out what happened to that hero who raised that poor orphan like a daughter."

"Good read," Clemmie says, opening a drawer to

pull out a small flashlight. "It's only six-ish but already dark outside." She hands the light to Rippa, then undoes the snap and reaches into her small clutch. "I meant to check on Ames's house one last time since we've been gone most of the day. Here's the key and code."

Rippa accepts the items. "Oh, hey, thanks. Be back in ten."

****

It's actually closer to fifteen minutes when Rippa appears at the back door into the kitchen. "We need to call Detective Fontenot." Blood stains her dress and trickles below her right knee.

My heart hammers, and I suck in a breath before jumping to send my wooden chair clattering over. "What happened?"

Davison is closer and stands, then gently takes Rippa's arm and seats her. I hurry to the sink and wet a paper towel.

Rippa pulls her hem back to expose her knee. "I…I was upstairs looking for my book. It wasn't where I thought I left it. The next thing I knew, I heard guy voices downstairs." She rubs the side of her nose. Her tell that she's distressed. "Étienne and Aldo. They sounded drunk. Étienne insisted the door was unlocked and the lights were on because the stupid carpenters were on a dinner break. Then they started arguing over the gold signet ring. It had belonged to Aldo's grandmother. He wore it on a chain around his neck. The chain broke, and he lost it the night…the night they forced their way in looking for the treasure and accidently killed Mr. Renaud."

Clemmie gasps. "Ames's death was an accident?"

Rippa nods. "That's what Aldo said. Then he

started crying. Étienne's voice got really mean. 'Your hand was around the ice pick. I just tried to take it from you. Besides, Honor won't have anything to do with you when she finds out you murdered that Moffat woman.' Then Étienne said he didn't care about the ring; he wanted to look for the treasure. And since the cops had been all over the first floor, he wanted to check out the second floor and the attic."

I'm busy dabbing at Rippa's knee. A quick inspection shows that's the source of her bleeding, and it's not as bad as I thought. Stella hands me a first aid kit. I'm trembling as I rummage through it. I stop. "Wait. There's only one way to get up or down from the second floor. How did you get past them?"

Rippa gives a wobbly smile. "Didn't wait around. I crawled out the window and down the scaffolding. Made a mess of it. Not something you want to do in a dress and in the dark. I also probably made enough noise that they're long gone. I think I heard footsteps going down the stairs."

I hug her hard. "You are amazing."

Clemmie kisses the top of Rippa's head. "Davison called Detective Fontenot. He's on his way. Can I get you something stronger than tea?"

Rippa laughs. "Diet cola over lots of ice, please."

I can't stop patting her, lessening my own fear about her close call. "Wow. Wrong place, wrong time. But it's over."

Clemmie's hands are trembling too. "It's not over until they're caught and punished. Poor Ames. Accident or not, he's still gone."

Rippa's face sobers at the assertion, but she doesn't say anything.

Stella gets her the cola. "I never cared for Étienne, but Samuel thought he just needed some stability, some growing up. I don't know much about Aldo. He keeps mostly to himself." She sighs. "So sad. Two lives lost and the families of those young men never the same."

Neither sister has mentioned the unfortunate Ms. Moffat. Ames Renaud's death holds a more substantial place for them.

Rippa rubs below her elbow where a bruise is starting to appear. "Can we take five minutes and change into some comfortable clothes at the rental?"

I lean to retrieve my heels from under the table. "Great idea."

"I'll walk you over. Just in case," Davison says.

Rippa pops out of her chair. "Oh. I left the key and code on a box, along with my book and the flashlight. Can we get them and lock up the house on our way?"

Okay, Rippa seems to have weathered her ordeal. Not sure going back into the Renaud house, even with two others and the police en route, is a choice *I'd* want to make.

A second flashlight is produced, and I head for the front door.

Rippa calls after me. "The back way around the hedge is shorter."

I wave my shoes. "Not putting these on again. Going to have them bronzed so I won't have to. We need to take the front steps and sidewalk to the rental. I'll wait outside the Renaud house while Davison accompanies you to get your things, then close it up."

Rippa shrugs. "Let's hit it. It's chilly outside, so we'll hurry, but I really want to be comfortable when the detective gets here."

****

An unremarkable gray sedan is parked at the curb near Stella's house. Fontenot has arrived. In the kitchen, Stella stands in comfortable slippers. She has also traded her tea for the reddish-brown liqueur she favors. Clemmie and the detective sit chatting.

He pops up from the table when we enter. "Miss Parkes. I understand from Mr. Ashurst that you overheard a conversation pertinent to our murder cases." He holds a hand toward the chair nearest his, a calm smile on his face.

Rippa doesn't hesitate. "Are you looking for them? Étienne and Aldo?"

The catch in her voice is new, and my stomach lurches. A delayed reaction after her initial shock? "I thought you said you heard footsteps going back down the stairs. Which means they couldn't have seen it was you. Did you think of something else?"

Clemmie stands and walks to Davison, leaving the chair on the other side of Rippa empty. I sit and put my hand on Rippa's arm.

She shrugs. "Not really. It's just that, well, when I was busy finding my next footing on the scaffolding, one of them could have gone back down the stairs while the other one looked out the window and saw me. Once outside, I couldn't hear everything going on in the house. Or when they hurried out the back, they could've looked around the side of the house and seen me running back here." She shrugs again. "You know, who's to say they didn't?"

I've been so busy thanking my lucky stars she escaped it hasn't occurred to me she may not be safe. I look at Fontenot. "Well?"

"Yes. As solid persons of interest, we're looking for them."

Rippa lets out a shallow breath. "Oh, good. That makes me feel better."

Me too.

Fontenot pulls out his notepad and pencil before sitting. "Now, tell me where, how, who, and what you heard tonight. Be very specific."

Rippa grins. "Just like a real mystery."

The detective nods. "Just like that."

She repeats her story, adding that she took off her shoes before going out the window and dropped one in the dark. The streetlight helped her see better once she was outside.

Fontenot interrupts. "Wait. Why was it dark upstairs? If you thought you were alone when you went into the house, why didn't you turn on the light in the bedroom?"

Nice he picked up on that.

Clemmie sets her cup on the table. "I think I know. The repairmen asked for permission to turn off the power to that room. The water leaking around the window frame soaked the old plaster and lath and compromised the wiring in there. It was a fire waiting to happen, so I said yes."

"That's why nothing happened when I hit the light switch," says Rippa. "I had just turned on the little flashlight when I heard the cousins downstairs. I turned it off right away."

The detective smiles. "You're very lucky that light switch didn't work, Miss Parkes. And I stand by my original assessment of your intellect and observation skills. I think you would make an excellent witness.

Especially as the gold ring was mentioned. Its ownership will be easy to verify."

Rippa nods at the compliment but rubs at a spot on the table, seemingly distracted. The detective continues making notes when someone knocks on the back door. Everyone except Fontenot starts.

Davison lets in the tall, blond, young officer we've seen twice during our stay. This time I notice a name tag—*Cole*. He grins and tips his head at Rippa until the detective clears his throat.

"You have something you want to share?"

"Oh. Yes, sir. We found two sets of adult male footprints leading from the back porch. They look recent and made in a hurry."

Fontenot taps his pen on the table and leans slightly toward Rippa. "My thought, from experience, is the Chappelles are going to be too busy making themselves scarce to worry about bothering anyone they *might* have seen at the house. Besides, if they thought it might be a carpenter upstairs, they wouldn't be as likely to want a confrontation." He glances at the Ashursts and Stella, all still dressed in their wedding finery, then back to Rippa. "I assume the wedding is over. How long do you plan to be in the city? I need to get this interview down and signed before you leave. You also might be asked to return to testify if there's a trial."

I really appreciate the detective is soft-pedaling Rippa's possible exposure to any retribution from the cousins. If they had seen her. "We're here for three more days," I say. "We're staying at the Sandoval house. You have my number if there's any news."

He stands. "Great. I'll get this into the system while I can still interpret my own notes." He nods at

Rippa. "Can you come down in the morning to read and sign your statement? Any time after nine?"

"I guess so," Rippa replies, then faces Stella. "Since we didn't find a treasure in Mr. Renaud's house, maybe we'll find one in yours. Would it be okay if we come over fairly early to start on the library? There's, like, a ton of books in there."

Stella nods. "Of course, dear. Why don't you take a house key on your way back to the rental?"

"Perfect," Clemmie says. "Because I've been in touch with Mr. Radnor, an estate sales coordinator who specializes in rare books. He'll be here Tuesday morning, first thing. With Julianne and Rippa starting work on the library in the morning, leaving time for their other errands and attending Ames's interment, Stella can use the day to help out and decide about Harlan's other collectibles."

Stella slumps. "Oh. With all your offered help, it's only fair to give some thought to your plan." She smiles weakly and takes a sip of her drink. "Otherwise, in a very short time, I will be sitting in a house I can't afford, surrounded by things I could sell to save it. Which is rather stupid."

Clemmie hugs her sister. "Not stupid. Just holding on to too many memories. But it'll work out. You'll see. This will give you some breathing room to maybe decide on a roommate. You always said you admired Geneva Preston's cooking skills. And she's recently widowed."

Stella grins. "Let's put a pin in that. She's this town's worst gossip."

I laugh. "So two things in her favor."

Fontenot is edging toward the front hallway. "I'll

just let myself out. Thank you again, Miss Parkes. For your help in solving these murders. Actually, the help you all gave."

We nod, and sighs of finality fill the room.

Davison stretches his arms sideways. "I know it's early, but I would like nothing better than to get out of this wedding gear and take my lovely wife home for a hot buttered rum. First though, I will escort Julianne and Rippa to the Sandoval house." He holds up his hands. "For my own peace of mind."

Raif chuckles. *A really nice guy, Cara.*

True. I'm glad Davison is nearly thirty years older and the love of Clemmie's life. Because under different circumstances, I would make a play for him myself.

Rippa pops up. "Missing the next chapter of my book. I'm ready."

Our reason for coming here, Jilly's wedding, is over. Unfortunately, I'm expected back home and received an email earlier this afternoon from the insurance company I work for. They have a new case for me to investigate, and the attached documentation folder holds lots of pages.

"Me too. Well, not a book, but reading to catch up on. Davison, I thank you for your offer and take you up on it."

We troop out of Stella's to our rental. The Sandoval house is quiet and locked up tight. Just as we left it.

Chapter Twenty-Two

Another night of good sleep is followed by a call from Clemmie.

"Hi, Julianne. I'm so sorry getting you up at this hour, but I just heard from Honor. Her family received an early morning visit from Aldo Chappelle. He was frantic and terrified. He admitted his involvement in the deaths but claims both were accidental. She said his story was heartbreaking."

I'm groggy and try to equate heartbreaking with a guy who's been a party to two murders within a week. It doesn't compute. I slide my feet out of bed and sit on the edge. Clemmie wouldn't have called unless she needed something. "What can we do?"

She continues. "Honor called and talked with the police after he left. They asked her to come in this morning and give a statement. She wants to tell us Aldo's story before she tells Fontenot and hopes we can accompany her to the station. She also wants to see if there's any way we can help him."

"Is Aldo turning himself in?"

"All the deGrandpre family tried to convince him, but he said no."

"Okay. Is Honor coming to your house, or are we going there?"

"She'll be here in a half hour. She's going to skip her morning classes. I thought since you, and especially

Rippa, have been involved, you'd both be interested. Honor agreed."

I yawn. "Very true. Will drinks from Davison's espresso machine be available?"

Clemmie's warm laughter comes through. "Of course."

"We'll be there." I end the call.

Rippa appears in the bedroom doorway. The curls she wore up as part of Jilly's lineup are now down and in disarray. "Did I hear Davison's espresso? What's the occasion?"

"We're meeting Honor there."

"Honor? Why? Is she okay?"

"Physically, yes. Emotionally, not so much. Her family got an early morning visit from a distraught Aldo Chappelle. He confessed. Told them the whole stories about Ames Renaud and Ms. Moffat. Then he ran. According to Aldo, both deaths were accidents."

****

Rippa and I dress warmer this morning. Although yesterday turned out perfect for Jilly's wedding, today is cool and cloudy. Like the Pacific Northwest weather we're used to. Which is a plus since we'll be working in Stella's stuffy library.

We arrive at Clemmie's right on time, as Honor is just walking up.

She's pale, but the set of her shoulders shows determination. "Thank you for helping. Again."

I nod. "I'm not sure we can do much, but we're anxious to hear about what happened with your friend."

Her eyes are downcast. "Yes. Even with everything, he's still my friend."

Clemmie greets us at the door and squeezes

Honor's hand before leading us to the kitchen.

The room is warm, and Davison is filling lungo-sized cups with espresso. Rippa and I both have serious sweet tooths, but Davison's blend and deft hand make his pours delicious without the bitterness associated with the larger size. The aroma alone packs a punch. Rippa's gaze darts to the cake on the counter. It's sliced and has a stack of plates, forks, and napkins next to it.

She tips her head toward the green, gold, and purple sugared top. "That's fancy for this time of the morning."

Clemmie hands her a plate. "Help yourself, honey. It's a King cake. A Mardi Gras tradition. Davison and I can never finish a whole one by ourselves."

Rippa and I help them out by each bringing a slice to our seats.

Our hostess brings the cups to the table and sits next to Honor. "We know what Rippa overheard, but that wasn't a voluntary version. Thank you for offering to share Aldo's confession. It has to be unsettling. And take your time. We don't have to leave for the station for a little bit."

Honor sips her drink, then sighs. "I wouldn't have believed it if he hadn't said it himself." Her expression darkens. "I blame Ètienne."

This should be interesting. I wonder if Honor's feelings toward Aldo's cousin color her perspective.

Rippa slides forward. "Wow. I mean, I don't like Ètienne either, but that's harsh, blaming him for another guy's actions. Especially murder."

"Let me explain," Honor says. "I've already told you about Ètienne's narcissistic personality. Well, part of that is the need to be in control. If he can't control you, he won't waste his time."

"Then why's Ètienne wasting his time with you?" Rippa asks. "No offense to your study, but from what I've seen, he hasn't any control there."

"That's true," Honor admits. "But being with someone he perceives as his equal brings him up in stature to others. It's kind of twisted but true. On the other hand, Aldo's submissive personality made him the perfect target. Aldo told us all the steps taken resulting in tragedy this past week were his cousin's idea."

I'm not one hundred percent convinced. "You believe that? It could be a case of 'he said, he said.' Each of them directing the blame toward the other. Then Aldo grows a conscience and freaks out at what he's done."

Honor's face softens. "I believe Aldo. *Pepa*'s known him for a long time. He says it would never enter Aldo's mind to get drunk, barge into an old man's house, tie him up, and threaten him to get information about a so-called treasure. The same with threatening Ms. Moffat to relinquish her claim on the Renaud house. Aldo just doesn't have it in him."

Clemmie cuts a glance at Davison who is standing quietly by the counter.

"I have a question," he says. "If his cousin exerts so much control over Aldo, where is he now?"

Good point.

Honor responds directly to Davison. "Aldo said when they ran out of the house after hearing someone on the second floor last night, they split up, and he hasn't seen Ètienne since."

Someone. So they didn't know it was Rippa. She

sits straighter.

Honor continues. "Ètienne works when he feels like it. Mostly for older women and widows. He's very good at what he does, just doesn't devote more than a dozen hours a week to it and padding those hours. No pension, no savings, and always on the lookout for an easy dollar. Someone else's dollar. That's where poor Mr. Renaud's *treasure* came in. Ètienne told Aldo when they found it, Ètienne and I would be together. He figured out Aldo had a crush on me but convinced him that Ètienne and I as a couple would make me very happy, and that's what counted."

I feel a frown forming. "Wait. How did Ètienne plan on taking the treasure and still leaving Ames Renaud alive? Did they wear masks? His death sounds premeditated rather than accidental."

My question results in a sharp intake of breath from Clemmie.

I reach to pat her hand. "Sorry."

"Yes, it does," says Honor. "Would you like me to leave the part of his actual death out?"

Clemmie shakes her head. "I'm okay. Tell us what Aldo said."

Honor nods. "It all started when Ètienne saw me with my boyfriend, Clément, and was furious even though, as I've told him repeatedly, I have no interest in him. Aldo didn't know this.

"The night Mr. Renaud died, Aldo and Ètienne got really drunk and knocked on his back door. He answered, and they grabbed him and dragged him to his library, tying him to the chair. Aldo said there was no plan beyond questioning him. They weren't wearing disguises or anything. Ètienne was really pissed when

Mr. Renaud said over and over he didn't have the treasure but told them how he was looking for it in books. And about his journal entries, all but one of the journals being in his safety deposit box. The last one in plastic in his freezer." She frowned. "That sounds odd, but that's what he said."

Davison's hand is on Clemmie's shoulder. Her hand is on his.

She nods at Honor. "Poor Ames. He must have been terrified."

Honor lowers her gaze. "Possibly after Ètienne got more sober and angrier. Aldo said he tried once or twice to calm Mr. Renaud, but Ètienne told him to stop. Finally, he told Aldo Mr. Renaud must be lying and to go chip every last bit of ice out of the freezer to see if he was hiding something else. When Aldo finished, he came back into the library and said there was nothing more. Ètienne said to give him the ice pick and he would get the truth from Mr. Renaud. Aldo refused. They struggled, both having hands on it, and with one last pull, drove it into Mr. Renaud, accidently killing him.

"Aldo said he cried because Ètienne kept saying everything was Aldo's fault. That he was a murderer. He wanted to leave, but Ètienne said he came to get something and he wasn't going to leave until he did. Then he started laughing, saying he'd teach the cheap old hag next door a lesson by planting a dead neighbor in her garden. 'Get it? Planting in her garden?' he'd said.

"That's when they made the body switch and Aldo lost his great grandmother's ring in the mud."

Clemmie's eyes are bright with anger. "Étienne is

despicable. He's just as much or more to blame for Ames's death."

I feel the same way. "I think Detective Fontenot will agree with you. I wonder, since Aldo and Étienne split up last night, if Ètienne's been taken in yet."

Honor clasps her hands together. "I know it's wrong, but I almost hope Aldo just disappears into the swamps like he plans. He wouldn't be able to stand prison."

I raise an eyebrow. "Most inmates probably share that sentiment."

"No. I mean he would literally go crazy. He has crushing claustrophobia. That's why he works on the docks and lives in a shotgun house with tall windows and skylights."

My own claustrophobia is mild and annoying, but I deal with it. I scrunch my face and huff a breath. "Sorry to hear that. It's like double the punishment."

Honor pats at her damp eyes. "Mr. Renaud's death might have been considered an accident, but add damaging a corpse and then Ms. Moffat's death... He made the only decision he could face. Unfortunately. And if he does disappear, the only one left who was there is Étienne, and like a true narcissist, he'll blame everything on Aldo."

Rippa has been quiet. "That's so sad. What happened with Ms. Moffat?"

A tear rolls down Honor's cheek. "Étienne told Aldo how unhappy I would be if Ms. Moffat's challenge won her the house and that he should go and confront her. Use intimidation and tell her to back off."

"How did he know where she was? The police couldn't even find her."

Honor lifts a shoulder. "He drove around the outskirts of the city, drinking beer to get his courage up and looking for her fancy yellow car. He said he was about to give up when he spotted it and followed her into a motel parking lot. When he approached her getting out of her car and tried to talk to her, she got very angry and came at him. She called him ugly names and kept slapping him and trying to scratch at his eyes. He wasn't making it up. His face and arms are covered in scratches, and she even bit him a couple of times. Aldo said he meant to leave until she started in on me. Calling me and my great-aunt awful names, telling him she would make me pay through the courts for her inconvenience.

"Aldo said he snapped. Pushed her hands away and grabbed her by the shoulders, yelling, 'Stop it.' He shook her back and forth like a rag doll. She slipped and fell back, hitting her neck hard on the top of the open car door and slumping to the ground. He'd heard the snap and realized what had happened but didn't want to leave her on the dirty parking lot, so he pulled her car door the rest of the way open and laid her inside. Nobody confronted him, so he got the idea to mess up her room, to make it look random, then left and drove around the rest of the night, thinking. He came to us because he wanted my family to know how much we mean to him and how sorry he is for his actions."

Wow. Rippa and I both suck in breaths at Honor's retelling. I try to imagine what goes through someone's head, even drunk, that triggers their response to another's attack. Aldo chose to ignore her gibes about himself but couldn't allow her to defame Honor and the deGrandpre family.

Clemmie squeezes her hand. "Do you know how to contact him?"

"Not directly. I guess *Pepa* could get a message to one of Aldo's family members. You mean in case we can help him?"

"I'm not sure that's possible," Clemmie says.

Davison speaks up. "I read about a recent court case where a criminal with a chronic phobia was sent to a secure mental ward for an attempt at desensitization. You know, increasing his exposure to his phobia over time until it no longer paralyzes him. A good percentage of the time, it's successful."

Honor perks up. "I've heard about desensitization in my studies, but I didn't know it could be part of a sentence."

"I would think it'd depend on his lawyer and how the judge and/or jury felt about that type of punishment," he says. "If it did work, he would eventually be sent to prison."

Her dark eyes cloud again. "When he came to us this morning, he spoke with an underlying desperation that his only option was taking his own life. He kept saying he shouldn't be alive with two innocent people dead."

"Two people he didn't start out intending to harm," I say. "It's too bad Aldo won't tell his version to Fontenot. The detective seems like a reasonable man. Unfortunately, two second-party versions of the events, yours and Rippa's, will probably, as you said, not be verified by Ètienne. If Aldo has escaped to the swamps, the only one with a direct statement, at least about what happened in the Renaud murder, will be Ètienne, and no doubt in his favor."

Rippa sips her espresso. "Do you think Detective Fontenot might let us listen to the interview? Like we did in New York? I could, like, let him know if Ètienne's stretching the truth about what I overheard."

"Oh," Honor says. "Do you think we could? We want Aldo to have every chance."

In my opinion, Aldo's planned escape means he's gone for good, despite Honor's hope he can be helped. "We can always ask the detective, but we don't even know if Ètienne's been picked up yet. He might have made himself scarce."

Rippa pales at this, even though she supposedly wasn't seen last night. "With lots of people still in the streets, it would be easy for him to disappear. He's from New Orleans, so there might be someone willing to help him."

"I don't think so," the pretty brunette says. "Besides Aldo, I've never seen Ètienne with anyone socially. He isn't well liked because he uses people."

That makes perfect sense to me. "Guess we'll find out when we get to the station."

Clemmie glances at her watch. "If we finish our coffees and cake, we can leave in plenty of time. I'll also call Stella and let her know what's going on."

Honor turns to Rippa. "Your visit and wedding functions have been interrupted by lots of drama. I'm sorry for that."

Surprise crosses Rippa's face. "Are you kidding? Centuries-old houses with mysteries and hidden treasures. Murders to solve, nice guys and narcissists on the run. Right up my alley."

Honor's mouth is slightly open, and her dark eyes widen at Rippa's pronouncement, then she smiles. "Uh, glad we could entertain?"

Clemmie, Davison, and I laugh out loud.

****

The station Fontenot works out of is on Royal Street. We arrive in the area and, after some searching, find a parking spot. Inside, Honor checks in at the desk, then returns to our little group, expelling a big sigh. She sits, looking nervous.

Clemmie pats her hand. "Are you okay?"

Honor's face starts to crumple. "It's not me I'm worried about. There are parts of the swamps that are so dangerous. Even as a big strong guy, Aldo's personality leaves him vulnerable to getting hurt because he trusts people."

"Does he have relatives or friends who live out there?" I ask.

She rubs her hands up and down her jeans-clad thighs. "Not that I know of."

That can't be good, Cara.

No, it can't. And I'm saved from expressing this as we spy the detective coming toward us. His brown suit has been replaced by khakis and a navy long-sleeved T sporting a "Back the Blue" logo. His outfit would make him look ten years younger if the lines in his face weren't deepened by the artificial lights.

Nevertheless, he greets us with a smile. "Good morning, ladies. Thank you again for your help. NOPD really appreciates it."

He singles out Honor. "I understand one of the two suspects identified by Miss Parkes, Aldo Chappelle, came to your house early this morning and confessed to the two murders."

Honor winces. "Aldo told us they were both

accidents. I believe him."

The detective nods. "Then that's how we'll proceed."

Smart move on his part, putting her at ease. Even if the charge turns out to be murder.

A woman with a badge on her belt stops beside Detective Fontenot. "Congrats on solving the Carrolton double."

"Thanks, Sheila."

I wonder if that's referring to the double homicide he got called away to on the same afternoon as his investigation of Ames Renaud's murder.

His glance finds Honor again. "You were asked when you first called in if you know where Aldo Chappelle is located. Have you since learned of his whereabouts?"

Honor wrings her fingers. "I wish I did. I'd give anything to talk him into turning himself in, but he was determined to head for the bayou. That's all I know. I don't care about Ètienne."

The detective steps back. "In that case, can you come into an interview room so I can get the details of his visit?"

Honor stands, and Clemmie is right beside her, pinning Fontenot with a stare. "Moral support."

Faced with a statement rather than a question, he nods. "I think I can talk the lieutenant into letting me make an exception. This shouldn't take long." He starts to turn.

Rippa pops up. "Ètienne hasn't been found yet? They're looking for him?"

"Afraid so. He seems to have vanished. Of course, the Mardi Gras crowds could easily swallow a half-dozen suspects." He gives a reassuring smile. "He's local and, from what you told me, not a planner. We'll catch up to him."

We watch Clemmie, Honor, and Fontenot head into the inner hallway of the building.

"I like the detective's confidence," I say.

Rippa sits back down. "I guess I do too. Just creeps me out that Ètienne's out there wandering around. He knows the city and could be anywhere."

Some distraction might help. "Creep outs aside, let's list the places he's not likely to be."

"What?"

I nod. "He's not likely to be here at the police station because, well, he's not the type to turn himself in, right?"

She folds her arms. "Now you're talking to me like I'm five."

"I'm serious. Think about it. We're going back to Stella's to sort books after this. Since that's one of his workplaces, do you think he'll be there?"

"No. Stella would see him and let us know or report him."

"So that's probably safe. After that we're going to Ames Renaud's mausoleum to attend his interment."

She smiles. "Ètienne probably won't be hanging around the cemetery, either. He's not even aware that's on our schedule."

"Then my guess is he won't be in any of the places we'll be. He may not even be in the city anymore."

She raises a shoulder and gets up to investigate a display of vintage police equipment when tall, blond Officer Cole we've seen twice at the Renaud house comes toward her.

"Miss Parkes?"

"Yes?"

"Um, Detective Fontenot said I could give you your statement to read and sign if everything's correct. Do you have time to do that now? Because I could bring it to your house if I need to."

Rippa holds out her hand. "Now's okay."

While she reads her statement, he nods to me, then more or less stands at attention and watches her.

She finishes and smiles. "Got a pen?"

He's prepared with one in hand and gives it to her.

She walks to the main counter, signs it, and hands it back. "Is there some way I can have a copy? It would be cool to frame it for my room back home."

He looks crestfallen. "Back home? You don't live in the Garden District?"

His obvious and heartfelt disappointment has her blushing. "No. Western Washington State. Near Seattle. I'm in town for a wedding."

He shakes his head but doesn't make sustained eye contact. "And now you're a witness in a murder investigation."

She grins outright. "Just lucky, I guess."

Officer Cole looks nonplussed. "Um, I can make a copy of your statement."

"Thank you."

As he walks away, I make a mental comparison between him and Ètienne. Both are physically attractive and well-mannered. However, Ètienne uses his to get his way. Officer Cole uses his manners out of respect.

He returns and gives Rippa her copy. "See you around." Then heads for the back of the area, giving one last wave.

She returns his wave. "He's nice. I'm going to miss New Orleans."

****

Ten minutes later, Detective Fontenot escorts Clemmie and Honor to the front of the station. He shakes hands all around, nodding to Rippa and me. "Safe trip home, ladies, and please come visit again. It's been a pleasure."

"Wait," Rippa says. "If you catch Ètienne today or tomorrow, can we watch the interview? You know, just in case he lies about what I overheard."

Fontenot's gaze travels over her shoulder. "I'm afraid *you* can't, Miss Parkes. It's policy. The information gained in the interrogation could color your testimony if the case goes to court."

Disappointment washes over her face in the form of a frown. "How about Jules? She has an investigator's license and everything."

The detective's expression remains stern. "Even if her observation was allowed, your aunt would not be able to tell you anything that transpired."

Clemmie and Honor stand quietly, eyes wide, as Rippa fists her hands and cocks them on her hips.

"That makes sense. Now, what if we help in his capture?"

Fontenot's eyebrows take on a life of their own. "I believe we've already covered this. No chasing, confronting, or crossing the line. That includes capturing. Otherwise, you are subject to a charge of obstruction. Understood?"

Rippa lowers her eyes, taking it down a notch. "I remember. And we wouldn't do any of that. I mean *helping* in his capture. Giving the kind of information that leads to you guys getting him."

The detective leans forward and tilts his head. "Noted. My concern is how you go about gathering that information. We've already interviewed his family and Miss deGrandpre who are, apparently, the only people close enough to guess where he might head. There are no other avenues of enquiry we're aware of. I'm afraid you'd be wasting your time."

Her lips pressed together, Rippa stares at me, wanting an ally.

We always have each other's backs, so I'll give it a try, although I don't imagine I can be any more convincing than her. "You haven't said no, Detective. If I give you my word as a fellow investigator that we'll stick to a virtual means of helping, would that do it?"

Fontenot heaves a sigh. "Can't stop you. And seeing as how a direct order after all you've contributed would be discourteous and a blot on our reputation as a friendly city, be my guest. And I will request that Ms. McCarren be allowed to view Ètienne Chappelle's interview if it happens in the next two days."

Rippa's eyes shine. "Then that's settled."

For all that he's likely betting on nothing happening in the next two days, our help notwithstanding, Fontenot gives a curt nod, turns, and leaves.

Chapter Twenty-Three

Clemmie drops us off at Stella's, promising to change into more casual clothes to help in her sister's library. Stella has sausage and egg sandwiches ready to heat and sweet tea to go with them waiting in the kitchen. Interestingly enough, her tea doesn't look dosed, but her demeanor is downcast. Jilly's permanent absence may be sinking in.

"This looks great," Rippa says. "Especially since it's been a really hard week for you. Is there anything we can do?"

Stella sits and pats Rippa's hand. "Thank you, dear. I've come to the conclusion it's change that bothers me the most. I don't do well with one thing changing, and to have four or five going on at the same time is a skosh overwhelming." She taps the kitchen table. "Starting with the library and the clearing out of some of Harlan's things, I'm turning over a new leaf." She frowns. "After poor Samuel's interment tomorrow."

I realize, with all the murder and mystery and wedding prep, I haven't thought of Samuel Guillory since they took him to the morgue. The poor man saved and saved for his week in the sun, and after two days and part of one night, he's replaced by a murder victim, then shunted off to be forensically inspected and interred.

I take a sip of tea. "Rippa and I have limited time

the rest of today and tomorrow, so if you'll give our regards to the deGrandpres, I have an idea for us all to remember Samuel by."

Stella smiles. "Of course, dear. And whatever your idea, I'm sure it will be lovely."

Fifteen minutes later, Rippa polishes off her last bite and stands. "Ready to look for valuable books."

"Davison and I have been busy," Stella says. "Hopefully it will help us get started."

I walk into the library and find it cleared of chairs and rugs, with tables along one wall.

"We were going to label the tables, such as nineteenth or twentieth century publishing dates, signed by author, or first edition," Stella says. She laughs. "Then we realized one book could fit in all the categories. Plus, the book's condition has to be considered. Unfortunately, as I already said, none of them have been take care of, so I'm not overly hopeful you'll find any of great value."

Clemmie comes in and points at the library ladder. "Oh, my gosh, you didn't make my poor husband haul that heavy thing in here from the ceiling of your storage shed?"

Rippa runs her fingers along a rung of the tall, mahogany ladder with brass fittings that's hooked to the rail running around three of the walls. "That is so cool. Are we going to start with the books at the top?"

Stella steps around her sister and heads for the library door. "It was his idea, Clementine. Would you like some iced tea?"

Clemmie grins. "I'll need it to wash down the dust."

A Rippa-worthy eye roll from Stella. "Since y'all

are going to Ames's interment, maybe we should work on the lower shelves. I've dusted them a lick as far as I could reach. Later this afternoon we can do the upper shelves and have something for that Mr. Radnor to evaluate."

I really hope we find some gems in here for Stella. "Good plan. Let's get to it."

Rippa gives a last glance at the top shelves and reaches for the book closest to her. "Hey, these look old, like the ones next door." She blows a film of dust from the top and opens the cover. It crackles. "*Captain Stormfield's Visit to Heaven* by Mark Twain, published in 1909 by HarperCollins. First Edition. Wow. It's over a hundred years old."

I hand her a microfiber dusting cloth.

Stella brings in Clemmie's iced tea and clears her throat. "As I mentioned before, neither of our parents were readers, and Grandfather Farrol had such poor eyesight the only thing he did in here was smoke his pipe."

Rippa wrinkles her nose. "Not good for books but there are ways of reconditioning them if they're worth it."

I huff a breath. "I did some online searching about how to recognize valuable books. Apparently, just being old doesn't count. The main thing has to do with scarcity. Famous author, famous titles. The print runs could've been in the tens of thousands or more. That and most of what Stella has already mentioned, which edition, is there a dust jacket, is the book signed or initialed with a date?"

Rippa looks her book over and lays it on the nearest table. "So how do we help?"

"There are valuation and auction sites…"

She is hot on her phone and tips her head toward the screen. "EBay has more than seventy of this title available. The most expensive has the original dust cover. Stella would be lucky to get fifty dollars for hers."

Stella smiles. "Over a thousand books on these shelves. If that price is an average, I'm ready to clean house. What's next?"

I shrug. "For starters, we could make two teams. One person can pull the book, clean it, and call out the title, author, condition, dust jacket or no, and edition. The other person looks it up. If they think Mr. Radnor would be interested, it goes on this table."

Stella snatches a book off the shelf next to her, the quick motion belying her usual relaxed pace. "My house. I want Rippa on my team."

Well, that hurts. Stella's known me a lot longer than Rippa. On the other hand, my niece does have mad online skills. I wave my hand between Clemmie and me.

Clemmie laughs. "She's right. It's her house."

Stella cranes her head upward. "That's true. In which case, I have news."

The rest of us follow the arc of her glance.

A chuckle from Raif. *Ghosts in the attic?*

"The attic. I'd almost forgotten," Stella says. "There are more books up there. Boxes of them surrounded by old furniture." She brings her gaze back down and shifts a shoulder. "Sorry."

Clemmie sighs. "When Stella and Harlan got married and moved back in here, he thought the mostly Victorian furnishings were…"

"Ugly," Stella inserts. "He thought they were ugly. He used to say the attic was a good place for Victorian furniture to go to die."

They were already married the first time Jilly had me for a visit, and I thought the traditional furniture in the most-used rooms was at odds with the house and the furniture in the guest rooms but never said anything.

"I have a plan," Rippa says, her eyes wide.

Of course she does. A new area of possible intrigue or treasure is on the horizon. Are we ever going home?

She continues. "First we make room on the lower shelves in here. Then we go to the attic and sort through those books. If they look promising, we bring them down." She snaps her fingers. "And while we're up there, we can see if any of the antique furniture is in good enough shape to be sold along with the things from Mr. Neely's collections and golf stuff." She swings her hand to include Clemmie, Stella, and me. "Not me. On looking over the furniture, as Jules already knows, I couldn't pick out a demi lune from a full-on lune. But you guys can."

I like where she's going with this. "I'll bet Mr. Radnor could refer Stella to an antiques dealer who does consignment sales."

Stella presses her hands on either side of her face. "Wonderful ideas. I have all the time in the world now to shampoo upholstery and wax wood trim. I'm certain I can pay some industrious young men to carry the larger pieces into the formal parlor. I'm also certain there are some original Victorian and Edwardian pieces."

Happy to see Stella getting into the spirit of helping herself.

****

Two humid, dusty, but successful hours later, we break. Clemmie heads home, and Rippa and I to go to the Sandoval house to clean up for Ames's interment while Stella makes everyone a quick lunch before we go.

Neither Rippa nor I expected to attend a memorial service while we were in New Orleans, but knowing the weather at this time of year is inconsistent at best, I put on black slacks and a thin, knit, gray sweater. Rippa wears a black denim skirt and long-sleeved tan button-down. Sober neutrals for a sober occasion and we head out.

Stella's kitchen smells of hard-boiled eggs. A plate stacked with egg-salad sandwiches sits on the kitchen table, and small bowls of fresh fruit are at each place. A pitcher of iced tea and cold glasses are also available. Linen napkins imprinted with cherries and bluebirds make the center of each plate cheery.

Rippa and I are just sitting when Clemmie and Davison arrive. They are more formal in dress, both wearing gray suits. His is dark, accented by a snowy white shirt and teal silk tie. Hers is lighter, with a pink silk blouse underneath.

Davison seats his wife, then reaches for her hand. Her red-rimmed eyes are hard to miss.

"We're it," Clemmie says. "Only four people to attend Ames's interment. And he never even knew two of them." She dabs at her eyes with a linen handkerchief. "I like to think you two would've gotten along well with him."

Rippa squeezes Clemmie's hand. "I know I would've liked him. Those puzzles are very cool. Plus, he believed in treasure. My kind of guy."

This makes Clemmie smile. "Thank you, dear."

Lunch is quiet, everyone probably thinking about the hours to come.

Rippa is the first to break the silence. "Do you all think we have enough shelf space in the library to check out the boxes in the attic after we get back?"

The mysterious lure of treasure. I know Rippa, and she's not in it for the value. It's the chase.

Stella sips her tea. "Good idea. I haven't been up there in decades. If we poke around, at least we'll know what kind of room we'll need."

That settled, we clear our dishes and head for Davison's car and St. Louis Cemetery No. 1.

We pull into the same parking lot we used the other day. When we get out, a couple dropped off by a taxi walks ahead of us. Since the entrance gate is on the wall around the corner, I have to ask the question. "How come they aren't driven to the front?"

"Common practice," says Clemmie. "Many drivers won't stop at the gate."

Rippa frowns. "Why not?"

"Because they think the ghosts of the dead may leave by the gate. This cemetery is known as the 'City of the Dead.' "

An apt image. One that makes Rippa's lips part.

We're met at the gate by an administrator. As we enter, the cemetery holds its occupants in the same gloomy atmosphere that enveloped us the other day.

Still crowded, Cara. Lots of French-speaking, um, presences.

I'll bet.

Rippa gives me a strong sideways hug. "You doing

okay?"

I chuckle. "Raif says it's crowded and most of them speak French."

She slaps a hand over her mouth, her eyes crinkling at the corners.

We approach the Renaud family mausoleum, and I notice a difference. It's been cleaned and appears much more fit to hold remains than the other day. Probably paid for by Clemmie and not by cemetery maintenance. The top burial chamber is unlocked in anticipation of Ames Renaud's interment. Its solid iron door exhibits a faint crest. I expect the hinges to creak loudly as Davison opens it, but they don't.

Rippa peeks inside. "Oh. I thought…"

"That it would be fancier?" Davison asks. "No. This is pretty standard for the time period. Narrow sides and bottom with a flat or curved ceiling."

Our inspection is interrupted by the squeaking wheels of a metal trolley with a burnished wood coffin atop it, being pushed and pulled down the walkway toward us.

A soft note signals an incoming message on my phone. It gets Rippa's attention too. I wince. It needs to be turned off. We pull out our phones and silence them.

The men working with the trolley are having a tough time due to the unevenness of the walkway. The administrator steps toward them, I think to help, but veers away to stop and talk to a guide giving a tour and coming in our direction. The guide immediately quiets her group, promising any time missed will be made up.

The trolley reaches us, and the beautiful coffin is raised and slid into the top chamber. The administrator and helpers stand by quietly since the mausoleum needs to be sealed after we leave.

Clemmie clears her throat, her handkerchief crushed in her hand. She faces our small group. "We're here to say good-bye to Ames Sheridan Renaud. He ascribed to no formal religion, so this farewell will be from a friend instead of an officiant or relative, as he was the last in this Renaud line. My friendship with Ames stemmed, at first, from a common interest but was no less genuine. His unnecessary, untimely death made no sense and had no benefit. He chose to follow the wishes of his uncle and leave his estate to Honor deGrandpre, his uncle's unrecognized granddaughter." Tears spill over as she lowers her chin and casts a last glance at the coffin. "Ames was a kind, funny, and warm man, his only idiosyncrasy his obsession with a supposed Renaud treasure. He will be terribly missed and leaves a hole in our lives. Davison?"

Davison pulls his wife closer to his side and hands her his handkerchief, his glance also taking in the mausoleum. "I didn't know Ames well, but he was welcome in our home. He appeared quiet, well-mannered, and…" He kisses the side of Clemmie's head. "He made my wife smile. You can't ask more than that from a friend. Yes, he will be missed."

Wow. Makes me want to go back in time and meet Ames Renaud.

Clemmie sighs. "I guess that's it. I just wanted to make sure he had someone to remember the kind of man and friend he was and how he lived his life."

Chapter Twenty-Four

It's close to two thirty by the time we get back to the Garden District, change our clothes, and return to Stella's. Clemmie has begged off for a while, pleading a headache, and no one objects to her absence.

We climb the steep steps into the attic. Stella's not a physically active woman, and getting her up the stairs through the narrow opening takes Rippa up front and me behind giving encouragement.

With the single bulb dusted and turned on, I get the view I dreaded. The attic is jam-packed. Mostly with furniture but a good number of boxes too. The overwhelming smell is of dried paper, with musty upholstery thrown in. Poor ventilation and disinterest make it a time capsule very rarely opened. "Where do we start? Any ideas?"

Rippa pulls out her cellphone and turns on the flashlight to get a better look. I turn my phone on too and see I have a voicemail. It's local, but I don't recognize the number and decide to wait and call it when we get back downstairs.

"Not all the boxes are full of books. Maybe scoot those to the light, one at a time since it's crowded in here, and see if we want to take them down?" Rippa asks.

I have a question for Stella. "Did Harlan bring the boxes of books up here at the same time as the furniture? And since the library is already full of books, where did these come from?"

Stella's eyebrows draw inward. "It wasn't Harlan. And Great-Grandfather never got rid of anything. I vaguely remember stacks of books in the library on the floor when I was a child. Father never got rid of anything either. He must have brought them up here."

Not helpful at all. I sigh. "So they could be older or pulled off the shelves for some other reason. Like Ames Renaud and his search."

Rippa is nodding. "Some of the books are in wood crates too heavy to take down the stairs. I see a smaller box. We could transfer books a little at a time, and they'll be easier to carry." She shrugs. "Have to agree with Mr. Neely on the furniture, though. Not my style at all."

Gentle way of saying she thinks it's ugly too.

I'm at the point of offering to pay for someone to come and do all the heavy lifting while we just sit in the library and sort. "Let's go down and talk about the tack that will work best. It looks like we've taken on a lot, and we may be doing more harm than help. There must be local bibliophiles or people who know more than we can find on the internet."

Nods all around and we troop down the stairs.

Back in the library, Stella smacks her hands clean and pats at the dust on her day dress. "I agree. Spending countless hours, since that's what it would take, and finding out we're not doing it correctly would be a big waste of time. A middleman sounds good."

Rippa pulls up Google. "I had planned to go to the Historic New Orleans Collection tomorrow before that Mr. Radnor looked over the books we'd chosen. I want to check into the Renaud family history and put together something for Clemmie. I'll go this afternoon instead."

I like that idea. "It'd be worth it to hire a real expert to look at what we've already done. That way, we'd know if we're on the right track and not wasting Radnor's time. And ours."

Stella checks her watch. "It's past three o'clock. We've been working or celebrating or investigating nonstop. I say we take the rest of the day off, have a nice dinner and a good night's sleep."

Rippa bobs her head. "I second that. I want to borrow Mr. Renaud's journals from Clemmie for a look-through before tomorrow, though. I hope she feels better."

I pull out my phone and tap the mystery number. "I have a call to return, then I'll meet you at the Sandoval house. Give Clemmie a call before you go to her house, okay?"

"Okay."

My call is answered. "Canal Street Hotel. How may I help you?"

"This is Julianne McCarren, room 208, returning your call."

"Let me connect you to the manager."

Wonder what this is about.

"Ms. McCarren. Thank you for responding. I'll get right to it. I agreed to extend your stay, but not on the condition that you allow someone else to occupy the room."

News to me. "I did not. Let me check with my niece."

I wave my hand to get Rippa's attention and cover

the phone's speaker. "You didn't agree to let one of those kids in the next room at the hotel stay in ours, did you?"

She wrinkles her nose. " 'Course not. Why?"

"The manager says someone's been staying there. Do you think Miles is back?"

Rippa shakes her head. "According to what he said, he's already left for Arizona."

I pick up the conversation on my phone and put it on speaker. "Hello. Neither of us gave anyone permission to stay there. What does this 'someone' look like?"

"I spoke to him this morning. He's tall, dark hair, nice-looking, and charming. He knows your name, your niece's name, where your home is, where you have another rental in the city, etc. He most definitely stated you gave him permission to stay there and talked one of our younger, more gullible housekeeping staff into letting him in. She admitted her part in his deception earlier. He's also running up a room-service tab that as the legal occupant you have to pay."

This is all I need. Someone taking advantage of my empty room. Rippa had a chat with Miles while I was gone that day he used our shower. He could've found out that information and passed it on to any of his buddies or someone on the street. "Thank you for letting me know. You can toss him out on his ear. Neither of us has any knowledge of, or given permission to, another person to stay in—"

Rippa waves her hand in front of my face. "Wait. Don't do that. I think I know who it might be."

I put my thumb over the speaker again. "What? Don't have him thrown out? Why? Who is it?"

She's bouncing on the balls of her feet. "Just say you'll call him back in ten minutes."

I do as she asks, then hang up. I am not a happy camper. "What is going on? Did you give our other location to Miles?"

"No. Listen. I think it's Ètienne."

A chill camps in my stomach. "How? The description matches, but he's never been in our hotel room. *Has he?*"

She shakes her head vehemently. "No! But when he and I were walking after dinner, we came around the corner of the street where our hotel is. I pointed to the guys acting out on the veranda and mentioned our room was right next to party central. He already knew about the Sandoval house, and the rest of that came up in conversation. I bet he's been hiding there since he and Aldo ran from the Renaud house last night."

Almost too good to be true and I can't get a full breath. "The police probably have a picture of him from his driver's license. I'll call Fontenot and see if he can have the guy checked out. If it's not Ètienne, at least they can remove whomever it is from the room."

Rippa is shaking. "I hope it's Ètienne. I'd feel much better with him in jail."

I huff a sigh and call the police.

Our favorite cop picks up. "Detective Fontenot."

"Detective. This is Julianne McCarren. We think we may have located Ètienne Chappelle."

Silence.

"Hello?"

"In six hours. You found him in six hours."

"Not sure it's Ètienne, but someone of his description talked one of the housekeeping staff at our hotel into letting him into our room. He knew it was ours and empty. Said he was a friend and we agreed he could stay there. If it isn't Ètienne, it's someone who's staying there illegally and needs to be put out anyway. We thought you could send over a couple of officers with a picture before the guy decides to take off. He might, since the manager spoke to him this morning."

"Which hotel and room?"

"Canal Street Hotel. Room 208."

"Thank you."

I let the manager know what's going on just in time. Fontenot calls back in twenty minutes. I put my phone on speaker.

"Ètienne Chappelle was the man in your hotel room. He's being brought in for questioning." The detective pauses. "I've explained your and Rippa's involvement and help, not only on the Renaud murder, but the Moffat murder to my lieutenant. I asked his permission for you to watch his interview via closed circuit. Since you have an investigator's license and you'll be leaving town soon, he's agreed. Which is a first for him."

"Thank you, Detective. Will that be today?"

"In an hour."

"I'll be there."

Rippa resumes her happy bounce. "That's great. I talked to Clemmie too. She said I could come get the journals any time after dinner."

****

I take an Uber to the police station as it's too far to walk and almost dusk.

After checking in, I head for the seat I sat in this morning, but Fontenot comes out to greet me right away.

"Thank you for being prompt." He smiles. "Our detainee is getting cranky."

I return the smile. "Hopefully, that temper will have him giving you what you want."

He pulls in his lips for an instant. "That's the plan."

A short walk through the inner sanctum leads to the space designated as the homicide unit. Anyone expecting the area to be other than ordinary office décor would be disappointed. Cop rules and slogans adorn the walls, and family pics, awards, and personal items cover the desks in the semi-open cubicles. Since it's the weekend, most of the desks are empty. However, the upholstery of some of the chairs belonging to smokers waft a lingering odor in the air. As I pass, I am stared at or ignored equally.

Detective Fontenot approaches a desk outfitted with a large monitor and a man leaning back in his chair with eyes on the restless figure of Ètienne Chappelle.

The man stands and holds out his hand. "Lieutenant Tynan, Ms. McCarren. You understand our allowing you to watch this interview means none of what you hear can be relayed to your niece. You are here to give additional insight from your interactions with our suspect. Are we agreed?"

Right to the point. Works for me. I shake his hand and tip my head. "Agreed."

Tynan speaks. "You're going solo on this, Geoff. Nobody else available to back you up. Sorry."

The detective rolls a shoulder in response and slides a chair toward me. "Let's see what Chappelle has to say for himself."

Lieutenant Tynan and I sit and watch Fontenot enter the smallish room with a manila folder and a pad of paper.

"Thank you for your patience, Mr. Chappelle. Have you been offered coffee or water?"

Ètienne smirks but nods.

Fontenot ignores the attitude. "Mr. Chappelle, have you been advised of your rights?"

"I don't understand."

"You don't understand your rights?"

A huff of impatience. "Yes. I understand those. I don't understand why they were necessary."

"We're getting to that. Do you know why you're here, and are you willing to talk to me on record?"

Ètienne curbs the start of an eye roll. "Yes, I'm willing. To start with, there's been a miscommunication. The hotel room I was rudely dragged out of is rented by a friend, Rippa Parkes, and her aunt. Rippa gave me permission to use it."

The detective opens the folder. "That's not the reason you've been brought in, but just to clarify, you have a local address. Why would you want a hotel room?"

"Rippa and I've dated. One of the big parades was routed down Canal last evening. Since my folks' house is crowded with out-of-town relatives, she offered me the room. She was supposed to watch the parade with me but never showed."

Fontenot frowns. "Miss Parkes and her aunt were at a wedding reception until dark yesterday, and neither claims to have given you permission to use the room. That also doesn't explain why you stayed the night and today until you were brought in." He closes the folder.

"But that's not why you're here. You're here to answer questions regarding the murder of Ames Renaud."

I'm watching for a reaction, as I'm sure the lieutenant and detective are. We aren't disappointed. Ètienne's face registers the barest flicker of consternation, replaced by a warm smile and a shoulder shift.

"You must be talking about my interest in his house. I mentioned it to several people after Mr. Renaud was killed. I figured the house was empty and I could indulge my hobby of learning more about Civil War Era homes." His smile turns into a grin. "Rippa ran with the notion she could impress me by giving me access, I guess. It didn't work out. She's pretty immature, and I kind of dumped her. Maybe that's why she set up the parade viewing. Knowing she wasn't going to show. That's it."

Lieutenant Tynan cuts a quick, sideways glance at me. Yeah, I heard it too. Girl crushes on boy; boy doesn't feel the same way and dumps girl. She gets her revenge by accusing him of murder. At the very least, it makes Rippa's statement look weak or even fabricated. However, the three of us know Rippa was the witness from last night; Ètienne doesn't. He's still stuck on her not giving him permission to stay in the hotel room.

Fontenot makes a note but doesn't look up. "Let's talk about this hobby of yours. There are a few houses from that era that are open to the public to tour. Been in any of those?"

Ètienne rocks back in his chair. "No. It's a new hobby."

"Have you ever been in the Renaud house?"

I can almost see the wheels turning behind those

pretty dark-brown eyes and chiseled features. "Where is this leading, sir?"

The detective shows no sign of impatience. "As I said. You're being questioned regarding your knowledge of the Ames Renaud murder."

Ètienne leans forward, a slight frown in place. "I think I *can* help. Have you considered Mrs. Ashurst? I understand he left her in charge of his estate. If she knew she could get her hands on a bunch of antiques and valuables before everything was turned over to the rightful heir…" His frown relaxes. "That heir would be my girlfriend, Honor deGrandpre. Anyway, Mrs. Ashurst was very friendly with the victim. Maybe her husband should be questioned too."

Knowing Clemmie and Davison, I almost laugh at the absurdity of his conjecture. However, I can see our young Creole friend is a master of misdirecting blame. A classic "I'm not the guilty party you're looking for."

Fontenot taps the table. "We're aware of those relationships. But let's get back to you. We have statements from the witness on the second floor of the Renaud house who overheard you last night and your cousin, Aldo Chappelle, stating you were involved in the kidnapping and murder of Mr. Renaud."

Ètienne presses his lips together, then shakes his head. "Poor Aldo. His mind has never been strong. He does foolish things and hides behind me. He's my cousin, so I protect him. I guess I can't do that this time."

"Meaning?"

Another shoulder shrug from Ètienne. "Aldo drinks too much. Then calls me. I have to come help him out. Usually, it's a bar fight. Lately, it's been his mania with the Renaud house treasure. Samuel overheard the sisters, Mrs. Ashurst and Mrs. Neely, talking about how Mr. Renaud was obsessed with finding the family treasure in the house. Aldo called me that night to say he had the man tied up and wanted me to come help. There had been an accident, and Mr. Renaud was dead."

"And did you?"

Ètienne's growing irritation is displayed by his slouch and jiggling knee. "Did I what?"

"Did you go to the Renaud house to help your cousin Aldo?"

More wheels engage. "Look. I feel responsible for Aldo. I don't want to get him into trouble."

"That doesn't answer my question. Besides, you just said you couldn't protect him this time. And since he's already admitted to being partly responsible, I'm asking you. Were you in the Renaud house that night?"

"You keep using words like partly and involved. I had nothing to do with the death of Mr. Renaud. My only participation was as an act of kindness. To help out my cousin, who was entirely responsible for what happened."

Don't worry. He'll get what's coming to him, Cara.

Not soon enough for me. I hope they throw the book at Weasel Boy.

"So you *were* there. But only to help out. What weapon was used?"

"You'll have to ask Aldo. He'd already untied Renaud and dragged him to the back porch by the time I had arrived."

"Let me interrupt," Fontenot says. "Why didn't Aldo just leave? There were no witnesses, and the only person who could identify him was dead. Why would he call you? And here's the best question. Why would he want to switch Ames Renaud's body with Samuel Guillory's? From the information we have, he and Samuel were friends. Besides, it took two people to trade those bodies out. So, you see, trying to place the blame on your cousin, alone, doesn't float."

This seems to be a lot for Ètienne to absorb. But no. His pinched expression clears. "I tried to talk him out of it. I really did, but Aldo was still drunk and freaked out over Renaud's death. He said Samuel had been stuck out there in the rain for three days. He was soaked and people laughed at him and took silly pictures. They didn't respect him. But people would notice if there was no body. He thought the perfect solution was to trade bodies, then wrap Samuel up and put him on a dry porch."

Ètienne's gaze wanders the room while the detective scratches on his notepad.

Then he re-engages. "Sounds like pretty clear thinking for a freaked-out drunk guy. Let me make sure I have it right. Aldo went to the Renaud house to try and get information about the supposed treasure, things went sideways, and he accidently killed Mr. Renaud, but you don't know how or with what. Then he called you, and you helped him switch the bodies."

Fontenot's good. He's quietly, patiently, and most of all skillfully drilled down to the essential reason for the interrogation. His suspect has admitted being at the scene of the murder.

Ètienne's gaze lands on the door to the interrogation room. He pulls his mouth to one side. "Yes, that's it. That's all of my involvement. So I can't be an accessory."

The detective shakes his head. "I never said I meant to charge you as an accessory. I am, however, looking into desecration, abuse, or tampering with a corpse. There are differences in the terms, and the prosecutor's office will make the determination, but the charge is solid. Now, let's get back to the statements from the two witnesses alleging you were fully involved in Mr. Renaud's murder."

I can almost see the first fissure in Ètienne's disdain for this interrogation show light. His blinking increases, and a sheen appears on his forehead. He raises his chin in an apparent effort to take control.

"I've explained about Aldo. He's soft in the head and very emotional. He's killed twice and is afraid of the consequences. He's terrified of small spaces and will do anything to avoid prison, so he made up the story he told the deGrandpres. As far as that other thing, that deal about the corpse abuse or whatever. That wasn't my idea."

Fontenot sighs and rubs his hands together. "Your cousin admitted everything to his friends. His part in the accidental Renaud murder, the body switch, and his assault resulting in the death of Ms. Moffat. The sticking point you and I have is your part. Both Aldo and the witness on the second floor of the Renaud house last night were specific as to your involvement in the first murder. You've already admitted you helped switch the bodies." He holds up a hand. "Doesn't matter whose idea it was, it's still against the law."

Ètienne glances at the camera in the corner of the room, up near the ceiling. I'd bet big bucks his mind is digging for some way to discredit the witness from the second floor of the Renaud house. He crosses his arms. "Look. As far as that other guy, that other witness, he must have misheard us. We were pretty hammered and not talking clearly. The hammered condition is why I let Aldo talk me into going in and looking for that stupid gold ring."

Great. The gold ring Rippa spotted in the mud is also accounted for by Ètienne.

Fontenot doesn't challenge or contradict him but does make a few notes on his pad. "Speaking of your cousin. Why did you split up when you left the house? Have you seen or talked to him since? Please don't bother lying. We can get a warrant for your phone call records."

Our person of interest's jaw muscles twitch. My guess is he doesn't much like the intimation that he is a liar, although everything that has fallen out of his mouth has been a lie.

"Splitting up was Aldo's idea."

Of course, it was. Bad ideas equal Aldo; good ideas, of which there are none, equal Ètienne.

The detective waits a beat. "Again, have you been in contact with him since then?"

Ètienne dips his head. "For about a minute. He was sniveling and crying about the innocent people he had accidently killed. He didn't deserve to live, so he was going to lose himself in the swamp after he talked to the deGrandpres. I told him not to drag me into his confession. Apparently, that didn't do any good."

"Apparently not," Fontenot says. "But that clears up your cousin's version. The witness on the second floor of the Renaud house was more specific. They said your cousin cried about the death of Mr. Renaud and you reminded him you only had your hand around the ice pick to take it away." The detective leans forward, hands hanging between his knees. A "we're just guys having a friendly chat" pose. "That part was confusing for us. Were you trying to take it from Aldo to keep him from assaulting Mr. Renaud?"

I hold my breath, and Lieutenant Tynan cracks a smile. Fontenot is offering Ètienne a lifeline tied to an anchor. This is where the guilty party who thinks they are smarter than the police usually step in it.

Eager acceptance has Ètienne leaning forward. "That's it. He went crazy when the old man said he couldn't tell us where the treasure was."

This admission puts Ètienne squarely in the action. He said *us* when talking about trying to force Renaud to disclose the whereabouts of the treasure. Unflattering brown suits notwithstanding, Fontenot is a rock star, and it makes me happy he's been assigned to this case.

The detective straightens. "Yeah. That probably pissed Aldo off, but it sounds like you were there trying to help and got pulled into the accident. That's the only thing that makes sense."

Ètienne's face loses color as he seems to realize he can't go back. He makes an effort, anyway. "You're trying to make me say I did something I didn't." His eyebrows underline his frown. "Wait. You keep talking about this guy who's supposedly a witness. I think it's a setup. We left the house last night without ever seeing anyone else, so they didn't see us. If they didn't see us, how can they identify us?"

A second glance by Lieutenant Tynan in my direction and my nerve ends pulse. I don't think Fontenot will come right out and say Rippa is the witness, but if he tells Ètienne his voice was recognized, that narrows the pool considerably for the young suspect.

Detective Fontenot pulls back his shoulders. "I never said you weren't seen. The light from the back porch was on. And even though the alarm was off when you two entered, the video was still running. It's a new system, and the images are very clear. You accompanied your cousin into the house."

I let out a slow breath of relief as Ètienne has no immediate comeback for this bit of news. His gaze rolls up slightly, as if trying to see the glare of the porch light.

His frown morphs into a mask of anger, which is a good thing in my opinion. When anger takes over, clear thinking fades.

Ètienne slaps the table. "Aldo has already confessed. My hand was on the ice pick, but only to try and stop him. If you were as smart as you think you are, you'd be looking harder for him."

Fontenot flips some pages in his notepad. "We'll get to that. But speaking of the ice pick, it, a copy of the family land grant, and Mr. Renaud's last journal, gouged out of the ice in his freezer, were all taken the night he was killed. Where are they?"

The young Creole folds his arms. "I keep telling you that whole scene was Aldo's idea. He used those things to threaten the old man. Afterward, he said he was going to get rid of them at the docks. That's all I know."

The lieutenant raises his eyebrows, giving me a slow smile. "What d'you think?"

I shrug. Tynan has probably seen lots of soulless

creeps like Ètienne who prey on others with no awareness for what they inflict. Anger doesn't quite express my feelings, and I squirm a little in anticipation of Ètienne's downfall. "In the last couple of weeks, he hasn't been able to gain either of his goals, Honor deGrandpre as his girlfriend or the Renaud house treasure. That could put a chink in what he thinks about himself." I pull my mouth to one side. "But I doubt it."

Tynan nods. "We get a lot of 'throw the other guy under the bus; I was only trying to help,' statements. But it's not usually about family. This guy's a real hard-core jerk."

I second that, Cara. Ètienne's sense of fairness starts and ends with himself.

I tip my head, and we refocus on the monitor.

With Ètienne's second admission he had his hand on the murder weapon, Fontenot is probably close to finishing. He scratches a few more notes, then looks up. "I'll pass that suggestion on to the detective who's investigating Ms. Moffat's murder. Although I'm told there's been a possible sighting and all efforts are being made to bring your cousin in."

Ètienne visibly relaxes at this. "Then are we done here?"

"Not quite," Fontenot says. "I'm placing you under arrest for felony murder." He stands and opens the door to a uniformed officer.

Chapter Twenty-Five

Wish I'd been allowed to take a picture of the look on Ètienne's face. Confusion followed by an angry smirk. He slaps the table again. "How stupid are you? You haven't been listening. I want a lawyer right here and right now."

Fontenot nods to the officer, who steps toward Ètienne with cuffs.

"You gave up the right to have an attorney present at the beginning of this interview," Fontenot confirms. "You'll receive court-appointed representation before your arraignment."

Ètienne jerks around, tussling with the officer, his face red with effort and anger. "When they hear my side, they'll help me sue this department for false arrest and imprisonment."

It's a little unnerving that, faced with incontrovertible proof, including his own admission, Ètienne's still convinced he is in the right.

The detective walks out of the interview room and over to his lieutenant and me. "I'll get it transcribed and put into the system."

"Nice job," Tynan says. "Works almost every time. In order to place the blame on someone else, they give details of the crime and sink their own boat."

"Page out of the narcissist's handbook," I say. "Everything unpleasant is blamed on someone else.

Difference is they get the other guy to believe it's their fault. Ètienne probably used that every day on his cousin. And according to my source, narcissists don't invest their time in anyone they can't control. That's going to be a tough gig if he goes to prison."

Fontenot and Tynan raise twin eyebrows.

"Good-looking kid," Tynan says. "But the 'I'm better than you' attitude will be knocked out of him in short order. If I was him, I'd go with the crazy defense instead of blaming everything we see with our lying eyes on his cousin."

I have a question for the detective. "Did you make up that remark about a possible sighting of Aldo Chappelle?"

He shakes his head. "No. His car was found abandoned on the Manchac Swamp Bridge this morning. Someone saw a man matching Chappelle's description walking along the side. They thought he was out of gas. The bridge is almost twenty-three miles long, and by the time the Good Samaritan decided to turn around and go back, the guy had disappeared."

I suck in a breath. Swamps always bring to mind alligators and snakes and unsavory characters. "So you think he jumped? Or?"

Fontenot holds out a hand. "Anybody's guess. He could have, or he got a ride from a stranger, or he arranged to get picked up by someone he knew. In any case, I think he's gone for good unless he decides to come in on his own."

"Sounds like you've written him off."

Tynan tips his head toward his detective. "What Detective Fontenot didn't say was the number of people who disappear into thin air in and around New Orleans each year. Or that a few of the swamp's inhabitants have been known to shoot at the police for sport. Both these cases have been solved, even though Aldo Chappelle remains at large. We'll continue to look for him, but essentially, we're ready to turn our information and interview over to the DA's office."

Tynan indicates the folder on his desk. "Unless you can add something we've missed that will help."

I shift a shoulder. "Might advise whoever gets the case to prosecute that he or she needs to bone up on personality disorders. Get an insight. Ètienne will no doubt lean on the 'my cousin's a killer who's guilty, and I only tried to stop him' defense. He can be very charming and always plays to the person he wants to manipulate. That being said, do you think Rippa will be called back to testify if it goes to trial?"

Lieutenant Tynan answers, "We'll add that personality insight to the case notes. As far as your niece is concerned, her testimony would be required and much stronger in person. Luckily, we have the cousins entering the house on video to back her up. Even so, the defense could insist she made up the story to get back at the guy who dumped her." Tynan leans forward. "Unless our suspect is lying about that. Is he?"

I sigh. Ètienne's danger quotient goes up when his word is challenged. And that's exactly what Rippa's testimony will do. Glad we will be thousands of miles away. "Ètienne used Rippa. He talked up his interest in Civil War Era architecture, but only in the Renaud house. When Mrs. Ashurst turned down his request, Ètienne saw Rippa had a crush on him and asked her out. We think to get access to the Renaud house key. During the one date, they ran into Honor deGrandpre with a male friend. Pissed off Ètienne and he left Rippa to get back to the house alone."

Fontenot is scribbling away. "Nice guy. Sounds like we're in for a 'he said, she said' toss-up in regards to what she stated she heard. We'll let the DA's office know about Mr. Chappelle's charm factor. If it does go to trial, and from what I've seen, that's what he would prefer, our strongest point is his confession, twice, that he had his hand on the murder weapon. That and his cousin's confession that they were there to force Mr. Renaud to give them his treasure. Unfortunately, that could be considered hearsay and not admissible in court. Although we might be able to use Miss deGrandpre's testimony about Aldo Chappelle's confession due to Ètienne's admission during interview that he knew about the conversation."

Looks like Rippa will have to come back and testify if it goes to trial. Does not give me the warm fuzzies. I thank Fontenot and his lieutenant and head out.

Chapter Twenty-Six

Once in motion with a goal, Stella shines. When I return after picking up coconut shrimp and a side of coleslaw, Clemmie, Davison, Rippa, and I are in Stella's kitchen to eat dinner. As we're setting places, I glance down the hall and see Stella's formal parlor is packed with old furnishings and dusty boxes.

I raise my eyebrows at our hostess. "Wow. How long was I gone?"

Stella follows my gaze. "Being on the board of the Garden District Association has its benefits. One of the homeowners is entertaining two strapping nephews from Chicago, here for Mardi Gras. They were loaned to me for an hour in exchange for cuttings from one of my prize-winning rose bushes. Everything large or too heavy has been brought down. Only small house items and a few boxes and small crates of books are left."

Clemmie is pale but looks rested. She smiles. "Our book sorting should go faster with your and Rippa's help. We'll at least have a good starting point for Mr. Radnor. We can work with the furniture after you've left."

Rippa came in about the same time as me. She is nearly vibrating with excitement as we all sit. "How did it go at the station? I know you can't tell me what was said, but is Ètienne in jail?"

"Yes. He's been arrested on a felony murder

charge."

She starts to say something, then gapes at her plate. "Oh, my gosh. These shrimps are fantastic. Remind me to find a good source when we get home."

Okay. Her one-track mind has jumped the rails. And since Ames's interment was only a half-dozen hours ago, and Clemmie is still hurting, I change the subject from his murder. "Find anything interesting at that New Orleans History place?"

"The Historic New Orleans Collection. Really cool building. Yes. You guys won't believe what I found."

I finish chewing a truly excellent coconut shrimp. "Remind us what you went looking for."

"History related to the Renaud family. And guess what?"

Everyone has stopped eating.

Clemmie frowns. "What? Why? Not the treasure story?"

"Yes and no," Rippa says. "I took the copy of the land grant Mr. Renaud gave Clemmie." A blush tinges her cheeks. "You know, research for a keepsake with some family history so she would have something in addition to the land grant to remember Mr. Renaud by."

Clemmie reaches to pat Rippa's hand. "That is one of the kindest things anyone has ever done for me. Thank you."

I agree, Cara. Family history seems very important to Clemmie and Stella.

My niece tips her head. "You're welcome. That's not the best part, though. Everyone has made family history assumptions based mostly on word of mouth. Not records."

Stella wipes her fingers on her napkin. "The

Farrols have a long oral history. Nothing wrong with that. In addition, the written documents, including a family Bible, go back over a hundred years."

"The thing is," Rippa says, "Renaud family records go back even further. I think I found a connection. The Farrols and Renauds are related."

"You found something about the Farrols while researching the Renaud name?" asks Clemmie.

Rippa bobs her head. "French guy named Renaud sailed from France with a wife, two small sons, and his younger brother in the early 1840s. He spent the next twenty years making a fortune in timber and cotton. Nearly lost it all in 1862 when the Union Army captured New Orleans. Lots of records disappeared during the three-year occupation and the end of the war in 1865. Afterward, many families donated their records and Bibles to the city to keep their histories alive."

Clemmie is pushing food around on her plate. "Where did you get all this information? I read Ames's and his uncle's papers and journals. There's nothing in them that goes that far back or refers to a family Bible."

"I know," Rippa says. "But I took a chance, and there it was, a Renaud family Bible with lots of letters tucked in the pages. There's even a description of the land grant." She points to a folder on the kitchen counter she must've put there coming in. "I got copies of all of it."

Davison leans forward, his mouth slightly open. "They let you go through the Bible and letters and make copies?"

Rippa grins. "Oh, no. I was allowed to make copies of the JPEGs they have online. The real stuff is kept in a climate-controlled room or vault or something."

Stella looks lost. "What was that, dear? It's on a peg?"

Clemmie rubs her sister's forearm. "I'll explain later."

Davison is not done. "This is fascinating. So where's the Farrol and Renaud connection?"

"The younger brother, Emile Phillipe Renaud, and his wife had one child," Rippa explains. "A daughter, Charlotte Marie Renaud. Her marriage to Stephen Gardner Farrol was recorded in the Renaud family Bible. Both her parents died not too long afterward." She waves a hand around the kitchen. "And apparently, the Farrols have lived here ever since."

My niece is amazing. Although Stella and Clemmie's father was the last of the male Farrol line, they'll have this family history to pass on to Jilly.

Rippa finishes chewing a shrimp. "When I get home, I'm gonna dive into the Parkes family history. So cool."

I glance at the folder and back to Rippa. "Do you think maybe the legend of the treasure tied to the Renaud house and a book could be their family Bible?"

She follows my gaze and presses her lips together for an instant. "Nope."

Laughter breaks out at the table, and I look around at the smiling faces. This trip has turned out substantially different than planned, but I'm feeling pretty good about my and Rippa's part in the whole "catch a bad guy" investigation.

"May we see your research after dinner?" Clemmie asks.

"I wanted to put it together nicer," Rippa says.

"But sure."

****

Rippa's Reader's Digest version of the two families' connected histories is backed up by the copies she brought back. Sailing-ship passenger lists, Renaud and Sons financial documents, land-parcel descriptions, personal letters, and birth, death, and marriage notations in the Renaud family Bible all add to the story that tragically ended with Ames Renaud's murder last week.

Stella and Clemmie are all smiles. Especially Clemmie.

She runs her fingers over the copy of the Renaud family Bible page. "Ames would have loved seeing this. All he had were the journals, and this would've filled in some blanks for him. Not toward finding the treasure exactly, but as a clue to his past."

I'm happy Rippa's digging has produced something Clemmie and Stella will value. "Speaking of treasures, if it will only take a few minutes, maybe we can clear out the last of the books in the attic now so we'll have an idea of what we're facing tomorrow morning."

"Good idea," Stella says. "The heaviest boxes of books have been put in the library. If you and Rippa bring down the rest, maybe Clemmie can help me get a head start sorting through the furniture that was brought down. Luckily, the good pieces were covered in dustcloths."

"Sounds like a plan," Rippa says. "I'm in."

Considering the calories in a half-dozen coconut shrimp, a mound of coleslaw, and that it was my idea, I sigh, stand, and stretch.

Rippa laughs and takes my elbow, dragging me

toward the stairs to the attic. "C'mon. Ten more minutes and we can go back to the Sandoval house and do laundry for the trip home. Yay."

I roll my eyes and groan. "Way to make it sound fun, Parkes."

When I clear the last step up, I am pleasantly surprised. Only a half-dozen boxes and one smallish wood crate are left. The floor is smeared with large footprints, drag marks, and various-shaped spaces in the dust. I have new respect for Stella's negotiating skills.

Rippa puts her fists on her hips. "Grab boxes and pull them over here for easy handing down?"

"Okay by me."

I slide the farthest box over, and Rippa does the same with one nearby. I test the weight by picking a box up by the corner. "These might be easier to carry if we take out half the books and come back to reload."

Rippa nods and starts making a stack of books to one side while I drag two more boxes forward. She disappears down the steps with a lighter box, and I follow suit.

After three more trips, we have the cardboard boxes empty.

Rippa heads for the wood crate. "Looks like the same thing here. Unload and take down two boxes, then the empty crate, and we're done."

She starts pulling the crate by the side, and it more or less disintegrates, spilling books out and splintered boards popping sideways.

Well, that didn't help.

Rippa makes an *aaarrgh* sound and drags an empty cardboard box to the mess. The crate was up against the eaves on the long side and is in shadow from the single light bulb by the stairs. She loads the box half full and slides it to me.

I unload the books in the library and peek into the formal parlor where Stella and Clemmie are directing Davison as he moves a very pretty petite Biedermeier secretary. I love the soft, elegant lines. "That is gorgeous. Mom and Dad are getting a bigger townhouse now that they've decided to stay in the southwest permanently. Let me know how much the furniture appraiser sets the value at. I'm interested in having it shipped out for Mom's birthday next month."

"Helloooo! Anybody there?"

Rippa's voice has me twisting toward the hall. "Uh-oh. Stern taskmaster."

Stella smiles. "I'll give you the best price I can, dear."

My niece is standing at the bottom of the stairs, one eyebrow arched in my direction. "Shopping?"

I pull on my "guilty as charged" mask. "For Grandma Parkes."

"Oh. In that case, it's okay."

Being the only grandchild, she is the apple of two pairs of eyes. Grandma and Grandpa.

Shopping permission granted, I follow Rippa up the stairs to the attic. "Load the pieces of the crate, bring them down, and we're done?"

We reach the top, and she turns on her cellphone flashlight. "Yes. Then we're done."

I hold the light as she fills her box with scraps, then hand her phone back and fill mine. I start to carry my box toward the stairs when Rippa stops.

"Wait. You forgot a piece."

I squint at where she's shining her light. A board is

leaning crooked against the joint of the wall and eaves. "I think that's part of the house structure. Maybe it got knocked loose when the crate was shoved there."

Rippa is shaking her head. "Then something got left behind. I see dull shine and color."

She bends down and taps her finger against something that sounds metallic, then moves the board away and pulls out a long, deep, flat box covered mostly in grime.

I chuckle. "It's the treasure. Too bad it's in the wrong house."

I can't actually *see* her eye roll, but I can hear it.

She lays her find on top of her box. "Very funny. It looks cool, though, so I'm taking it down to Stella. Maybe she'll know what's in it."

We make our way down to the hallway and hang a left into the kitchen to leave our boxes of broken wood on the back porch, minus the treasure Rippa has found. In the kitchen light, it changes from dirty and slightly dented to interesting. On closer examination and after brushing off some of the dirt, the box has a lid, sealed all around with wax. Wax that is cracked and broken to bits in places. The color and shine that attracted Rippa's attention turns out to be hand-painted flowers, suns, and moons on a red background, with a tiny fleur-de-lis in gold on one corner.

Rippa runs her fingers around the edges. "It looks really old."

"What does?"

Rippa and I turn to see Stella standing in the kitchen doorway.

"Dusty work in there. I came in to make refreshments." She tilts her head. "What's that?"

We move to one side so she can get a full view.

I point to Rippa. "We were hoping you could tell us. Rippa found it stuck behind one of the boards where the eaves meet the wall in your attic. It seems to be a very old, hand-painted tin box sealed with wax."

Stella turns and calls out, "Clemmie, Davison, can you please step in here for a moment?" Then walks to the table.

The Ashursts appear in the doorway a moment later. "What is it?" Clemmie asks.

Stella points to the box. "Rippa and Julianne found this in the attic. I've never seen it before." She tips her head at Clemmie. "Do you know what it is or what's in it?"

Clemmie and Davison approach the table.

Clemmie picks it up. "I have no idea. Looks like it's been sealed for a while."

"Maybe it's full of valuable confederate money. Hidden there during the Civil War for emergencies," Rippa conjectures.

Davison reaches in his pocket. "I have a small pocketknife. I can try removing the wax holding the lid in place without disturbing the paint if you want."

Stella is wearing a half-frown, thoughtful expression. "Good plan, but please wait a few minutes. I'm going to find the box of white cotton gloves Harlan used when he polished his watch collection." She sighs. "And his golf clubs. If the box or contents have any value, I'd like it protected."

Excellent idea. Body oils can do damage to paper and even some metals.

Rippa stands on one foot, then the other. "So does anyone know if Confederate paper money is worth, like, the paper it's printed on?"

Good question. Clemmie pulls her lips in and out. "If I recall my history, there wasn't just one kind. Some states and even counties had their own. I imagine some, because of the scarcity, are quite collectable."

"Then I hope that's what this is," Rippa says, hot on her cellphone. "Guess what? See the gold fleur-de-lis on the corner? That used to be the exclusive insignia of the French court. Depending on who the former owner was, the box may have been passed down or given to someone of high social standing. The royal line ended in 1870."

Royalty? That's pretty exciting, Cara.

Stella reappears with a dark blue box of disposable cotton gloves. "Would anyone who will be touching the box or contents wear these, please?"

Heck. Who doesn't want to touch the mysterious contents? We all take a pair and put them on. Then Clemmie slides a sheet of parchment paper under the box.

Davison gets a nod from Stella and takes out a small Swiss Army knife. They're very handy. I have one in my bag.

The next half hour is an excruciating time-suck as Davison carefully chips away the dirty wax seal. When he's done, he slides the box toward Stella.

Metal on metal screeches as she carefully works off a lid that's been sealed more than a century. Stella lays it, shining inside up, on a second sheet of parchment paper.

Davison sucks air through his teeth. "Good choice for a box. Tin is resistant to corrosion."

We all crane to see what looks like a deep stack of

ecru-colored paper.

Rippa is the first to break the silence. "Why would anyone go to the trouble of sealing a bunch of old papers?"

I peek around Stella's arm. A couple of smaller sheets of rough-edged paper sit on top. The faded writing is in French. I turn to the group. "Can anyone read French?"

"I'm decent at it," Davison says. He turns to Stella. "Unless you'd rather?"

She shakes her head. "I used to be, but I'm afraid I'm too rusty at this point. Please go ahead."

Davison removes the two sheets and lays them side-by-side, squinting at the words. " 'I, Jacques Louet, am responsible for the theft of this manuscript penned by Alexandre Dumas.' "

Exclamations spring from everyone in the room.

"Are you kidding?"

"Holy cow."

"That's amazing, if true."

"This is crazy."

"So happy for you."

I agree. It's pretty amazing, Cara.

Stella is standing with her mouth slightly open, her eyes wide. As if the next words will be "gotcha, just kidding."

Davison nods. "It looks genuine. Ready to hear the letter?"

Stella's gaze stays on the box. "Yes. Thank you."

Davison has a nice, deep, radio-announcer voice and speaks into complete silence.

" '1850

" 'For fifteen years, my mother and I worked in the

household of the famous Alexandre Dumas. After many years of questioning, my mother told me Monsieur Dumas was my father. As with others who made this petition, he denied the claim.

" 'I convinced my mother our fortunes lay in the Americas, and we spent our savings to book passage. The night before we sailed, I stole into the study of Monsieur Dumas. Because of the heartache he caused my mother and me, I took something he valued. This manuscript.

" 'Sadly, my mother died during the voyage, but not before telling me she lied about Monsieur Dumas. I sealed the box and kept it with me, intending to save for the fare back to France and return the manuscript in person, even if it meant prison. The Civil War broke out, and shortly, New Orleans lay in the hands of the Northern Aggressors. All the money I had set aside was spent keeping body and soul and my family alive.' "

Davison turns the first sheet over. It's blank. He points to the second one. "The ink color has changed to black and looks more recent than the first page.

" '1865

" 'My fortunes have changed since the end of the war. Although I am an educated man, I have been hired as a carpenter in charge of the renovation of a Monsieur Renaud's home and the building of his brother's, next to his. I have much respect for this man, and although he is not especially kind, he pays well. His younger brother has a more modest nature and is kind as well as amiable.' "

Our interpreter squints at the bottom of the second page. "His writing has changed. It's spidery and made with effort.

" '1870

" 'I am of failing health and may not see the spring. Monsieur Dumas, once the well-to-do prince of Paris society, has passed. I cannot know whether this manuscript would have made a great difference in his wealth, but it seems my fate all along was to pass it to one who deserved it. My intent is to reseal the box with this letter inside and disclose the location to the younger Monsieur Renaud for his many kindnesses toward me.

" 'Jacques Louet.' "

I look in the box, my heart pounding. The top sheet of a stack of velum several inches thick reads *La Femme Soldat by Alexandre Dumas.*

"An amazing find," Davison says. "I can't imagine it's not genuine. The title translates to *The Soldier's Woman*. Congratulations."

Rippa peers into the box. "It's the treasure."

I laugh. "She's right. It's old, it's a book, and it was in the Renaud house."

Davison gives his wife a quick, sideways squeeze as Clemmie's face crumples a little.

"A century and a half, then eight months and a week. Ames might still be alive," she says.

Stella hugs her sister full-on. "Oh, Clemmie. I'm so sorry my pride wouldn't let me do this sooner. You lost a dear friend because of me."

Clemmie returns her sister's hug. "It mightn't have happened at all without Julianne and Rippa helping. I have a feeling this was all meant to be for Honor and you. Two good women in need of a hand reaching out from the past."

I don't envy the headache and notoriety this find

will visit on Stella and her calm surroundings. "I see a high-profile entertainment or literary lawyer and maybe a Dumas scholar in your future. If the book's finished."

Stella's hand goes to her mouth. "Oh. The box is full. I…just assumed."

Davison's expression is somber, his face almost blank. "We wouldn't want to just tip the box over and dump the contents or push a hand down inside. I have an idea. Will you help me?"

Stella, her eyes wide, nods.

"Okay, open your hand against the table at ninety degrees. Block the edge of the table with your other hand. I'm going to carefully tip the box, turning the manuscript upside down. I'll hold the pages together from the top, you hold them from the sides. Once they're all out, I'll turn over the last page. That way we don't have to unstack each page and take the chance on damaging any. Ready?"

Stella takes a deep breath and does as Davison asks.

He very slowly tips the box, but the rough paper doesn't slide much. When it's empty, he lets the box tip back onto the table, slides off the top page and turns it over. He grins and holds it up for everyone to see. There is one word.

Fin.

Epilogue

Rippa and I receive email updates from Clemmie every couple of days. This morning's has a little bit of everything, so I call for Rippa to come into my office. "Wanna hear the latest from New Orleans?"

She enters, nods, and says, "Sure," around a bite of bagel.

"Jilly and Hugh are back and well rested from their honeymoon in Fiji. They're looking for a house on the fringes of the Garden District to gut and restore. Jilly will work on the house while Hugh joins a new medical practice.

"Things are going at a mad pace for the sisters but especially Stella. Turns out James Radnor is a widower and smitten. He has spent every spare minute with her, making sure the library collection is evaluated and having several furniture appraisers in to see her antiques. She is selling most of the traditional pieces and replacing them with some that were in the attic. Minus the petite Biedermeier secretary I bought for Mother.

"Stella seems to be smitten with James too but has been generous in lending him to Honor to help her with the Renaud-house books and other content appraisals before her house goes on the market."

I smile. "The wrought iron garden bench I had sent with the brass plaque reading 'In remembrance of

Samuel Guillory' arrived. Stella loved it, and Honor cried when she saw it.

"A Dumas scholar flew in from France, and the manuscript has been authenticated. The handwriting and age of the work matched perfectly. Stella asked why Dumas didn't just write the book over since it was already finished. The scholar claimed Dumas was extremely prolific, due to the fact that he loved the high, expensive life, and worked on several projects at a time. It was very possible he might have been bored with an already-done book and just moved on."

Rippa is now reading over my shoulder. "I wondered the same thing. Did you know one of his stories was serialized in a French newspaper and found, almost finished, at the end of the twentieth century? It was completed by a Dumas scholar and published in France in 2005, then in 2007 in English in the US. It's called *The Last Cavalier*. I wonder if it's the same scholar who visited Stella and Clemmie."

I shrug. "Could be. Stella is trying to make the decision of which international auction house to accept. She's had offers from Sotheby's, Christie's, and Bonhams so far. Tough decision, but she's getting help from James and Davison and Clemmie."

Rippa points to a lower paragraph. "Oh, look. Étienne accepted a plea bargain. Wow. That's hard to believe. Clemmie talked to Fontenot and says it's because Étienne got a real hard-core legal representative who convinced him admitting to having his hand on the murder weapon during the stabbing pretty much guaranteed a guilty verdict if he went to trial. Even if he claimed he was trying to prevent his cousin from harming Mr. Renaud. Especially as the prosecution had video showing them entering the house and a solid witness to his conversation with Aldo about both murders and the reason for the break-ins. Yay. Looks like I don't have to go testify."

"Doesn't look very likely. They still haven't found Aldo even after a couple of forays into the swamps. Nobody's talking."

I point to an email I've opened from Mack. "Look at this. The end of the saga that was Ms. Moffat. She had no will, but she and her partner in the staging warehouse had a surviving partnership agreement, so he got all of that. Mack located a cousin in Minnesota who flew to New York and hired a lawyer to claim her considerable assets. The cousin had her cremated and interred in the same cemetery as her mother."

Sad end to an angry person, Cara.

Rippa plops down beside me. "Say hi to Mack for me." She grins. "Stella and a boyfriend. That is so cute. Can we go back if there's a wedding?"

A word about the author...

DeeAnna is a freelance editor and writer of romantic suspense, women's fiction, children's picture books, and mysteries. She teaches elements of the writing craft for the love of it and has never met a dog she did not want to pet.

~*~

Find DeeAnna online at:
http://deeannagalbraith.com